DIRTY WHITE COLLAR

JULIUS MELNITZER

DIRTY WHITE COLLAR

ECW PRESS

Published by ECW PRESS
2120 Queen Street East, Suite 200, Toronto, Ontario, Canada M4E 1E2

NATIONAL LIBRARY OF CANADA CATALOGUING IN PUBLICATION DATA

Melnitzer, Julius, 1947–
Dirty white collar: a novel
ISBN 1-55022-510-3
I. Title.
PS8576.E4714D57 2002   C813´.6   C2001-904071-7
PR9199.4.M44D   2002

Editor: Michael Holmes
Cover and Text Design: Tania Craan
Production and typesetting: Mary Bowness
Printing: UTP
Author photo: Gail J. Cohen

This book is set in Columbus and Franklin Gothic

The publication of *Dirty White Collar* has been generously supported by the Canada Council, the Ontario Arts Council, and the Government of Canada through the Book Publishing Industry Development Program.

DISTRIBUTION
CANADA: Stewart House, 195 Allstate Parkway, Markham, ON L3R 4T8

UNITED STATES: Independent Publishers Group, 814 North Franklin Street, Chicago, Illinois 60610

EUROPE: Turnaround Publisher Services, Unit 3, Olympia Trading Estate, Coburg Road, Wood Green, London N2Z 6T2

AUSTRALIA AND NEW ZEALAND: Wakefield Press, 17 Rundle Street (Box 2066), Kent Town, South Australia 5071

PRINTED AND BOUND IN CANADA

ECW PRESS
ecwpress.com

To the memories of my sister, Roslyn

&

my old friends, Brian Kelsey and Hans Arndt

"HURRY NOW, THE PLANE LEAVES IN TWO HOURS."
She found it hard to believe. Since saying good-bye to her father at the airport more than six years ago, she had been hoarding time like the coins in her penny jar, waiting for the moment she could trade its contents for something that really mattered. All the while she hadn't been sure that what she'd saved could be contained — the jar was too large and too small at the same time.

Now, finally, the time had come. It had happened suddenly.

"We're going to meet Daddy," her mother announced a few days earlier.

"Why?" she asked.

"Because he's finished his work and it's time for us to be a family again."

"Then why doesn't he come home?"

"He's found a better place for us to live."

"Will we stay there?"

"Yes."

"Forever?"

"Forever."

What the little girl did not ask and what her mother did not tell her was why they were leaving almost everything behind.

PART ONE

CHAPTER ONE

JEROME WYNDHAM COULD JUST AS EASILY HAVE BEEN practising law again, holding court even when court was out. His visitors, three cops who arrived unannounced that morning, had no way of knowing that his Polo shirt — without a name tag — was in breach of prison regulations. That small defiance, and the seat at the head of the table in the large conference room adjacent to the warden's office, were habits that two and half years in jail hadn't changed.

Jerome's thoughts strayed from his company and their conversation. In his own office, he was always thinking ahead; now, too often, memories distracted him.

"You with us?"

Almost from the moment Sergeant Adam Portland arrested him, they'd shared the unique friendship of intended adversaries, bartering Jerome's cooperation for a silent acknowledgement that he wasn't all bad. Good cop/Bad cop was a game Jerome recognized from the hundreds of confessions his clients made to countless detectives before they bothered calling him. Still, the Mountie's motivations mattered little.

Portland didn't share the wariness of the few friends who stayed in touch after his arrest. The cop had taken the trouble to call in the early, dark days. Left messages, really, because prisoners were freer to return calls from police than they were from their lawyers. And they could do so in privacy, to ensure someone didn't bludgeon them for talking to the Man.

"I'll drop by when you clear max," Portland told Jerome, and he did, visiting soon after the lawyer arrived at Fairlawn, much maligned in the media as Correctional Services Canada's minimum security country club.

Portland wasn't like the two other cops in the room, despite the standard dress code: all three Mounties wore unyielding earth tones, except for their black shoes and Superintendent Gunnar Einarson's oversized, glaring, diamond-studded tie pin. He had worn it every day for eight years since Marta had made it a 20th anniversary present.

Mind you, drab goes nicely with those glasses Gunnar's wearing. I've never seen lenses so thick.

Thinking back on two decades as a criminal lawyer, Jerome couldn't remember a detective in a blue suit, except maybe for senior officers in the big cases that attracted photographers. Mounties were the worst, as if they were bent on disowning the scarlet tunic of Sergeant Preston or disguising a collective embarrassment over the Musical Ride.

But unlike the shop-bought, shopworn formality of his companions, Portland slumped right into his clothes: his contours melded with his jacket and pants as if he had been blown into them, each crease an effortless intersection on a natural grid; his tie curved gratefully over the soft hint of handles around his torso and waist, enticing companions to a childish face with the comfortable lull of a lazyboy. Jerome had long yearned for that easy image, a tall order, he knew now, for a man who had spent most of his life seeking happiness by trying to be all things to all people.

The trace of a bemused smile on Jerome's face caught Gunnar's eye. "What's so funny?" The senior officer in the room looked across the boardroom table at Inspector Tom Yu, his second in command.

"Nothing, just thinking about FBI shows and best-dressed lists," Jerome said.

"What?"

"I'm sorry. There's a lot to think about."

"Well, what's your answer?" Gunnar was unable to repress 35 years as an investigator.

"It's scary."

"Christ, it was your idea."

"A year ago. Now, I don't know. I'm not finished hiding from the past, so I don't think it's such a good idea to hide from the present."

"You've turned into quite the philosopher."

Jerome didn't like Gunnar. In the old days, he would have walked out.

"What the fuck do you know?"

"We've got a roomful of files on you, Wyndham. Half of them newspaper clippings. Lots of lowlife shit, nothing about philosophy."

Jerome stood up, coming to a stop behind the seated Gunnar, but talking to Portland. "Now you know why I said I'd only work with you, Adam. I can't find another cop who's a human being."

"Take it easy," Portland said. "It's been a long day. Everybody's tired. Remember, you made the offer."

"It expired. And it would have helped if you had given me some warning. You don't just disappear for a couple of hours around here without people suspecting you've been talking to the IPSO or the cops. How am I supposed to explain being in the warden's quarters on a Sunday?"

"You'll manage, Jerome. I have every faith you haven't lost your old skills," Gunnar said.

That hit its target, but neither his vulnerability nor the horrors of arrest and prison had dispelled Jerome's instinct for one-upmanship.

"Right. Tell me again how Dirk showing up as my next-door neighbour isn't a coincidence."

Gunnar twitched, then tried to hide it by glaring back with the insolence of a witness caught in a lie.

"Not that it ever took that much to make monkeys out of cops like you," Jerome continued. "Lawyer to liar. Liar to lawyer. Liar to liar. That sort of thing. You know what I mean, don't you, Gunnar?"

"Look," Portland intervened, "why don't we take a smoke break?" Portland, who hadn't smoked since university, still appreciated the opportunities for tactical solitude that came with the federal govern-ment's recent crackdown on tobacco.

"All right," Gunnar agreed, "but this is a waste of time. And the two-hour drive here was no picnic for any of us. Police officers have families too, Mr. Wyndham."

"I wouldn't know. I haven't had one for a while."

Gunnar hadn't meant it that way. Portland had warned him that anything remotely touching on the dead kid was off-limits. His atten-tion to detail had served him well in his rise through the RCMP's Criminal Intelligence Directorate, though rumour had it that deterio-rating eyesight, which a decade past had cost him his driver's licence, would force him to retire.

"I'm sorry," Gunnar said into his neatly trimmed beard. "Really."

But as he and Yu rose to leave, he couldn't look at Jerome, who didn't believe him anyway.

■

"You all right?" Portland asked, as Jerome removed his glasses and stared through them at the ceiling. "Never saw you in glasses before."

"Would you have cut me a better deal if you had, Adam?"

He'd had them, his first pair, for almost a month, wearing them more than he needed to. When he finally saw himself in a mirror, he wrote a poem. Surprising yourself, he had discovered, was much bet-ter than fooling yourself.

> *In prison, they gave me glasses, free,*
> *to help me see, for I could read*
> *in languages not clear to others*
> *or to myself.*
>
> *Now, looking up from my book*
> *I can see the hills beyond the fences*

thanks to their glasses
it's clear where I am.

The lingering silences, Portland thought, were new — and useful if Jerome agreed to come on board undercover. At the first interrogation, Portland and his partner hadn't asked a half-dozen questions, just let the tape run. With Heidi sitting by, Wyndham laid it all out for them without the benefit of a single document or note, and without once looking at his wife. The elegant blonde's crispness, even as her world crumbled, convinced Portland that she wouldn't stick around for long.

When the identification officer was fingerprinting him, Jerome announced his intention to be in jail before spring. Six months after his arrest, he was. It made Portland's career, and he was promoted to Staff Sergeant before the year ended. Still, he wondered whether the lawyer had merely figured out a way to keep people off balance and himself in charge.

Jerome heard about the search at Heidi's parents' place in London, where the annual family gathering had become little more than a chance to pool their grief over Sarah. He flew back, surrendered before Portland could get an arrest warrant, and confessed. His dispatch made him an excellent candidate for bail, and he didn't spend a single night behind bars before he was sentenced.

Jerome waited a few weeks before hiring a lawyer, then cut a deal at the second bargaining session with Crown Attorney Barbara McGowan. The sentence wasn't light. From the outset, Jerome told the few friends he had left that he was looking at ten to 15 years. He got twelve; his wheeler-dealer squash partner, Scott Lewis, who had dreamed up the scheme, got nothing, having chosen to disappear — presumably to the same destination as his share of the proceeds of his crime — when Jerome agreed to plead guilty and testify against him. Still, the sentencing judge noted, although Jerome had been a transient player who benefited relatively sparsely from Lewis's activities, he was in a position of trust and his participation before withdrawing from the fraud had made Lewis's laundering of millions possible, and perhaps facilitated his escape.

In return for his cooperation, Portland, McGowan, and the Judge recommended him for minimum security and early release. If everything went well, Jerome would do three or four years before he made parole. He was eligible after two, but he was sure the Board, always courting public opinion, would turn him down at least once.

Portland had never met anyone so mysteriously open. Both light and darkness, he had read somewhere, were disarming: if that were true, Jerome had raised the contradiction to a lifestyle. Which was why Portland believed Jerome when he said he was broke, and why Portland was not one of many self-appointed commentators on the case who professed disbelief at why someone *so together,* even after the death of a child, needed so desperately to ruin his life.

He remembered when Jerome, with the very momentary stare he had perfected for cross-examination, looked up from the stacks of paper he had been organizing effortlessly into the paper trail that would explain his activities to the police and their accountants. *I'm doing your job for you, Adam, better and faster than you could do it yourself. Warmth in the guise of friendship is all I ask, and who's to say I'm asking?*

"In case you're wondering, Adam, the allure of happiness is that it invites complacency, which in turn invites chaos."

"What?"

"Write it down. I'm giving you motive."

"I don't think it'll sound that good to the judge."

"What my lawyer is going to tell the judge has nothing to do with motive."

◼

They were a couple of hours into their third all-day session. Jerome's lawyer, silently acknowledging that his client was perfectly capable of looking after himself, left the room without a word soon after the interview started. He wasn't about to waste the limited time he had allotted, at $400 hourly, to the $20,000 flat fee that Jerome paid him from funds Heidi borrowed from her father and mother. They had retired in considerable comfort after selling their interest in a small boutique investment house to Barclay's Bank; then, as before, they could never do enough for their daughter.

"Someone's got to make a proper show of selling the done deal once we agree how long my vacation's going to be," Jerome told Portland the first time they were alone in the lawyer's office, by way of easing the Mountie's discomfort at an accused spilling his guts in the absence of counsel.

"Sure you're not setting up some Charter argument?" Portland had asked only half-jokingly.

"Want me to sign something? Or do you trust me?" Jerome responded, no more serious than Portland.

Portland did trust Jerome. Not just because he was making a full breast of it; that was a common enough cover for people who still had something to hide or seeking to ingratiate themselves with the court. It was the haste with which Jerome wanted to get to jail that set the lawyer apart, suggesting that an inner cleansing had been unleashed by the relief of his arrest.

The funny thing was that Jerome seemed unable to admit to anything as noble as remorse. His punishment — whether for his crime or for letting Sarah die — was incomplete without self-flagellation, effected through penetrating rationalizations designed to confirm the public perception of a smart, but scheming and self-centered man.

Jerome didn't talk about how sorry he was. Instead, he explained that high profile, white-collar clients did harsher time on the street before trial than they did in jail.

"Not only do my job, my reputation, my routine, and my property disappear, but every move I make is open season for the neighbours and even the press. By comparison, jail's a sabbatical. It isolates guys like me, shelters us from the shame we dread more than anything else.

So here's how I figure it. Five years before trial and a six-year sentence means it's seven years from arrest to the time I get out. Six months before trial and a twelve-year sentence makes it less than five years before I can get a life again."

Most well-heeled white-collar crooks made things as expensive as possible for the state. Their lawyers maneuvered until the prosecution and the media found new fish to fry; then, when their cases were no longer on top of the Crown Attorney's pile, they did their deals. Old cases, Jerome used to say, make short sentences.

Portland was of the same mind. From his perspective, there wasn't much to distinguish the Canadian system from the American mess anymore, especially now that the lawyer as celebrity had arrived north of the border. Which reminded Portland, a vegetarian, that his distaste for some of the American ways began with his trip to Las Vegas for a police conference, where he observed that the city's most popular carnivorous restaurant, Gutsy's, had chosen a stuffed steer as its emblem.

■

Gunnar and Yu still hadn't returned.

"I don't understand," Jerome snapped. "I'm almost out of here. I hardly know the guy."

"Exactly. He's chasing you. He needs a friend. He hasn't had a visit since we picked him up."

"Because he doesn't want to jeopardize his wife and family," Jerome said.

"You know that only because he trusts you." Portland was gentle, anxious not to provoke the give-and-take Jerome hid behind on the rare occasions answers didn't come to him instantly.

"There's no time," Jerome said as Yu reappeared, holding the door open for Gunnar. "I'm up for parole soon. Are you saying I should stay here to help you?"

"Don't worry, we'll take care of that," Gunnar said. "You'll get parole and so will Dirk Mueller. It shouldn't surprise anyone. You'll remember, I'm sure, that the system treats drug offenders and white-collar criminals the same way."

"Our mutual release should warm the hearts of the Canadian Alliance," Jerome said.

"The dealers are never on the street long," Yu replied.

Jerome thought better about another diatribe against the forces of the law. "So Dirk gets out," he said instead, "and then?"

"He's out, but he's stuck in Canada," Gunnar said, taking control of the conversation, as if he couldn't bear to hear Yu speak with authority. It wasn't the first time Portland had observed something off-key in their relationship, which was odd considering that Gunnar had been Yu's mentor, arranging for his promotion every time Gunnar moved up the ladder himself. But Portland knew little about Yu, who never mentioned his personal life, not even when they were in the same study group at the Canadian Police College in Ottawa. He hadn't married and if he had a social life, Portland hadn't heard about it.

"From what I hear," Gunnar continued, "Mueller can't go back to Colombia. And his wife and kid can't move up here until the money's washed, because he needs her to look after things at home. She's also got to close down the business, sell the ranch. Meanwhile, he has to find a way to clean up that money for when they need it."

"And what do I do for him?"

"Help. You'll have more freedom, more connections, and everybody knows you have a stash waiting that also needs some tidying up."

"Fuck you, Gunnar. You think ratting on Dirk is some scheme to help myself? Don't you read your own goddamn files anymore? If you did, you'd realize that I didn't even know Dirk when I called Adam. And the only reason I called him was to do something about the kind of people who gave Sarah the drugs."

Again, Sarah's name stopped Portland and the others cold, as if some hidden force had inhabited Jerome in mid-conversation. Jerome paused too. A pause Portland recognized — barren, white, turning

Jerome's round face into a full moon without craters.

"Getting a few less drug dealers off might have helped. Maybe your daughter would still be alive," Gunnar said.

Jerome was all over the Mountie before anyone could move, shoving him so violently he fell backwards to the floor. Portland and Yu reacted in chorus, though barely in time to divert the kick aimed squarely at Gunnar's head. Somehow, they all crashed down on Gunnar, who had recovered sufficiently to punctuate a string of obscenities with hollow battle orders and futile counterpunches intended chiefly to resuscitate his dignity. Portland dragged a still-shaking Jerome off Gunnar and stood him up; Yu held off his boss, who eventually settled into craning his neck and dusting himself off.

"What's the matter with all of you?" Jerome's whisper commanded the room. "Sarah never even smoked a joint as a kid. No booze, no cigarettes, she choked whenever she tried to inhale. Does that sound like someone who'd OD on heroin? When she was in school in Montreal, she called us all the time. She talked to us. If something was wrong, we'd have known. And who are you to judge, Gunnar? Your make deals with drug dealers, crackheads, addicts. You trade dope for information, and then when you have what you want, what do we get? A plea bargain. You don't even have the guts to get on the witness stand. Doesn't matter. The arrest's the thing. Why should a cop believe in anything?"

"Let's all sit down," Portland said.

They did.

"Be fair, Jerome," Portland said. "You didn't tell anyone that you'd changed your mind."

"I offered. You declined. Normally that's the end of it between consenting adults. In case you haven't noticed, I'm paying my debt to society. I don't owe you guys anything. And I never said I'd take out a friend."

"You offered to help as an undercover drug operative," Portland said. "You had no target in mind. We had no target in mind. And why would a drug dealer, any drug dealer, let a white-collar guy on parole inside his operation? But when we learned that Dirk was your friend and that his real purpose in Canada was to launder his money, your offer became practical — and attractive."

"What makes you so sure that Dirk wasn't here just to complete a drug deal like he says?"

"We have our ways," said Gunnar, who had collected himself. "And we believe that your friend has some very dirty business making its way through some very fancy laundromats including a few occupied by your former colleagues. Maybe you ought to charge Dirk a fee."

"I can see you've got an open, trusting partnership in mind," said Jerome, wondering what the cops knew about Dirk that he didn't. The uncertainty steadied him. "Sorry. Informing in here is suicide."

"We're not going to do anything until you get out except collect information," Portland said.

"Right. You think you're talking to a ballerina? What if Gunnar changes his mind and decides I should be a little more aggressive in my inquiries? Do I spend the rest of my time in the hole? Or gather up my neighbours and ask the Warden for a pass so I can stage a protest on Parliament Hill? Maybe a new life in your Witless Protection Program? That's what the cons call it, you know."

"You could always make me laugh, Jerome. That hasn't changed . . . I'm glad."

"Well, keep laughing, because I'm out."

The finality reminded Portland of Jerome's determination to expedite his case. He sighed as he rose to open the door.

"Gentlemen, I don't believe there's anything left to discuss."

"That's my decision," Gunnar grumped. But he got up with the others and left.

CHAPTER TWO

DUSK HAD FALLEN WHEN JEROME ARRIVED AT THE IRON LATTICE barrier by Two Control, Lorimar's central security post. Simpson, the Internal Preventive Security Officer who had escorted him to the meeting through the back door of the administration building, had let him out the same way. Through the smoked glass, the solitary guard smiled and greeted him with a wave. Jerome leaned toward the document pass-through to hear what the man was saying.

"No movement. They're having trouble with the count. It's always like that on Sundays. Short staff. Big visitors day today, even with the bad weather. Might be a while."

"They probably forgot me," Jerome shouted back.

"No, no, I got you, counselor. You're not someone we'd forget."

"That used to be a compliment," Jerome replied. Both men laughed. Jerome leaned easily against the orange barrier. Putting on his glasses, he pulled out the paperback that was in his coat pocket as a hedge against prison's vacuums. *That's the nice thing about prison clothes. Always too big. Lots of pockets for hiding stuff.* There was as much light to read by as there was shadow to think by, and Jerome did both. He had long noticed that contrast was closely associated with clarity. That observation, always there, forced him to read, and live, in the detached condition that follows on the urge to instant analysis. His mind worked much like a camera: focusing, closing the shutter, focusing again. In the end, he got a perfect picture, a perspective he could hold in his hand without ever running the risk of joining the crowd.

Nearly everyone at the medium-security prison, where he had served most of his time, knew Jerome — or of him. He was as notorious for his refusal to return to a minimum-security institution as for being a criminal lawyer who had joined his clients. In the maelstrom that was the last 15 years of his life, success, mobility, and escape had travelled hand-in-hand; it was in confinement that Jerome had discovered that movement could stunt growth. He liked it at Lorimar, where there were few lockups, almost everybody was civil, and the guards didn't bother him. Despite the limited options, he spent more of his day doing what he wanted to than he had on the street. The food stunk, but George, the adult ed teacher, was the best boss in the joint. Instead of wasting time being jealous of criminals more competent than he was, George embraced the "pro-social" inmates, turning their otherwise wasted skills to his classroom's, and his career's, advantage.

Helping illiterate felons gave Jerome an uneasy satisfaction he hadn't experienced previously — uneasy only because, when Sarah died, he forgot how to be comfortable with any good in himself. Although the job could be frustrating for a 47-year-old man with a history of unrelenting ambition, the demand for Jerome's computer skills, which he had picked up almost idly in prison, got him out of the classroom for a couple of hours every day.

Jerome got along with most of the people at Lorimar. It didn't start out that way. When he arrived at the classification centre in Milgaard, the maximum-security penitentiary that was his first prison, he bore the twin curse of privilege and privilege lost, a pariah on both sides of the wall.

To the public, decrepit Milgaard was "Disneyland." Its medieval towers and turrets had surprised travelers and their children halfway to their destination on the main highway between Montreal and Toronto for years. The prison of choice for those who touted punishment as rehabilitation, Milgaard double-bunked its windowless 53-square-foot cells where prisoners ate, slept, talked, fought, and masturbated when the female guards took their turn at count. Once a day, the prisoners were marched lockstep past the central dome to the gym for a one-hour exercise period beneath shotgun-bearing guards, who strolled back and forth on the catwalk with sombre relish, pointing their weapons down ever so slightly in defiance of regulations. Otherwise, prisoners left their cells only for communal showers and telephone access on alternate days.

Jerome's discomfort at Fairlawn was more of his own making. The camp's spacious, cottage-country setting with guards in civilian dress, real rooms with real doors in chalet-like structures, and common areas with cloth-covered chairs, had earned the institution its Club Fed reputation. Jerome arrived there only two months into his sentence; most hardened cons waited for years to make it to camp. As Jerome's interest in criminal law hadn't touched on the details of the prison code — *criminal lawyer is a misnomer* — he didn't know enough to keep his good fortune to himself.

Like most criminal lawyers, Jerome's clients interested him most before they formally became criminals — while they were "the accused, against whom the allegations have not been proven in court." He forgot about the majority, though, right after the judge sent them off to the joint, at which point most could no longer pay the bills for the services they needed in prison. Ninety percent of Jerome's clients, the norm, plead guilty or were convicted, so the list of the forgotten was lengthy, at least until they came back for more of the same. What they did in between visits didn't concern Jerome. His secretary knew enough to forward letters from the pen directly to a handful of "prison lawyers," a vanishing breed inexplicably committed, in the eyes of their peers, to lost souls, worn-out causes, and a lifetime of scraping by financially.

Now, living in the strata of his ex-clients, Jerome envied the prison lawyers. Their causes were people. His causes, in the early years, were about principles: fair process and a vigorous defence for everyone, even when Legal Aid wouldn't pay for the time and money he spent hiring investigators, bringing motions, and launching appeals no one thought he could win. But as his career blossomed and cash clients flocked to him, it became easier to fight the good fight when he was being well paid for his efforts. Somehow, though, the cash clients didn't seem as worthy of the principles, which made abandoning them when they no longer had any cash a no-brainer. As his stay in Lorimar unravelled his roots, Jerome realized that he had started to dislike his practice even before Sarah died.

None of that got through to him at Fairlawn, where he could have done easy time on the fast track to early parole: reading, writing, watching TV, listening to music, pretending to work in the camp's school where he indulged his new fascination with computers, playing the indoor racquet sports he loved in the winter and spending the summers sunning himself on the clay tennis courts with partners he chose from a cosmopolitan crew of killers, reformed rapists, and wayward professionals of his own caste. But Jerome didn't know how to do easy time. Soon he was living as he had on the street, albeit on a smaller scale and in a smaller economy. He fought the system at every opportunity, using his legal skills to win minor victories for himself and his friends, blowing his own horn as he did, in case someone had missed the show.

Fairlawn's stand-alone dining room, log cabin style, featured sweets prepared by Hans, a former pastry chef at a trendy Toronto restaurant who had decided to expand his horizons by sampling the forbidden delights of underage fruit. What bugged Jerome was that the guards dined before the inmates, who constantly lamented being reduced to leftover delicacies. When the guards ate all the Florentine cookies Hans had baked in return for a bit of legal advice from Jerome, the ex-lawyer — ever the scholar, ever the pragmatist, and ever-torn between the two — buried himself in the prison library. Two days later, he emerged with a grievance in hand: *Regulation 187, subparagraph 39.1(d)(4)(iii) prohibits preferential access by staff to goods and services intended for inmates when the said goods and services are available to inmates.* The Warden dismissed the grievance, but Jerome embarrassed him by appealing successfully up the CSC ladder. From then on, the guards ate after the inmates, and Jerome ate as many

Florentines as he could, taking what he couldn't eat back to a room that felt like the isolated lodge where he stayed on his heli-skiing trips in BC's Bugaboos.

When the Florentines started doing their job, Jerome supplemented his tennis with a weight-lifting regimen. He skipped lunch and got Hans to serve the Florentines for dinner. Arriving at the recreation complex, which included a regulation-size basketball court alongside well equipped aerobic and weight rooms, Jerome discovered that the guards had appropriated the gym for their own lunch time exercise.

"And don't get huffy on us again," said Brendan, friendly only because Jerome had agreed to share the investment expertise the guard believed all lawyers possessed — even criminal lawyers — by way of nighttime chats on Brendan's graveyard shifts.

"The Warden checked this out after your dessert caper. Legal told him the gym isn't available to inmates at mealtimes. Not that they're entitled to anything, if you ask me," he added as a sop to colleagues within earshot.

Jerome went back to the books. Prisoners at Fairlawn didn't have to stay in their rooms if they skipped lunch, he discovered. They could roam the camp at will so long as they didn't enter prohibited areas. The gym wasn't prohibited. The guards were out, Jerome was in. Already admired for his impact on the dining-room fare, he quickly became Fairlawn's star attraction.

Still smarting from his losses, he embraced the spotlight. But it made him no more a part of his new society than he was of his old one. No matter how much his own coterie respected him, Jerome always had something to prove. The feeling had been around since his father told him God wouldn't listen unless he prayed loudly enough to be heard above the congregation. It got worse when Sarah — just 19 — died in Montreal.

Overdose, my ass.

Jerome cried only when alone. He comforted Heidi on the rare occasion she let her guard down and at first, pushed ahead with his cases, doing what everyone expected of him.

■

Heidi had been Jerome's only visitor Down Under, though it was more than a month after Jerome's sentencing that she summoned up the will for her first visit. He couldn't help but notice that she had combined seeing him with a visit to friends in Montreal. She hadn't come to the Don Jail, where he spent two weeks awaiting transfer to the penitentiary, even though it was barely 20 minutes away from their refurbished three-storey Annex home, oversized and empty since Sarah died.

Heidi had wanted to move, but he wouldn't. "Of course you won't, because you'll never move on," she had screamed.

She always moved on, he thought. That's why it was so hard for her to see him in prison. The visitor's drill was especially gruelling: it began when her taxi took her past the barbed wire that topped Milgaard's external fence as far as the internal gates, similarly bedecked; then she'd stand in line in the outdoor cage reserved for waiting guests amongst society she had only read about in books, having silently conspired with Jerome never to burden her with the details of the clients he called "files."

He saw her from the window in the prisoners' holding area adjacent to the cage. Even on this grey day, her sexuality swirled about her like a light wind tugging at a miniskirt, drawing stares that mingled with the hostility due an attractive intruder. The abrupt female guard, whom Jerome knew and disliked, was young enough to be playing peace officer. She forced Heidi to empty and leave behind the contents of her purse, and her newspaper. A second female frisked her, though not as abruptly as he suspected his wife might have wished. He lost sight of her as she went inside.

■

It was another 20 minutes before they let him in. The visitors' room was perfectly square, meant for 40 but holding at least 50, where the non-smokers were the exception by far and all the heated whispers swelled into a roar.

Inmates and visitors must keep their hands above the tables. The words appeared on the small sign on each perfectly square small table as well as on much larger signs at the entrance and on all four walls. A single sign, probably an administrative afterthought, hung on the windows surrounding the glassed-in, raised office looking out on the proceedings: *No more than one inmate or visitor shall sit on one side of a table.* Dutifully, each table had four chairs, one on each side, except for the tables along the walls, which had two or three.

She didn't see him come in, so intent was she on a young couple sitting a few tables away. As Jerome walked silently towards his wife, the woman, about 30, washed but dirty, angled her chair ever so slightly toward her prisoner and much too tightly toward the table. Her partner did the same, leaning back, nonchalantly spreading his legs and arching his hips, now within arm's length of her. She cupped her chin in her hands, her elbows on the chair's armrests. He spoke animatedly, while she said little but shook her head constantly. Agreeing, disagreeing. Like electricity, the motion passed through her right hand and forearm, maneuvering her elbow off the armrest and ever nearer its target's centre of gravity with more grace than this place deserved. The guards, behind the glass answering questions and dealing with visitors, were too busy to notice or too studied in reality to waste their time trying to stop what couldn't be stopped. Prohibition, Jerome had mentioned in one of the letters to which Heidi had not replied, no more deterred ingenuity here than it did in proper society.

It was over in less than a minute. The prisoner smiled. The woman settled back in her chair. Jerome, now behind Heidi, sensed her titillation. It aroused him. Startled by the body she sensed much too close to her, his wife turned to him and for a moment, just long enough to haunt him, failed to recognize him in his greens. She forgot to kiss him, then remembered, shrugging off his bear hug as inappropriate affection here. The long wait at the prison meant she had only two hours to catch the three o'clock to Montreal.

"But visiting doesn't end until 4:30. Isn't there a train after that?" Jerome protested, his first challenge to her since his arrest.

"I don't know."

They touched, by the book, four hands on the table. She surprised him still, inquiring about the details of his confinement, his food, the guards, the other prisoners, exercise, but not asking if he needed anything she could send or bring. She was there, Jerome knew, because standing by him during the harshest part of his sentence was the right thing to do.

They had last made love six weeks before he went to jail, the only time since her lawyer told her about his mistress. It was lovemaking so solitary he felt the need to apologize. "Don't be sorry," she said, without pity, without kindness, without anger. It was then that he knew she was gone. Before that, the loneliness of their infamy — few could distinguish between Heidi's carefree spending and her visceral honesty — had heightened their lovemaking, if only because it was the first time since Sarah's death that Jerome didn't have a paramour or a one-nighter within hailing distance.

Afraid that the police would suspect that Dara was involved in the crime unless he was up front with them, Jerome told them that their relationship went beyond business even before they uncovered the payments he had made to her. Somehow, the media got hold of the information and pounced on it. Jerome speculated that he was paying in spades for building his criminal law practice on the backs of the local press, particularly the *Toronto Standard's* Buddy Ladner, who trumpeted his fall as sensationally as he had his courtroom triumphs.

Worst of all, the revelations snapped the furtive, frail bond of passion that had bound Heidi and Jerome since his arrest.

Heidi drove up to Fairlawn that first summer. She told him she was leaving him. He didn't argue. Still she explained. It wasn't the frauds, she repeated, it was the girlfriend. She didn't trust him. Did she love him? She wouldn't say. He didn't push that either. Later, after she drove off in tears, it occurred to him that she had answered his question. Or maybe he'd answered for her — by lying when she asked him if there were other women before Dara.

He hadn't seen her again. They'd talked once afterwards, when Heidi left a message just after Christmas. Jerome called back. How was he doing? She sounded alone, or he wanted her to. Was he lonely? Jerome was noncommittal, almost offensive in his pride. No woman had ever left him before. She was either relieved or took a hint he didn't mean. After he read about her new boyfriend a few months later in *Toronto Scene*, he could at last imagine how she felt when she learned about Dara; until then, he had been too wrapped up in fear of her leaving to think about it. He had the prison library cancel his subscription and waited for the divorce. It came quickly, robbing him of his most treasured trophy, the one he had so proudly worn on his arm even as Sarah's absence became their incremental divide.

What good does talking do, Jerome? Is there anything new to say?

Heidi reached in. Jerome reached out.

In the spring, just before the first anniversary of his arrival at Fairlawn, five cons couldn't hold down Jerome's six foot, 240 pound frame when he went nuts on the slender, but muscular inmate whose elbow accidentally broke his nose during a pick-up basketball game. Jerome's wild punches drew blood from his surprised opponent's face before his unexpectedly effective pummelling became a vigorous wrestling match. Both combatants were tiring when Jerome — on top of his adversary, his fist raised to the level of his bloody nose and the beginnings of two black eyes — noticed a prison-wise con conscientiously mopping blood from the shiny hardwood floor, removing the evidence before the screws arrived. *Only in the joint.* Jerome laughed out loud, got up and left, leaving his bewildered antagonist muttering at the sudden end to the hostilities: "Crazy bastard."

■

Two years later, the shock of the only fist fight of his life returned as the winter gusts chilled Jerome at the barrier where he waited. After a ubiquitous prison "rat" informed Fairlawn's Warden of the fight, the beleaguered administrator transferred Jerome to Lorimar. It marked the end of easy time. He was either too tired or too depressed to appeal the transfer. His passivity, contraindicated by everything in his files, caused his new keepers to put him on a suicide watch. Lorimar's psychiatrist took one look at him and prescribed 50 milligrams of Zoloft three times daily. Jerome, who usually avoided medication, didn't argue and dutifully took his dose. When the raccoon eyes disappeared, Lorimar's size took Jerome out of the prison's limelight. His unexpected pugilism even endeared him to the solid cons, especially when it turned out that his adversary had testified against accomplices as part of a sweet plea bargain.

Over time, Lorimar became comfortable, like Carlos Castaneda's "spot" on a hard floor, freeing Jerome of the constraints of life as performance. His obsessive helpfulness lost its manipulative edge. He learned to discourage the whiners seeking free legal advice without offending them; instead, he concentrated on his students, who couldn't read and weren't much better at expressing themselves. Shortly after he refused a transfer back to Fairlawn, Jerome noticed that some staff and inmates had taken a liking to him, even appreciated him. He suspected they harboured a fondness they could never articulate. *What a place to get popular.* No matter. It felt good.

That's what made the timing of his offer to Portland so curious and yet so predictable. Whenever Jerome found an anchor, even before Sarah's death, he headed out to a deeper sea.

CHAPTER THREE

WHEN THE EMPTINESS RETURNED, THE IMAGES WERE THE same. Sarah. Fine blond hair like her mother's, almond-shaped eyes like his, summer freckles. *Dad, don't embarrass me.* Or were they dreams? It didn't matter. Emptiness was much more seamless than life. Memories followed the images: of holding the baby girl after ten insufferable days of watching her from behind panes of glass as she struggled with premature birth; of the time she convinced him, with her mother's help, that a curfew was unfair; or the evening just before she left for Europe, when she told him, shyly, that she had spent her first night with a man. Each time, he was proud.

Daddy, do you think I could get 90s at school next year if I tried?

Sure, honey. Why do you ask?

You never pushed me or anything.

You once told me you didn't want to spend your whole life studying.

Yeah.

So why would I push you?

I just needed to know.

The visions of Heidi wouldn't go away either. Visions of the future that brought back the past. Of running into Heidi with a boyfriend and everybody being happy but him. Of finding a place for himself when he went back to the world. At first, the only place he could think of was with Sarah. That's why he had called Adam so many months earlier.

"I need to talk to you. In person."

"It's a long trip. Give me a hint."

"I can help you. Have I ever failed to do what I said I would do since you arrested me?"

Still, Adam seemed less than enthusiastic. Jerome attributed it to the inability of long-distance technology to give sincerity its due. "All right, sometime in the next month or so."

Jerome's plan was simple. Pretend there's hidden money. Go to the drug dealers. Make the deals. Keep the cops informed. Get even with the people who caused Sarah's death.

All he wanted in return was a new identity and a modest start, far enough away to bury the past. Not the formal Witness Protection Program, Jerome explained. Just a social security number, an address, a driver's licence, a passport, and a little money.

"Headquarters will want to know how much money."

"Enough so I don't have to call back, to give me a start."

"Why do you want to do this, Jerome? What's wrong with a normal life?" Portland asked.

"Empty isn't normal."

"Lots of normal lives are empty. Patience fills them up. I thought you said you'd learned patience in here."

"I need to do something. Even if I can't find out what happened to Sarah, I can punish the people who took her away from me."

"Isn't that how you got here in the first place?"

"Stop it, Adam. I've said what I have to say. Are you interested or not?"

"I'll have to check with CID."

"Gunnar Einarson?"

"How do you know Gunnar?"

"Any criminal lawyer who's dealt with CID knows him."

"Well, it's going to be his decision."

"Fine, as long as you make it clear I won't do this unless I'm working through you."

Too many weeks later, Adam called back.

"They're not interested," he said. "To put it bluntly, they think you're nuts. Obsessed. Also, we — you — don't have a plan or a target. Even if they didn't have concerns, they wouldn't know what to do with you, and creativity isn't their strong point. Maybe they'd be more receptive if you could name someone they could sting. Most of all, though, they don't have any kind of a hook on you. You know, something they can hold over your head."

"Did you push it, Adam?"

"I told them what you told me. Besides, I got the feeling they didn't think much of me being involved. I'm not an undercover guy. The intelligence people like to keep things to themselves. They prefer the handlers and the operatives to be a little unfriendly. They probably think you're too comfortable with me."

"Must be Stockholm Syndrome," replied Jerome.

"You need to get out of the joint."

Jerome wasn't a cop-hater, but a decade and a half as a defence lawyer had made him distrustful of police officers. Most were men on a mission, unlike Adam. In a strange way, he had wanted to go undercover for his friend — or else he was too frightened to do it without a friend around.

It wasn't long before Jerome put the idea away. When he had first proposed himself as an police operative, it seemed romantic, exciting, and comfortably vague: there were no real people in his scenario, and besides, he preferred the vagueness of a real but undefined job to the uncertainty of a life spent dredging up purpose. Jerome dehumanized his undercover idea, refusing as usual to face the risks until they materialized.

Now the Mounties wanted him to spy on a friend. But he had become wary of reliving the ugly feelings that came with deceit, sensing that the shadow of rectitude wouldn't make him feel any better about it.

He remembered watching his neighbour on Upper C Range, Unit 12, hunch over the steel desk next to the open toilet in his cell: how could he judge a man who found happiness in cutting pictures from magazines and combining them with his drafting skills to make collages for his daughter? The pictures of Sonia that cluttered the wall above Dirk's desk haunted Jerome almost as much as his own photographs of Sarah. Something of all children is alive in every child.

As their acquaintance touched on friendship, Jerome couldn't hide his feelings about drugs.

"I'm businessman," Dirk insisted, staring down Jerome with the disarmingly wicked smile that cupped his assertive aquiline nose. "I no criminal. I no do different from guys who sell alcohol and tobacco. Soon marijuana legal, later cocaine."

One night in December, when prison's special Christmas melancholy had set in, Dirk called Jerome over to see Sonia's homemade card. Inside, she had taped the last photograph taken of herself and her father, standing with their backs to the Andes at Bogotá's El Dorado airport.

"I'll be waiting at the same place," Sonia had written in Spanish. "Don't work too hard. Merry Christmas. I love you, Papi."

As he showed Jerome the card, Dirk pointed at the back of his head, his eyes welling. "They back here, kids, drugs, but I push away."

Jerome wasn't impressed. "New Year's resolution, Buga?"

Dirk ignored him. "Since when Sonia be born. I learn from my father. But my child, I not want in business. I find my money or make one more deal and then I be OK. Then finish."

One more deal. Hints. Tantalizers. To comradeship. To more conversation in forbidden territory. Jerome didn't answer the call. Still, by the time the Mounties returned with their own offer, Dirk was confiding in him regularly. It would have been easy to give the horsemen the information, filling himself with superficial redemption by working for the good guys and a notion that he was doing something for Sarah.

But the prospect of a daughter without her father was too tough for a man who'd lost his own. So Jerome had said "no" to Portland and his colleagues — recognizing all the while that he had yet to choose between the living and the dead.

■

The barrier moved, unlocking electronically and clanking over an ungreased track like an unruly cavalcade of chained men. The sounds of prison had become white noise to Jerome, like the smell of disinfectant to hospital people.

"Want the paper, Jerome?" the guard asked. "It's uncut."

Uncut newspapers or magazines were rare in prison. Junior custodians routinely combed inmates' subscriptions for copy that might affect the "peace and good order of the institution." That meant any news or commentary relating to the prison system, even the Chinese prison system; the decisions of appeal courts; crimes or cases involving sex offenders or informers; and ads for "deviant movies." Also anything else that didn't appeal to the scrutineers, which they promptly tossed in the trash, reasoning correctly that inmates wouldn't bother to grieve the censorship if they didn't know what they were missing.

Jerome took the paper through the pass-through without looking at it, waved to the guard, and walked straight ahead towards the two-storey, grey structures that comprised the housing for 700 inmates. He walked slowly, deliberately, his hands locked behind him, the newspaper in his armpit, welcoming the privacy and now even the cold air that rushed down the artificial wind tunnel, clearing his mind. Shadows danced at the entrance to the recreation complex. Probably the inmate set-up crew waiting to get into the gym; they reminded Jerome he had a racquetball game with Dirk in a couple of hours.

Dirk was lonely. Almost six years had passed since he last saw his family. Juliana, wary of leaving Colombia after her husband's arrest, was still in Bucaramanga with Sonia.

"If Juliana arrested, Sonia orphan," Dirk said.

Dirk had known Juliana when they were both kids. Emilio, her old man, supplied the Colombian marijuana that Dirk's father, a Dutch-born Canadian national who was the South American manufacturer's representative for a number of Western European construction equipment companies, first shared with his friends and then sold in Europe on his business trips. By the time Leon met Jenni, Dirk's mother, on a ski vacation to Bariloche, he had discovered that selling marijuana and cocaine smoothed out the havoc of an industry plagued by unstable and corrupt South American economies. Bucaramanga, Jenni's home, fit conveniently into his plans, as did the Colombian passport he eventually acquired for himself and Dirk to go with their Canadian papers.

Supplying dope was also a sideline for Emilio, who realized that the cartels wouldn't tolerate any expansion of his business beyond the direct sales of high-quality product his half-dozen agents made to the very upper echelons of European society. Leon became Emilio's best agent, then his best friend. As the kids — both only children — moved into the family business, romance and marriage merged neatly. Juliana was Dirk's equal from the beginning, keeping the circle tight in the time-honoured way.

In 1991, Pablo Escobar, drug lord of the Medellín cartel, surrendered to authorities. He subsequently escaped, but in the interim, the Cali cartel, Escobar's arch-rivals, stepped up to challenge the Medellíns as the world's premier cocaine traffickers. After a Colombian SWAT team gunned down Escobar in December 1993, the Calis' challenge became a rout, especially after the Pepes — the acronym for People Persecuted by Pablo Escobar — switched sides, retaliating for Escobar's wholesale, paranoid purge of his own organization as the end neared.

When the infighting ended, the Calis controlled over 80 percent of Colombian drug exports, valued in the tens of billions. Now a virtual monopoly, they were unwilling to tolerate the activities of even the smallest independent dealers. Dirk and Juliana found their profits incrementally squeezed by the cut the local Calis demanded, and he had the temerity to object when his oppressors sought yet another raise.

"Go home and tell your bosses to think about the respect my family maintains in this community," he told the collector.

Three days later, his new Mercedes blew up barely a minute

before he got into it. Even as he watched the pyre, the collector arrived on the scene.

"That car was five days old," Dirk fumed, covering his shock. His family had prided itself on avoiding the drug violence.

"Thank God nobody was in it," the collector answered.

Dirk and Juliana paid, that night, delivering the money themselves. But from that moment on, they focused on getting out of the country. With the passing of Juliana's mother, there was little in the way of family to keep them there.

Canada was the natural choice for their new home. Neither Dirk nor Juliana had convictions or arrests, and he was confident that, with a few properly placed bribes, Colombia's foreign office would omit any suspicions from their report to Canadian authorities. In the end, he and his family would be among the small number lucky enough to escape the chaos in their country.

Getting the family's money out was another matter. The Canadian authorities knew full well that few residents of Colombia could have amassed his family's fortune without some degree of participation in the drug trade. Even if he could convince them otherwise, he and Juliana would be under a microscope, their worldwide assets always subject to seizure under Canada's new laundering laws unless they could account for virtually every cent they spent after entering the country. Sonia's future might be safer, but no more secure, than in Colombia.

Their money had to be washed. With time running out on them, Dirk sought help from an old client in Luxembourg who also happened to be his banker.

"There is a man in Toronto, a lawyer, who can help you, Dirk," Ludwig said, in perfect Spanish. "But he is very professional, very circumspect. I know that he will not take your money unless you prove to him by deeds, not words, that it is indeed money that needs washing."

"Can't you tell him that for me?"

"I do not know him or his name."

"So what do I have I do?"

"I do not know the details of such matters. But I can give you a contact who will make the arrangements."

Dirk met the contact, an urbane young lady who went straight to the point without exchanging pleasantries, not even her name. She also spoke perfect Spanish. He guessed she was Ludwig's protegé.

"We must establish your good faith before we can handle your money. You may do that only by delivering a sufficient quantity of a product to be agreed upon that assures our contact you could not possibly be an agent of the authorities. Two and a half million American dollars is our minimum requirement. When we agree on the nature of the product, the amount, and the price, you must arrange for the delivery to Canada. Before the shipment departs, Ludwig will advise you that an appropriate escrow deposit has been made."

"What is my guarantee of your principal's good faith?"

"Ludwig. He cannot afford to offend his clients."

"And then?"

"Then you must go to Canada. Once there, you will confirm your presence with the recipient of the goods by calling a pre-arranged telephone number. Arrangements will be made for you to meet the man who will see your money safely to his country."

"I need time."

"The schedule is up to you."

"And how do I reach you then?"

She produced a typewritten card.

"You will not reach me. Here is a telephone number and a password. When you are ready, call the number and leave only the password. Someone will contact you."

Dirk and Juliana, anxious not to alert the cartel to their plan, amassed cocaine slowly, moving it to Europe without selling it. At home, they carried on business as usual, continuing the extortionist payments to the Calis. Without the income from sales, they used up almost a third of their cash. Eventually, however, they had three million dollars worth of cocaine ready to ship. They deposited several millions more with Ludwig, to be washed with the proceeds of the shipment.

Using his cover as a civil engineer and his Canadian citizenship, Dirk sent some outdated drilling equipment for customs clearance at Toronto's Pearson International Airport. A routine check on the recipient revealed that Holland Drilling Company's phone was out of service. The follow-up letter also came back: Dirk's customers had closed down their shadow operation without telling him. When the dogs didn't turn up anything, custom officers opened the boxes to find the cocaine sealed in hollowed-out drill bits. The Mounties, certain that someone would call about the prize sooner or later, had Bell hook up the original number, which they promptly tapped. When Dirk called, a female officer kept him occupied long enough to let the horsemen trace him to a pay phone at the airport, where on-duty customs officers arrested him as he left the booth.

Ludwig disassociated himself from Dirk immediately on learning of his arrest. And Juliana's attempts to contact Ludwig to get their money back precipitated an anonymous phone call threatening Sonia with dismemberment if she or Dirk did anything that might connect Ludwig to them.

Dirk told Jerome the story.

"I know is great risk," he said by way of explanation as to why he followed his delivery. "But I trust Ludwig many years. He trust me."

That Dirk felt compelled to explain made Jerome suspicious. Lies, he had learned, lose their cover when liars feel compelled to replace the uncorrupted faith of the listener with logic. The declining popularity of religious orthodoxy, Jerome thought, was the best example of that.

What was clear was that the cops were keeping tabs on Dirk.

"He's just someone I do things with in here. Soul-baring is the first no-no in the joint," Jerome told them.

"Sure, sure," said Yu. "You two spend all day together in the school, where you recommended your buddy be hired. Tennis and racquetball three or four times a week, with coffee right after, just the two of you, from 8:30 till lockup, always in your cell."

Ritual Nescafé on Candid Camera.

"We drink tea."

During the infrequent, monitored overseas calls permitted by CSC regulations, Dirk explained to Sonia, now eight, that her father was working far away, a lie that became ever more precarious as the little girl's eyes opened to the world.

"Don't worry, Dirk, you're her dad," Jerome said. "Sonia will believe what she has to as long as she has to."

"And if not?"

"She'll forgive you," said Jerome, unable to foreclose a comparison with Heidi's hasty retreat.

As a non-violent offender, Dirk was also eligible for early parole. But as a Canadian citizen with roots abroad, he was in a double bind. Canada couldn't deport him; as an escape risk who would be closely supervised, however, he would not be allowed to travel beyond the limits of Greater Toronto, let alone abroad. Without the cash to hire intermediaries, his situation made it virtually impossible for him to try to get his money back from Ludwig before his parole was up. And, as he well knew, getting it back after twelve more years, when his 18-year sentence expired, was a lost cause. His only recourse was to find the Canadian with whom Ludwig had promised to connect him.

To be sure, the authorities would allow his wife and child to join him, for humanitarian reasons. But even if Juliana tried to bring only what she still controlled — roughly four million dollars after selling their Colombian assets — into Canada, the feds could seize the money as suspect proceeds and ask questions later.

Meanwhile, their funds were quickly dissipating. On his arrest, their clientele would have disappeared, even if Juliana could have arranged for delivery on her own. But the cartel, which Juliana was still paying, would demand their due indefinitely. Dirk was desperate to retrieve his money and find a way to launder it quickly or at worst launder what was left.

But how? Ludwig was his only real connection to the world of money laundering: independents like Dirk and Juliana eschewed complex business arrangements, preferring to keep enormous amounts of cash stashed in safety deposit boxes all over the world, with the rest in numbered accounts in various safe havens. When, after a time, Dirk learned Jerome's story, it occurred to him that the ex-lawyer might be able to help.

Grey-haired in a way that suited his merchant sailor looks, and with a Master's degree in engineering, Dirk was charming in his roughness, witty, well travelled, well read, and cosmopolitan to the core. Though his thick accent and broken English made him hard to understand sometimes, Dirk was an irresistible commodity for Jerome, companionship that made the difference between dead time and a real life behind the walls.

Yet, even as Dirk's story leaked out by measures, letting Jerome know that he trusted him and could be trusted, the drugs kept Jerome at a distance. To be sure, his own crime had repelled him without deterring him; but after he did it, it digested his life. He had always been scrupulously honest — he even paid taxes on the proceeds of the crime — and to the astonishment of cynical customs officers, he always declared *everything*, even foreign editions of *Time* magazine, when he returned to Canada from trips abroad. *There's more to the criminal than the crime.* It was lame, but it sounded good, which was all Jerome needed to deceive himself. "You don't think the natural laws apply to you, do you?" Heidi had once observed.

After Sarah died, they did. He faked it pretty well for a while. But the drive and flair that had earned Jerome his high profile, high-paying white-collar criminal practice never came back. Accustomed to a lawyer who took all his cases to the wall, the Crown Attorneys saw it first, barely ahead of his clients, and the judges couldn't help but notice when the plea bargains started coming early and the acquittals stopped coming at all.

To the judges and lawyers, Sarah's death was explanation enough. But clients were a more suspicious lot, and word that illegal drugs were involved in Sarah's death spread quickly. A lawyer so touched by crime, Jerome's clients believed, was tainted, someone who could not preserve the moral neutrality required of criminal counsel doing their job properly. The irony, Jerome told Portland while reading over his confession, was that society had specifically entrusted lawyers with the job of preserving citizens' rights, only to castigate them when they did it too well or not selectively enough.

Jerome's income dropped severely, but he and Heidi could have managed except for the time and money that went into finding out the truth about Sarah's death. *What truth, Jerome? She screwed up or we screwed up. Live with it. Live with me.*

Jerome began spending his off-hours, then his office hours, investigating his daughter's life. His clients now waited hours for him to show up for appointments and days for him to return his telephone calls. With increasing frequency, he did neither.

When his preoccupation finally outpaced the time he could give it, he turned to Dara, the ex-cop turned private investigator who had done a good job fleshing out alibis or dirt on prosecution witnesses for him. Throughout, he insisted on paying her as if she was working on a client's file. Not admitting until it was too late that Jerome was her real fixation, his obsession became hers — though if she had thought about it or been asked, she would have said that he wasn't her type and that she certainly wasn't his. He was a man who, one way or the other, lived in the spotlight; she preferred to hide behind the aspidistra at cocktail parties.

The loneliness of his perseverance attracted her. She didn't do anything about it, though, until they were alone in his office one night, huddled again over the police files on Sarah. Frustrated by their lack of progress, he told her, on his way to the bathroom, that he wished he could move on with his life as Heidi had. When he returned, she was sitting on the couch, wrapped in the fulsome throw he kept there. He couldn't tell if she was dressed underneath it, but having to guess told him plainly what his choices were.

He never once told her he loved her. She felt better once she realized that Sarah, not Heidi, was their firewall. So she contented herself with the sex that soothed him and what Jerome called their "quest," saying it as if his daughter were still alive.

It ended with his arrest. It wasn't as if there was nothing but sex and Sarah between them. It was just that Sarah was their matrix, as her death was Heidi and Jerome's milieu. But that's not what Jerome told Dara. *I can't cheat on Heidi anymore.*

If he were honest, he would have told her that he was afraid.

■

A flood of light smoothed the shadows in the breezeway as the set-up crew entered the gym. *Rec up in ten minutes,* the loudspeakers blared. In no mood to socialize as he neared the living units, Jerome lowered his eyes to the front page of the newspaper.

Below the fold was a report of John Felderhof's violent death. Felderhof, a prominent but low-key immigration specialist known to the bar as a "lawyer's lawyer," had been shot in the underground garage of the Royal Trust Tower at the Toronto Dominion Centre. Police were looking for Paula Maydek, Felderhof's former secretary. After ten years of service, Felderhof had fired the 33-year-old single mother of two for "erratic behavior" and refused to give her a reference, meaning that she would never work for a prominent law firm again.

"It's crazier out there than it is in here," Jerome thought, just as the gym door closed and revived the shadows.

"Hey, maggot."

Jerome turned to the voice behind him, unsure of its object.

"Give *this* to Gunnar, you rat."

A blow to the back of his head from a flat metal instrument removed Jerome's doubt about the target of the insult. A second blow, a little further forward on Jerome's skull as he fell, removed him from his senses.

CHAPTER FOUR

THE HAWK HATED THE CITY HALL BEAT, ESPECIALLY WITH SUMMER coming on; he got out a lot more in his last job. After a decade covering big-city crime, Buddy Ladner had relished the promotion, his reward for two national best-sellers — though like most things Canadian, they hadn't made him rich.

But after a time, Buddy found that he disliked the posturing and the repetitiveness of the political cycle: he had been hoping to write about issues, but politics, like crime, was all about people. He liked people, all right. It was just that, after a while, cops and robbers seemed more real than politicians, who, Buddy thought, were sometimes further removed from their constituents than criminals were from their victims.

He wasn't about to complain, though — at least not to his colleagues at the Press Club. Half of them, it seemed, had lost their jobs or were on thin ice. Ironically, it was the thriftiness of the times that had allowed Buddy to keep tabs on Wyndham. When the paper moved him to City Hall soon after the lawyer was jailed, they let him follow the story — provided he waived his overtime.

The restriction wasn't burdensome, because Jerome had steadfastly refused interviews since his arrest. And except for the black eyes, there hadn't been much to report since Buddy finished his three-part series after the sentencing. But Jerome was coming up for parole soon.

The ex-lawyer's low profile went against the man's grain, thought Ladner, recalling Wyndham's bitter, flamboyant battles with prosecutors and police. Jerome had shocked Buddy by pleading guilty and accepting a lengthy sentence with barely a whimper. Still, he couldn't imagine Wyndham broke.

"No one ever explained why Wyndham stole the money. The statement of agreed facts that the Crown read at his sentencing said he got into financial trouble by overspending. Unexplained over-spending means a stash to a lot of people," Buddy told Portland a few months after Jerome was sentenced. They were having a beer at The Bombay Club, not far from the nondescript offices the RCMP occupied in downtown Toronto.

"Money is one thing," Portland replied. "Attention is another. Sometimes these guys have to spend all the money they steal to get the attention they stole it for in the first place. But Wyndham doesn't fit in either category. He was — he still is — like an alcoholic. His daughter's the booze and it's the only thing that talks to him."

"Is that an excuse to you, Adam?" Buddy asked.

"No. No more than alcohol or drugs or compulsive gambling or whatever brings crime on. But it's a reason."

"It never came up in the sentencing. Wouldn't it have saved him at least a couple of years?"

"When I asked him about his daughter, he told me that it was per-sonal, it had nothing to do with his crimes, and would I please respect his privacy. It was pretty clear — this conversation's off the record, right?"

"Of course."

"Everybody who worked in the criminal courts knew about her death, and pretty well everyone knew what it was doing to his prac-tice. The report we had from the forensic accountants confirmed that most of his overspending went to that obsession even while his income was disappearing, but Wyndham insisted that we keep the forensic report under wraps. He said — it was the first time I'd seen him come even close to losing his cool after his arrest — that if the report leaked to the media or if his daughter's name came up even once, there was no deal."

"What about the money that went through his trust account, and Lewis's disappearance? It's suspicious, no?"

"It is. But we haven't been able to find anything that suggests Wyndham has a stash."

"You haven't been able to find Lewis either."

"True enough."

"So Adam, do *you* think Wyndham has something put away for his old age?"

"I think I believe Wyndham — but I want to, so who knows?"

■

If the motive were as simple as the crime, it was undetectable for the same reason. In an uncharacteristically personal moment on the squash court that surprised even Scott Lewis, his longtime early-morning playing partner, Jerome, who had been losing more than his usual share of their matches, confided his preoccupation with the financial pressures that followed on the disintegration of his practice. A few weeks later, at the club, Lewis nonchalantly asked Jerome to notarize affidavits supported by the rental stream printouts the trust company wanted to remortgage his properties.

"I don't know anything about real estate, Scott. When I was an articling student, they took me out of the rotation after I spent two hours in the wrong line at the Registry Office."

"You don't have to know anything. You're just witnessing my signature."

"I know that, but look at all this shit. It's a lot to read. And I'm not sure I'd ask the right questions before signing the affidavits."

"Don't you have malpractice insurance?"

"Why don't you just take it to your regular lawyer?"

"He went on holiday after he drafted this stuff. I've got to get these documents in today. Do me a favour, Jerome. How long have we known each other?"

Long enough for me to avoid socializing with you. But you're a hell of a squash player.

"I couldn't do it now even if I wanted to. My notarial seal's in the office. Come by at lunchtime, oneish. I'll tell Gwen to expect you."

■

Lewis was waiting when Jerome arrived at 1:45.

"Sorry, Scottie. The judge gave us the choice of going late on a bail hearing or coming back in the afternoon. But now I can give you a little time."

Two hours and more than a few unanswered questions later, Lewis couldn't or wouldn't produce the leases supporting the rental figures.

"I need to see them," Jerome said. "The mortgage advances are based on the leases. What's the cap rate these days? Last time I looked, every dollar of rent translated to $100 of funding."

"Not quite, but I'll give you $10 of every extra hundred for every deal we do."

A few seconds passed before Jerome reacted.

"What are you saying? If you're saying what I think you're saying, I didn't hear you. And if you're saying what I think you're saying, get the fuck out of here. And call the club and cancel our next game."

"I'd think about it, Jerome," Lewis replied. "The phone hasn't exactly been ringing off the hook, and I'll bet there's nobody waiting outside."

"I told Gwen to hold my calls. Get out."

There was no one in reception.

■

Jerome was still furious when the phone in his office rang a few minutes later.

"Didn't I ask you to hold my calls?"

"It's Dara."

"Put her on."

"Am I interrupting?" Dara asked, in the way mistresses do to remind themselves and their lovers of their respective places.

"No, no, I'm alone. How'd things go in Montreal?"

"Sorry, nothing," she said cheerlessly. "But there are a lot of bills in the mail."

"I'll get them from you at your place tonight. I'm glad you're back."

"You mean that?"

"Around seven, then."

■

Jerome needed a drink, an urge he rarely had. But he didn't keep any liquor in his office. Later he would reflect that it would have been better if he had had a few before Scott called back that same afternoon.

"Sorry about that business," he said. "Let's play Friday."

"How about 15 percent?"

Lewis replied as if Jerome had agreed at the outset.

"You're on. What about the squash?"

"Bring the documents here about an hour before our game," Jerome said. "But just one thing, Scott. What if the trust company asks for the leases?"

"For the extra five percent, you'll draft what we need."

He did it once, pocketing enough money to get by for a while after paying down his overdrawn operating line and the second mortgage he'd taken on the house over Heidi's objections. It wasn't enough to merit twelve years, but Lewis's much larger share of the proceeds passed through his trust account, and he looked the other way as he followed his client's direction to distribute the mortgage funds to a series of numbered companies.

When Lewis approached him for a second round, he had already decided that he wouldn't do it again. On the verge of believing that no life was better than the one he didn't have, he almost turned himself in, stopping only when he realized that prison would end his search for Sarah.

Lewis was incensed when Jerome refused to help him out again, but there wasn't much he could do about it and it didn't deter him. The New Economy's attachment to digital facsimiles made it easy for Lewis to reuse Jerome's letterhead and duplicates of his signature over and over, cheating several institutions of millions more.

The roof fell in when Ali Sood, a management trainee with one of the trust companies Lewis was victimizing, took it upon himself to scrutinize each file's loan conditions while reorganizing the institution's real estate portfolio. Ali's initiative was in keeping with his upper middle-class origins in Srinigar, where he had worked in his family's successful export-import business before the violence in Kashmir led them to emigrate.

On discovering that none of the commercial leases submitted by Lewis had been independently verified, Sood ignored his manager's signature at the bottom of the page and telephoned one of the commercial tenants for confirmation. The tenant had never heard of Lewis or his building.

When news of the arrests broke, few distinguished Wyndham from Lewis. Just about everybody who read the newspapers assumed that Jerome, because he was a lawyer and because the proceeds of the first fraud passed through his trust account, knew exactly where Lewis was and that Jerome had been or would be well rewarded for taking the rap while his partner in crime celebrated in some remote hideaway.

■

Only the languid bluegrass of Alison Krauss coming from the MP3 player he had in his pocket had curbed Buddy's restlessness throughout the long evening. It was after midnight and Council still hadn't reached the agenda item he was covering. That meant another night away from the kids on Thursday. But this beat wasn't nearly as hard on the family as police hours had been, the Hawk told himself as he neared the media's watering hole a few short blocks from City Hall. And with Helen teaching piano at home, the girls got plenty of attention. On the weekends, he contentedly played housefather, quietly ensuring a harmonious future with his children by exposing them to as many sporting events as he could get away with. It was working: Hannah, eight, could argue the merits of the Raptors' starting five, and six-year-old Laura knew the Maple Leafs' roster by heart. But now, as after every Council meeting, a drink was in order.

His regular haunt, in the basement of one of the few older buildings left in downtown Toronto that hadn't been renovated, had served the media as a *de facto* press club for years. The recession had interrupted plans to move the venerable institution, leaving it as one of the rare out-of-fashion places where Buddy could escape the stifling chic of a city desperately trying to be New York. Like his colleagues, Buddy cherished the club's shabbiness as an antidote to lives spent hunting the new in the news. There, stuffed with liquid courage and unfettered by the filters of their trade, they talked about what interested them most — the things they couldn't print or broadcast.

Buddy picked his way through the protective cobwebs of the narrow staircase. Inside the crowded room with the low-hung ceiling and supporting pillars that made navigation an adventure, he wound his way to the bar, slowed by the chit-chat compulsory for arrivals. The bartender, without being asked, put a Blue in front of him. In minutes, Morris, his mentor at the *Standard*, waved him over: an unwritten rule said no one could drink alone.

"How'd it go tonight, Hawk?"

Buddy stood by the table with his Blue, looking around for a chair.

"Waste of time . . . I'm telling you," he said as he pointed to an empty chair on the other side of the room. The woman sitting beside it nodded.

"I wish I'd known you were coming over," said Morris, as Buddy squeezed the chair between the *Standard*'s reigning bisexual letch and Tony, young but a veteran photographer and Morris's latest preoccupation.

"Why? Planning to repay that 50 bucks you owe me?"

"I'd have brought that envelope over," said Morris — somewhat seriously, Buddy thought, noting the number of empty pitchers on the table.

"What envelope?" Buddy asked.

"I wouldn't even have mentioned it this late, because you'll see it in the morning, on your desk. But it does say 'urgent.'"

"Urgent started and ended with the Council meeting," Buddy laughed, settling down to his beer.

"I don't know. It's on your desk, not in your mail slot."

"Our ultra-efficient internal mail service probably sent it to the wrong person again and he put it on my desk."

"Maybe, but it doesn't have your name on it and it's not open . . . I think."

"From staff, then."

"Maybe. Must be some kind of joke, though."

"Why do you say that?" Tony asked, trying to keep the conversation going despite Buddy's lack of involvement.

"Our reference numbers don't start with 'FPS,'" Morris replied. "'FPS' and then a bunch of numbers. Beats me."

"Say that again?" said Buddy, suddenly awake.

"FPS something. That's what's on the envelope."

Buddy grabbed his coat.

"What the hell is FPS? Must be a big deal to make you abandon your beer," Morris said.

Buddy exchanged a smile with Tony. "It's all yours, Morris. 'FPS' is 'fingerprint system.' Cons' numbers. See you tomorrow."

■

Normally, Buddy would gladly have taken the 15-minute walk to the *Standard*'s new building by the harbour, especially after an evening sitting in City Hall gallery's uncomfortable chairs. But it was now raining and he was immersed in the urgency that always attended him when he sensed he was about to break a story. Cabs weren't easy to come by in the financial district this late, and he'd have taken the car if Council night hadn't coincided with Hannah's softball game somewhere in the boonies. He was more than a little wet when he arrived at the *Standard*, but felt better when he saw a tow truck hooking up a small vehicle whose unfortunate owner — likely from out of town — was unaware that the busy drop-off zone in front of the building was a favourite target for the towers who lurked around the corner.

No passerby could have missed the red magic marker invitation to curiosity over the entire front of the sealed, legal-size manila envelope that leaned upright against Buddy's computer screen.

URGENT

FPS 8 0 2 3 8 9 C

Buddy turned the envelope over. The same characters, in the same style and print, stared at him from the other side. Maybe Morris was pulling a fast one, getting even for the time Buddy produced a phony mock-up of one of his columns, edited just enough to drive Morris to the publisher in a rage. But the equally cryptic characters on the index card in the oversized envelope, its only contents, didn't help Buddy decide either way:

TNT 430486–51721

He stared at the envelope and the card until his legs ached, then sank into his chair, comfortable only because it was so well worn. Buddy knew that the FPS system was how the police, CSC, and the

Parole Board identified prisoners and parolees. But the second number meant nothing to him.

Aimlessly, Buddy examined the envelope again, inside and out, then the index card, with no idea what he was looking for. On a whim, he called 31 Division.

"Is it important, Hawk?" asked the dispatcher, who remembered Buddy from the old days. "Shane's putting together a lineup. He's been on that Scarborough murder since early this morning."

"Yeah, it's very important, darling."

"Same old Hawk."

Inspector Shane Whiteside was as friendly as always. "You need something, don't you? And I bet you need it right away."

Buddy tried to stay casual. "Ah, you know me. Everything makes me anxious."

"You're never friendly for nothing. You're too busy for friends. What do you want? I have ten seconds."

"That's all it should take for you to punch up this number on CPIC."

"Wait a second. I'm not at my desk."

On hold now, Buddy wished that City Hall had something like CPIC to keep track of politicians.

Whiteside came back on the telephone. "You know fucking well who that number belongs to, you old whore," he boomed. "What's going on? Did Wyndham escape or something?"

"I didn't know it was him," said Buddy, after a moment's pause.

"My ass, you didn't. Either you let me know what's going on or I call Portland right now. I told him to keep an eye on that guy. The money's got to turn up somewhere."

"What money?"

"The money you've been trying to find so you can win the Pulitzer."

"The Pulitzer's American."

"Even better. What else have you got?"

Buddy winced as he looked at the index card. Only his distaste for the generally accepted, which had contributed significantly to his journalistic reputation, muted his enthusiasm for the "stash" theories that were floating around. Still, he'd never abandoned his preoccupation with Wyndham and a crime he couldn't understand. *Or forgive if it comes right down to it.*

"You still there?" Whiteside growled.

"Nothing right now. Don't waste your time. I'll tell Adam myself."

"Fine. If anyone asks, remember I asked. You owe me a double. Soon." Whiteside hung up.

Buddy had never quite come to terms with the dividing line between journalistic scoops and good citizenship. In the early days, his reputation for hare-brained ideas left him free for frolics of his own; he lost his independence when the police started paying attention to him. Finally, he decided that if he wasn't sure and it didn't endanger anyone or screw up an investigation, the police could read about it in the newspaper. This was one of those times, he decided, just quickly enough to leave him uneasy about his decision.

■

Buddy arrived at First Canadian Place early the next morning, before the rush-hour queues formed at the skyscraper's elevator banks. Barry Northrop, the Executive Director of the Canadian Lenders Association, liked doing his paperwork before the phones started ringing. Not wishing to disturb that habit, Buddy hadn't bothered calling. He was betting that Northrop, whom he had featured in his series on Wyndham, would remember him. *Thank God for the flattering photograph.* Too many people blamed writers for "inaccurate reporting" to hide their discomfort over their pictures.

The doors to the stately offices, unchanged since he was last there, were open. The receptionist's chair, pushed away from the enormous mahogany desk, said that she was in, but elsewhere on the premises. He was tired enough to enjoy a few minutes of rest.

On his return to their small house in Toronto's Cabbagetown, Buddy had scanned the Internet. His search for a foreign bank that matched the TNT on the index card was fruitless. At dawn, he'd nodded off at his computer, awakening only when Baxter, the aging basset hound that Helen claimed was the true love of Buddy's life, decided to express his annoyance at Buddy's absence from the conjugal bedroom where he also slept. After breakfast, Buddy managed a few minutes alone with Helen to tell her about the envelope. A music teacher whose interests leaned to the abstract, Helen invariably provided a fresh perspective on the mysteries of human nature that rooted Buddy's incessant curiosity.

When he left the house that morning, Buddy took an uncharacteristic look in the full-length mirror by the front door. He was purposefully dressed in his only suit, a pinstripe job that belayed his daily habit of sports jackets. *If Northrop doesn't remember me, maybe he'll remember the suit.*

Fifteen minutes went by before anyone appeared.

"I'm so sorry, sir," said the middle-aged woman. "There were no appointments scheduled until ten o'clock this morning." Her emphasis on the "o" in "o'clock" restored the formality dislodged by her absence from her post.

"That's quite all right. I don't have one," Buddy said. *Quite all right. Can't believe I said that. Must be the suit.*

"Well, then, how may I help you?" the receptionist said in a pleasant tone devoid of interest.

"I'm with the *Standard*," Buddy replied as he presented his credentials. "I'd like to see Mr. Northrop, if that's at all possible."

"Was he expecting you, Mr. Ladner?" she said, returning his identification with even less interest than before.

"No. I was hoping he'd see me. I need his help for a story I'm doing."

"Oh, then you wish to interview him for the newspaper."

"Yes."

"Would you mind waiting?"

"Of course not." *Two minutes with this woman and I miss City Hall.* Buddy paced while he waited, staring blankly on and off at the appropriately Canadian art on the wall, about which he knew nothing, except that he liked animals and trees. Besides, for some reason, exhibitors and collectors always hung Canadian art too high, at least in Toronto and at least from the perspective of a five-foot-six reporter with short man's syndrome.

Northrop's prompt appearance signalled the man's expectations. "Mr. Ladner, what a pleasure to see you again."

"Likewise."

"How may we help you today?"

Two croissants and a cappuccino, to go. Keenly aware that Jerome Wyndham was the first thing people who knew about the case thought of when they met him, Buddy chose his words carefully.

"I was hoping that your organization might be able to help me with some information."

"Nothing confidential, I hope?"

"Of course not, Mr. North —"

"Barry," Northrop insisted.

"Of course not, Barry. You were clear about that the last time we talked."

"Regarding Mr. Wyndham, I presume."

Don't you mean Jerome?

What Buddy had wanted to talk about the last time he interviewed Northrop was about how members of his organization had managed to fuck things up so badly. *If someone at Terra Nova Trust had made even one phone call to a tenant to check out Lewis's leases, Lewis and Wyndham would have been history, and a lot of people would still have their savings. But when Helen and I needed that second mortgage for the addition to the house so she could quit that stupid music store job and teach at home, the loans officer just about asked us to donate our organs while we were still alive.*

"Excuse me, Mr. Northrop," the receptionist said. "The gentleman you've been trying to reach at the Bank of Canada is on the line."

"I'll take the call in my office. Buddy, would you mind waiting here for just another few minutes?"

Buddy did mind, but he didn't let on. Northrop's casual disdain for his time brought to mind how callously Terra Nova Trust had treated Ali: after the company discovered the extent of its losses, Ali had been among the first employees laid off, and with a minimal severance package. "Those bastards gave new meaning to killing the messenger," Buddy thought.

He still got great satisfaction from his exposé of the company's mismanagement and Ali's firing. The story pressured Terra Nova into a generous settlement of Ali's wrongful dismissal suit. *Now that was a story. I'll bet the severance was the biggest a lowly clerk ever got from a bank.*

Tired of standing, Buddy moved to one of the upholstered armchairs opposite the receptionist. He had no interest in the business-oriented magazines in front of him or the morning newspapers he'd read on the way downtown. Restless, he opened his steno pad and began an outline of the points he wanted to cover with Northrop. It was a waste of time. Buddy wasn't inclined to structured interviews. He got as far as writing "Terra Nova Trust" before he took to doodling. He double-underlined the heading, then shaded in the "a's" and the "e's" before circling the capitalized letters. He was still wondering what suitable turn of phrase he could coin from the acronym "TNT" when the obvious hit him.

TNT. . . *Terra Nova Trust . . . No way! Oh, Jesus! Who'd have thought Wyndham would stash his dough with one of the companies Lewis robbed?*

But it didn't make sense. Although Terra Nova was only a minor player in the scheme of things, its losses were disproportionate to its capitalization. An ongoing recession, the bad press over Ali and the cost of his severance only hastened its collapse, though not before Ali got his settlement. Federal deposit insurance only covered the first $60,000, so most large depositors and investors lost a lot of money. If Wyndham had a stash at Terra Nova, it was gone, victim to his own crimes.

"No, no, no. No goddamn way," Buddy thought out loud, smacking his temple with the base of his hand just as Northrop returned.

"Oh!" the receptionist exclaimed, but unaccustomed to speaking out of turn, caught herself and blushed. "Excuse me."

Buddy stood up, and with one hand still supporting the back of his neck, took the crook of the banker's arm and led him through the doors to the inner office. Northrop, lost whenever the barest element of his everyday existence ebbed, complied meekly.

"Mr. Northrop . . ."

"Barry, please."

"I'm sorry, Mr. Northrop. Barry."

"It's quite all right. Is anything wrong?"

"No, nothing, nothing at all. I just need a little bit of help from you. It won't take a minute. Let's step into your office."

"I usually hold my meetings in the conference room, Mr. Ladner."

"Buddy."

"Buddy."

Northrop led the reporter into a large room where at least 30 chairs stood around an oblong table. "I thought we might be more comfortable here."

"That's fine," Buddy said, taking the index card from his jacket pocket. He showed the notation to Northrop.

"Any idea what that means?"

"No, I'm sorry," Northrop answered.

"What about TNT by itself?"

"Dynamite, perchance?"

"That's very funny."

"Humour rescues us in many situations, you know, Buddy."

"Not this one, at least not so far. Do you remember Terra Nova Trust?"

"Naturally. I see what you mean. But it no longer exists. Perhaps your information refers to a driver's licence number or other public identification," Northrop volunteered. "Are you going to quote me?"

"No, Barry, it's off the record. Not for attribution or print. I just need some help. But with your permission, I'll be glad to give you and your organization proper credit if this leads anywhere. Maybe we could use the same picture."

"Delighted, Buddy, delighted."

"I was wondering," showing Northrop the card again, "whether the numbers alone could be a bank account number or transit number or anything to do with financial institutions."

"I am of course only qualified to comment on the Canadian banking system." Buddy's hand returned to the back of his neck.

"And in that context, I do not recognize the number sequence or pattern."

"What about another context? Any context?"

"As I told . . ."

"I know, you're only qualified about Canadian banking institutions. Let's deal with the letters again. What makes you so sure TNT can't refer to Terra Nova Trust?"

"Because our former member no longer exists, and because our former member was never officially identified by that acronym."

"Says who?"

"Those who care to identify the financial institution correctly."

"What about 430046 alone? A transit number?"

"No. Even if it was a transit number, it would refer to a Schedule A chartered bank, not a trust company."

"How about an account number?"

"Alone, 51721 could be an account number. Together, the numbers are too long."

"What kind of account?"

"Probably savings."

"Probably?"

"Someone familiar with the system would be able to help you better. Someone at a financial institution."

"Can you give me a name?"

Northrop, who to this point had called up images of uncomfortable defendants under close cross-examination, stood fully upright.

"I would prefer to place a call in advance, Mr. Ladner. You were instrumental in effecting a precedent-setting settlement between Terra Nova Trust and its former employee, were you not?"

"You might say that."

"Not everyone in the industry would be favourably disposed to assisting, I imagine."

"I get the message, Mr. Northrop. Thanks for your help."

"Thank you. But before you go, Buddy, would you mind advising me of the subject matter for which you are seeking the information? For our records."

"For your records, I haven't decided yet."

The receptionist ignored Buddy on his way out. He took it as a compliment.

■

When Buddy called Ali's house, he got a referral; at their new home, Jasmine, though harassed by the wailing newborn in the background, was delighted to hear from him. Ali's generous settlement had helped him upgrade his technical skills. Trading on his experience in the family business, he now worked as the manager of a custom broker's database; there, Jasmine told Buddy proudly, Ali's impeccable memory made him invaluable and happy in a working environment where he conversed regularly only with a computer. In short order, he had also developed a reputation on the Internet for his anti-hacking skills.

Buddy and Ali met at a nondescript diner near Ali's office in Toronto's docklands. They had barely exchanged pleasantries when Buddy showed Ali the index card.

Amirali Sood spoke as meticulously as he worked, conjuring up checklists: the man was a researcher's treasure, but a reporter's nightmare.

"Buddy, no one, no customer, nobody inside Terra Nova, ever used TNT, whether speaking or writing — for obvious reasons. And I believe the press always referred to it as Terra Nova."

"How long did you work for them, Ali?"

"Forty-two and one-half months and three days. I read many documents. I would not have forgotten such a usage if it was ordinary. If it was unusual, it would have remained with me."

"OK, how about the numbers?"

Ali thought for a moment.

"There is one possibility. It is correct that the last series could be a savings account number. And the man who told you that the first six numbers could not be a trust company transit number is generally correct."

"Generally?" asked Buddy.

"There were exceptions, but I am not clear on them."

"What kind of exceptions?"

"I'm not sure."

"Guess, Ali, for me."

"I believe that in special situations and perhaps with respect to certain international transactions, transit numbers were more than five numerals. I cannot answer your question. I know only that I remember exceptions, my friend."

"Well, that gives me something to go on. By the way, Jasmine brought me up-to-date on the baby and the new house, and the new job. But I'd like to hear it from you."

"Buddy, you would not listen. I understand the significance of Mr. Wyndham's situation to you. We may talk about myself on a less pressing occasion."

"Thanks, Ali. Maybe I should learn from you. You know as much about me as I do about you, and you never ask any questions."

"Perhaps that is because your profession is your shield and your questions are your sword."

"Perhaps," Buddy smiled.

Ali ordered for both of them while Buddy was on the phone with Morris, who was now a business columnist, his cushy pre-retirement reward for years of scoops as an investigative reporter. Bay Street was hardly amused when their nemesis became their gadfly, but his chatty columns, full of barbs wrapped in forgiving humour, charmed its denizens by nudging them to laugh at themselves, if only for an early morning moment.

Having Morris onside always helped Buddy relax a little. So he managed to stretch a cool bowl of soup and a limp tuna sandwich into a 20-minute conversation with Ali, mostly bringing him up to date on Wyndham. After a quick cup of coffee, he paid the bill as Ali hailed a cab for him.

Buddy waved as the taxi pulled away. *I should make time for people like you.*

■

"Providenciales? What the hell is that?" Buddy asked Morris, who was staring out his office window at Toronto's Harbourfront, across the room from Buddy's precarious perch on the arm of the couch.

"Most people call it Provo," replied Morris. "It's part of the Turks and Caicos in the Caribbean — actually it's in the North Atlantic southeast of the Bahamas. They're still a British overseas territory, a couple of hours from Miami by plane, half an hour from Grand Cayman."

"And?"

"And Provo's not nearly as fashionable as the Caymans. The population is only 15,000 or so and it's popular with scuba divers who like out-of-the-way coral and lately, with tax dodgers — especially Canadians — who like out-of-the-way money and consider Switzerland and the Caymans too high profile. Their currency is U.S. dollars and the official language is English, which is handy. Most of the lawyers on the island are Canadian. Making a fortune, I'm told."

"And the numbers in the envelope?"

"From what my contact told me, money's pretty safe in Provo because the place is still low profile and because fees from offshore financial activities are a major source of government revenue. But she did say that six-digit transit numbers are common for Caribbean financial institutions that are subsidiaries of foreign banks."

"That's not much help. Terra Nova doesn't even exist anymore."

"But when they did, they had a branch in Provo. My contact looked it up. Terra Nova's still there, but it has a different name — Island Trust — and technically, it's still a subsidiary of the Canadian shell. Except the Canadian shell doesn't exist: a numbered company bought it, gave up the trust company charter, and absorbed the shell, presumably for the tax losses."

"Wyndham, or Lewis, or both," said Buddy, as he slid off the armrest into the couch.

"Makes sense. Because it doesn't take local deposits or make local loans, and because it's a foreign subsidiary, Island Trust doesn't have to report very much down there."

"So they're unregulated?"

"No, technically they report to their home government through the parent institution."

"Which doesn't exist in this case."

"Exactly."

Morris checked his notes as he spoke. "They renewed their filing last month and verified their transit number. It matches. Their only retail branch closed down about the time Terra Nova went under, but local law requires them to have a physical office and at least one full-time resident employee. Otherwise, nobody knows much about them, if they ever did."

"Anything else?"

"Nothing."

"Maybe I should make a trip down there," said Buddy, who believed that only hands-on reporting produced news that mattered.

"Why don't you talk to that cop first? You always said you could trust him."

"By the sounds of it, the RCMP would take years to get information by the book. Every rag between here and Fort Nelson will have the story by then. In the meantime, we've got nothing exclusive we can print."

Morris rubbed his lips, as if to remind himself of the pipe he'd given up only recently and, he maintained, at considerable detriment to his thought processes.

"Unless Wyndham helps, Buddy."

"What do you mean?" Buddy asked, sharp only momentarily. Over the years, he'd learned to listen carefully to the man after whom he'd modeled his career.

Morris crossed the room, sat next to his protegé, and rubbed his lips again. Buddy moved to the edge of the couch.

"Listen," Morris began, a word that meant he had been thinking hard for a while.

■

Morris was still talking when his editor called with some questions about his column.

"Got to go. It's easier to push editors around in person," he said.

Buddy went back to his desk and left a message at Portland's house. When Portland returned the call late that evening, they arranged to meet the next morning at the coffee shop across the street from his office.

CHAPTER FIVE

"FOR GOD'S SAKE, WHAT HAPPENED TO YOU?" HE SAID AS Wyndham walked into the small interview room in the rural Ontario Provincial Police post some ten miles from Lorimar. Before Jerome could answer, Adam motioned to the officer who stood in the doorway. "Take those things off him. He's in my custody."

Adam fumbled with his notebook, avoiding eye contact with the lawyer, whose baldness, disfigured by yellowish bruising on the side of his head, accentuated the metal restraints on his wrists and ankles.

Jerome rubbed his wrists as his escort freed him before leaving.

"They don't make cuffs like they used to. Mind if I sit down?"

The men's inquiring glances crossed paths. "And I thought this was a sympathy visit," Jerome said.

"I don't know what you're talking about. All they told me at the prison when I came last week was that you wouldn't see me. Then I got your message saying you'd meet me anywhere else."

"I got mugged on the way home last time, that's what. A fractured skull — in two places — for my trouble. I spent two months in the hospital. I still get headaches. My ribs ache, I limp, and I have double vision. I put compresses on my head all the time, so it's easier just to shave for now. Even that hurts. Anyway, that's why you didn't get a thank you note for the visit."

"Any idea who did it?" Adam asked.

"Someone who recognized Gunnar, probably when he was having that smoke break you suggested."

Portland ignored the barb.

"Someone must have recognized him coming or going . . . Put that pen down, will you, Adam, I feel like I'm being interrogated."

"Are you safe now?"

"Well, I've been out of the hospital and back in the joint for a month and no one's bothered me."

"Have you asked for a transfer?"

"Why? Every con in the system has heard about this."

"I'm surprised the Warden didn't transfer you."

"The screws don't know the attack had anything to do with your visit. I didn't tell them that the guy who took me out was a friend of Gunnar's."

"How do you know that?"

"He used Gunnar's name just before he hit me."

"Then maybe we can trace him. What if he decides to take another crack at you?"

"Stay out of it, Adam. Whoever it was made their point, don't you think? That's why we're meeting here. If he wanted to kill me, it wouldn't have been a problem."

"I suppose so," Portland agreed. "How are you otherwise?"

"Not great. I spend a lot of my time in my cell, in bed. But my parole hearing is in a couple of months, so that's an upper. Three years in the joint suddenly feels long enough."

"That's what I came to talk to you about," Portland said, reaching into his portfolio. "I wish I'd have know about that beating. It doesn't make this any easier."

Adam handed him a piece of unlined paper with a few lines of information centred on it, vertically and horizontally, in bold. Portland had typed it himself, convinced that the hard reality of a document was a much better sop to co-operation and even confession than words alone, which somehow — no matter how gently put — bespoke accusation and judgement to the detriment of fact.

It took Jerome only a second to read the simple notation:

TERRA NOVA TRUST COMPANY

PROVIDENCIALES, TURKS AND CAICOS ISLANDS

430486 - 51721

"My name is Jerome Wyndham and my lawyer told me I have the right to remain silent."

Portland said nothing.

"Bit lame, eh? So what are we talking about here?"

"Why don't you tell me?" Portland said quietly.

"Not a lucky guess on your part, is it, Adam? Have you known all along?"

"I can't answer that."

Jerome stood up and paced in silence for a while. He seemed more embarrassed than distraught.

"How long have you been saving it up? I underestimated you, didn't I?"

"All I can tell you is that we didn't know about this when you were sentenced," Adam replied, never taking his eyes from Jerome. "But I can say that offering to go undercover as a guy with a stash would have thrown us off the trail for sure, not to mention allowing you to access the money right under our noses. When this is done, you can give me the details over a beer. I'd like that."

Jerome pretended he didn't enjoy the compliment.

"Maybe I should make you prove how long you've known to a judge, who might just decide there's an abuse of process here because you've been holding out on me. Anyway, I don't suppose you'd believe me if I told you that's the only account I have. I guess I should put off my parole hearing."

"As far as the account goes, the answer might not interest me. About your parole hearing, it depends."

"On what?"

"On Dirk Mueller."

"Fuck you, Adam," Jerome hissed, pounding the table with his fist.

"I'd rather spend another ten years in here than kiss Gunnar's dick in Dirk's ass."

There was no response.

"Look at me," Jerome went on. "Look what I got just for talking to you guys."

"I've never lied to you, Jerome. Do you think Gunnar would have given up so easily last time if we had something on you?"

"Maybe you thought I'd change my mind on my own."

"If we were watching you that closely, we'd have known you'd been hit."

"Maybe you did. But how come Dirk hasn't gone to camp like he was supposed to?"

Portland had mislaid his basic rule, which was not to argue, especially with Jerome. Maybe he was getting too close to the man. Or uncomfortable with the strong-arm tactics.

"This is unfortunate. But it's your doing. You lied to us."

Almost imperceptibly, Jerome shook his head and smiled, as if in appreciation of an opponent who wouldn't go down.

"You've got a point there."

"Would you like some time to think about this? It's upsetting, I know."

"What's the downside?" said Jerome.

"What do you say, Jerome?" Portland asked. "You know better than I do. Another three, four years, total of 16 or so. And you'd be a repeat offender. No parole for another seven years maybe."

"You think that's worse than living a lie as a stooge?"

"You're living a lie now."

What remained of Jerome's smile disappeared, replaced by the detached tone Portland had come to recognize as the invariable companion to his rising but suppressed intensity. "I know. It bothers me, believe it or not. Aren't you going to ask why I did it?"

Portland, who knew better, found himself answering the question. "You probably weren't thinking too straight at the time. Maybe you were a bit scared of what was ahead. Maybe you felt you had to keep a little bit for yourself . . . maybe you just got greedy."

"You got it, Adam. But I wasn't as lost as I feel right now."

"I don't see that you have a choice."

"There's always a choice. I just make the wrong choices. Let me think about it. But we're talking full parole here, right, none of that day parole shit. Right?"

"That's fine. We can meet back here. How long do you need?"

"I'll call."

"When?"

"Before my parole hearing, no more than a month."

He paused.

"They knew what they were doing when they picked you to give me the good news, didn't they?"

"Gunnar thinks you trust me."

Jerome shrugged. Portland stuck out his hand. "We don't want you gone from Lorimar too long."

"I'll take a rain check on that handshake. Goodbye, Adam."

Portland stopped at the door. "Just one more thing. You can keep some of the money."

"Give me a break."

"I mean it. Gunnar's agreed. You can keep enough to start clean when this is over. Enough so you can live wherever you want, without working."

Jerome seemed unmoved. "And whose idea was that?"

"Mine. Gunnar wouldn't go along with it until I convinced him greed was the only thing that motivated you. It wasn't hard."

Jerome walked over to Portland, extending his hand. "All the money," he said.

Adam laughed. "Ingrate. We'll talk."

■

For the first time in a long while, Jerome was sitting freely in a car, albeit a police car. His two youthful escorts were much more relaxed on this leg of the trip — probably on instructions from Portland — even opening the Plexiglas partition between the front and back seats.

"We'll have to stop and put the cuffs and shackles on you before we get back," said the driver.

"Can I open the window?" Jerome asked.

"You can't, but we can," the driver said. "Can we?" he asked his companion even as he pushed the button, partially opening the window.

"Are you guys comfortable?" Jerome asked.

"Yeah, I'll open my window, so it'll be less noisy," the driver said. The other officer followed suit. Soon, all four windows were half-open.

The feel of the wind rushing through the cruiser was pleasantly distracting and uniform, unlike Lorimar's currents. There, the wind in the breezeway was always direct, cold, in Jerome's face, a reminder that at the end of the walk, a cell was his home. The wind in the courtyard past the breezeway, busy with the scents of inmate commerce, hinted of Bay Street business, its noise and its traffic, or the buzz of City Hall's criminal courts. But the wind in the yard, open on three sides but for the fence and the towers, and as big as two football fields, occasionally took him to the places he could never reach after Sarah died. Places that were open and free, yet contained enough to be soothing, like a solid cottage in the woods.

Back in the cruiser, the wind continued its work, unifying its occupants by extinguishing the barrier between front and back, guard and prisoner, cop and con. Whatever it gave on the way in or took on the way out, it gave and took from all of them, imposing a silence that was comfortable, one that meant Jerome didn't have to think about the meeting with Portland.

Instead he thought about Dara and his time in the forensic trauma unit. The unit was set up much like a cellblock at Lorimar, with a central station quartering the nurses and the guards. The hospital rooms had no doors and each, for security reasons, harboured one patient only. But alarms went off whenever the pressure on the bed springs fell below a designated minimum, meaning that the cons couldn't use the bathroom unless a guard stood by. Even so, maximum-security prisoners were cuffed to their beds and no medical staff, male or female, ventured into their rooms without security at the door. The precautions amused Jerome: if an inmate were well enough to move from his bed on his own, he wouldn't be on the unit.

He was in bed when a doctor he had never seen, without identification but walking like a doctor, came in the room. She stopped at the foot of Jerome's bed, picked up his chart, and began reading it.

"Are you new, Doc?" Jerome asked.

"No, just filling in. Could you help me read some information on this chart, please?" she responded, eschewing the exaggerated bedside manner that all but the most experienced physicians adopted when tending to cons.

"Sure," said Jerome, too weak to act on his curiosity but not too weak to welcome being within arm's reach of the attractive woman.

She did him one better, bending over so that her white hospital jacket opened. His eyes followed her hand to the vista afforded by the two open buttons at the top of her loose silk blouse. She fumbled, steadying herself by resting the clipboard on his chest, her fingers transmitting a universal code of fantasies as she pulled a square of densely packed paper from the orifice formed by the tightness of her breasts.

"It's from Dara," she said.

"Say what?"

"Take it."

And she left, pausing only to return the chart to its place.

What remained of her had caused the red ink on the first page to run, blurring the words.

JULIUS MELNITZER

Dear Jerome,
Please sign the visitor's form.
There's new information.

The note was unsigned. The second page was the document CSC used to vet inmates' guests, which Dara had downloaded from the Solicitor General's site on the Web. The form required personal details of the visitor, two passport-sized photographs, and the consenting signature of the prisoner.

This was the third time Dara had sent him a visitor's form to sign. She had included photographs with the first, but their unbearable immediacy convinced Jerome there was no sense in responding. The second time, he tore up the letter accompanying the application without reading it, a move he now regretted, wondering how long the "new information" had been around.

Assuming, of course, that the new information mattered. But then, Dara wouldn't have taken the risk of having her note delivered personally unless it was urgent, though she understood him well enough to know that just talking about Sarah substituted for news, sustaining hope almost as well, sometimes better; for his part, he understood Dara well enough to know that the conversations sustained her too, patching the void of the unloved lover with the diluted passion of communion.

When they parted after his arrest, over the telephone, he couldn't very well ask her to continue their search. Besides, continuing took money and there wasn't any. Constantly wary of revealing too much of himself to others, he admired Dara for not offering to continue on her own, for shunning the temptation to transparency.

Right now, it was a temptation he couldn't deflect. His admiration for Dara's restraint became his reason for signing the form: she wouldn't bother him again, he rationalized, unless what she had was important.

Battered and beaten, he couldn't see that he just ached.

CHAPTER SIX

HER SEARCH FOR SARAH ENDED WITH JEROME'S ARREST. But after the movers delivered her office's contents to her new place, Dara came across the boxes containing Sarah's files. Unlike her other archives, which she put in the basement, she stacked them in the space between her desk and the wall.

One evening, needing something to do while her high-speed Internet connection made another futile attempt to call up a busy Web site, Dara took the cover off the box closest to her and started reading. She had read the documents many times, but that night it was different, like the difference between photographs and movies. Photographs could convey the beauty of life and even its mysteries, but not life itself. Movies did that much better. Photographs were substance. Movies were process.

So she read just as carefully, but rather more aimlessly, than she had before. She could do it because the documents were no longer her present; when Jerome left, they had become her past. The past, she discovered, had more give than the present, letting her wander around Sarah's files at her leisure in the dazed confidence she would bump into the things that mattered.

At first, she read in the order that the boxes and documents came off the pile. Some days she started and couldn't go on; other days she couldn't stop. Many days she didn't read at all: her desperate urge to know and do had succumbed to the contentment of learning by feeling. No longer intent on understanding what had happened, she was free to watch it unfold.

After she finished reading everything, she reorganized the files.

When Jerome was around, they had been concentrating on Sarah's death, her movements, her friends, the forensic evidence, the witnesses. *That was the substance. But the investigation was so cursory, we never investigated it ourselves.*

It took her a few weeks, but eventually she had two new piles: one pile contained everything they had learned about the death and Sarah's activities preceding it; the other pile, considerably smaller, contained marginal administrative documents. So while the autopsy report was in the first pile, the visitor logs from the morgue were in the smaller group. When rereading the administrative pile revealed nothing, Dara went through it again, this time compiling an alphabetical list of all the people mentioned in the documents, whether they were involved in the investigation or not. Still nothing jumped out at her.

So she organized yet another pile containing the media reports: newspaper articles, newscast videotapes, and radio broadcast audios. She had used these materials as background, watching the videotapes and listening to the audios once, and then, in her thoroughness, arranging for transcripts, which she promptly cross-referenced. Eventually, the background went into the backroom.

She didn't know what moved her to listen to the audios and watch the videos again. The audios yielded nothing, but something on the local independent's tape caught her eye: three men got into the investigating detective's car as it left the scene. It seemed innocuous enough, but it was one cop too many, if it was a cop, and one body too many, if it wasn't. She recognized the two detectives getting into the front seat from her interviews with them. The shot of the third figure, getting into the back of the car and recognizable as a male only because he was wearing a suit, was too fleeting for her to make out, even using the pause and still functions on her vcr. Her calls to the detectives yielded nothing: neither remembered having a passenger.

Dara's purposefulness returned. She contacted a friend at a post-production studio and got him to digitize the video. But even the image he extracted wasn't clear enough to make out a face. So he sectioned off the photograph, producing blow-ups of every portion of the man's body.

"I can't get a fix on the centre of his chest," the technician complained. "It's too bright. The light's bouncing off something."

"Just give me what you can," Dara said.

Had Dara not loved Jerome, she might have dismissed the threesome entering the cruiser as, at most, an anomaly without meaning. Or, she could have let Jerome know without bringing the photographs to him, and taken it from there. Ultimately, it was the triviality of what she bore that convinced her she had to see him — either to ensure that the distance between them did not further diminish the little she'd found, or in the hope that their proximity would enhance it.

In either case, Jerome had already rejected her missives twice. Having spent the years since Sarah's death bedding and deceiving various women, he had, like most men, preferred suspicion of the opposite sex to suspecting himself. But Dara knew he respected action: "When you're on thin ice, take the direct route out," he had once said by way of explaining why defence lawyers so frequently resorted to advocacy by intimidation.

Dara was shocked when she discovered, not without considerable effort, that Jerome was in hospital, but his temporary relocation turned out to be a stroke of luck. Dara had many friends in Kingston from her undergraduate days at Queen's, where the amorphous meanderings of her liberal arts professors convinced her that a few years as a police officer would be a much better introduction to a career in criminology than a master's program. So did her boyfriend at the time, a handsome, self-assured junior professor in sociology who seduced her by locking his eyes onto hers even as he delivered his guest lecture on gender discrimination in the justice system to her second-year law enforcement class. But that was the only fond memory she had of him. He couldn't move beyond seduction in the year they were together, leading her to resolve that, in the future, she would do the seducing. *The son of a bitch didn't even take the trouble to come to Mom's funeral.*

None of the women she knew, including her mother and sisters, liked Darryl. Lucy Parrott, Dara's former roommate, who wanted to be a pilot but became a doctor by parental direction, was particularly vocal about him, but their friendship survived. After Dara joined the force, Lucy had envied what she saw as the excitement of her work, peppering her with questions about it whenever they got together. She would relish the opportunity, Dara knew, to participate in a covert endeavor.

When Lucy reported back after completing her mission, Dara realized that visitors at the forensic unit were subject to the same controls as visitors to the prison itself. She wouldn't be able to take in the blow-ups of the video.

"What about personal photographs?"

"Visitors may bring a reasonable number of personal photographs for inmates to view," the voice at the hospital told her over the phone.

"What size photographs?"

"A reasonable size."

"What kind of photographs?"

"Photographs that are not offensive."

■

At the entrance to the forensic unit, in a small booth that allowed some privacy, Dara waited as a dour guard — the kind of personality who gave a hard time to anyone she perceived as better-looking, an attitude that did little for her own appearance — examined the contents of the large envelope.

"I called ahead and they said it would be all right," Dara said.

"That's my decision."

"I'm sorry, Miss."

"The pictures are large. How big are they?"

"Eight by ten."

"They're bigger than we usually see here."

"They're enlargements of his daughter. My friend is interested in photography."

"Wyndham. He's the lawyer, isn't he? Should have stuck to photography if law wasn't good enough."

"Yes. Yes."

"Do you have a car in the visitors lot?"

"Yes."

"Give me your plate number."

"BASK-843."

"Sign here."

Dara couldn't help but notice that the standard entry form didn't have a column for licence numbers — and only her name had the plate figures squeezed in beside it.

The guard pressed a buzzer. Dara opened the door. Halfway down the hall, she remembered that she had left her ID on the table outside. The door behind her was shut, but through its small square window, she could see the guard on a cell phone, speaking excitedly as she read something off the visitor's form.

That seemed odd. The use of cell phones was prohibited in hospitals.

■

He was asleep when she arrived. She hadn't seen him since he and Heidi left for England before his arrest. Every memory, it seemed, was one of parting. Had he been awake, she would have fought off the tears, stifled the sobs, making constructive use of the lump that was in her throat when she thought about him, every day.

Not all day, though. Her therapist complimented her, by way of complimenting himself, on "getting a life so quickly." Her "life so quickly" meant selling the downtown condo she had earned with her hard work and personal thriftiness well before she met Jerome. Few shared that view. By and large, the public, and especially the lawyers among her clients, preferred the more succulent opinion that Jerome had been keeping her.

Ladner's version, published after Jerome went to jail, was much closer to the truth, but went largely unnoticed. His article established that the condo, the suv, and Dara's camera collection were all purchased before Jerome came on the scene. Drawing from the records of Jerome's trustee in bankruptcy, the newspaperman concluded that all the money Jerome paid her was for fees or expenses, and that she had no way of knowing the source of any of the funds. As Ladner wrote, "The other woman rarely has access to the truth. It is the myth, for the most part, that sustains her. Dara Addario was no exception."

She sold her suv, too, trading it in for a Geo, and shut down her office. Working from the townhouse she rented in Newmarket, north of Toronto — it didn't escape her that if Jerome changed his mind and sought her out, it would be easier to visit him without slogging through the city — she eked out a few references, put together a portfolio of sample reports, and quickly garnered the attention of insurance companies and adjusters, who were perennially short of first-rate, independent investigators, especially those willing to travel.

For some people, travelling was lonely. For Dara, travelling made loneliness comfortable. It was also the best time for easy sex.

"It's a different ballpark when you're out of town," she told her therapist.

"How so?"

"It puts men and women on the same level. If I spend a night with a decent guy in the city, he does the decent guy thing. He dances around seeing me again, he's extra polite, gives me a ride home if we're at his place. If he's at my place, he assumes I want him to stay for breakfast. It's all pretend. Like good fucking needs good soothing. But if I'm out-of-town, staying in a hotel, and leaving the next day,

I'm the one who wants it. And I do. The guy feels like I chose him, not like he chose me. That also makes it much easier for married men. So there's no bullshit, no casually personal conversation that makes me wonder whether he read about me in the newspaper or saw my tits on the Web. Just fucking till the cows come home."

"Does that make you feel good?"

"Great. I've had regular sex since I was 17, and I've never given up the habit. If there's no one in my life from time to time, I look for opportunities, not relationships. People who mix up the two don't get the best of either. Travelling is a great opportunity, partly because there's no confusion about what's going on."

"And when there is someone in your life?"

"I'm not one of those people who ranks sex number 23 in importance to a relationship. If the sex isn't good, I'm history. There is no life without good sex, whether you have a steady partner or not."

"Was sex good with Jerome?"

"Yes."

"And you still love him?"

"Yes."

"How does that figure when you're with another man?"

"I just told you, it doesn't."

"And with monogamy?"

"I am fiercely a one-man girl. I'm faithful from the beginning to the end. Sometimes that's a few hours, sometimes a few years."

"If you and Jerome were still together, what would you do about regular sex?"

"Trailer visits, I suppose."

"How often?"

"Every two or three months or so."

"Is that what you mean by regular?"

"Regular is whatever is worth waiting for, no matter how long you have to wait. When there's nothing worth waiting for, like now, I don't waste time waiting."

"But you still love Jerome, even though you're not together. So do you think about him when you're with other men?"

"I could only answer that if I did. And I don't."

"I see."

The therapist didn't see. From his unspoken perspective, Dara would put Jerome behind her a lot more quickly if she stayed at home and settled in with a new boyfriend.

I wouldn't be here with Jerome then.

His sallow complexion, almost lost in his bandaged skull and the oversized, white hospital pillow, drew her to his sleeping form. She reached for him, but settled for resting her hand lightly on the top sheet, where his breath was her first warmth since he left her. She stood rigid, like an inexperienced trekker on a mountain trail, unsure of her balance or her comfort zone, afraid that when he opened his eyes, the way would narrow and she would be too close.

Telling herself that she wanted to be ready when he awoke, she looked for a chair, which she found only in the hall. He had had no visitors, she thought, finding solace in the illusion that her presence was a singularity.

She took the chair and put it where she had been standing. Now seated, she opened the envelope and removed the pictures of Sarah. Carefully, she used her nails, which she had honed for the occasion, to peel the video stills from the invisible adhesive she had taped to the back of the pictures.

She was looking at the photos when he stirred.

"Dara?" he asked, squinting at her as he fumbled for his glasses on the night table.

"It's me, Jerome. Are you all right?" she asked softly.

"I think so, a little groggy, but better all the time. How about you?"

"Fine. But what happened to you?"

"I had a meeting with a couple of cops, and somebody at the prison punished me for it."

"What cops? Why?"

"It doesn't matter, honey," he drawled. "What have you got for me?"

"Me, to start with."

That woke him.

"I mean what did you bring for me?"

"Photographs of Sarah. Here."

He glanced briefly at them, a rare occasion when a photograph of his daughter hadn't focused his attention.

"You look so studious with glasses on," she said.

"Believe me, it's the rest of the outfit. How do these pictures help?"

"They don't," she said, reaching into the envelope. "But here are some blow-ups of stills from a video of the scene."

He looked at the dozen or so pictures carefully.

"I've seen this before. So have you. Not the stills and maybe not in this much detail, but so what?"

"Look at the stills of the police car. How many people are getting in?"

"Three."

"Does that strike you as odd?"

"No."

"When's the last time you saw three investigating detectives at a run-of-the-mill investigation into something that doesn't even look like a crime?"

"It's not run-of-the-mill to me."

"I'm sorry, Jerome, that's not what I meant. You know that."

"I know. I know. So there's one extra cop around justifying the annual increase in the police budget. Or maybe it's not a cop."

"It's got to be a cop, a prisoner, or a witness. A prisoner would be in cuffs with a cop escorting him into the back seat. A witness, maybe, but the police records don't show any witnesses going to the cop shop. What if we assume it's a cop? All I could think of was that if there were drugs involved, maybe Metro called in the horsemen."

"No. Nobody knew it was drugs until after the autopsy. Besides, you know as well as I that Metro doesn't call in the feds unless they have to, and even then they're kicking and screaming about jurisdiction. I wonder if there's some way to build a composite of that man's face."

"I'll check."

"It's expensive."

"I'm back working full-time. Accident stuff."

"You've done enough for me, Dara."

He'd said that before. On the telephone, when they last spoke three years ago.

"That's nice, Jerome. Gratitude is so versatile, isn't it? It just smoothes 'fuck off' right over. What's the matter? Are you afraid I'll do too much? That you'll owe me? Maybe I should do what Heidi does . . . nothing. Put Sarah behind me. It sure keeps you interested in your wife."

"Heidi's put me behind her too."

"Oh, God, I'm sorry, Jerome."

He flipped through the blowups again, slowly.

"What's this one about?"

"I wish I knew. My friend said maybe a headlight or a flashlight was pointing at something bright on the guy's chest. Look where his hand is, in that other picture. Maybe he was wearing a ring."

"What guy?"

"The third guy — the one who was getting a ride."

"What did you say?"

"The third guy."

"No, no."

"The one getting a ride?"

He beckoned her. But by the time she stood up and kissed him on the cheek, he was already deep in thought, where he remained for one of those moments, not necessarily long ones, which people remember as eternities.

"Dara, have you got a pen and something to write on?"

With the marker she produced from her purse, he printed instructions on the back of one of Sarah's pictures.

"Watch the adhesives around the side," she warned. "It's how I got them in."

He smiled, remembering the fleeting moments that made him think he loved her.

"Now where can we hide this?" he asked.

"Dr. Lucy tells me you have a favourite spot, even when you're semi-conscious."

He laughed, deeply enough to make them both feel good.

"She noticed, eh?"

"She loved it. I wanted to borrow her bra when she told me."

"Come here. Let me make sure we get this picture hidden just right."

He was still weak, but they surprised themselves, satisfying each other as best they could, without movement, without sound.

When they finished, he was still hungry, not spent as he had always been before. The change was enough to make her believe in a future. She would be faithful to the end, again, and then to whatever end came after that.

PART
TWO

CHAPTER SEVEN

BY THEMSELVES, THE FRONT CLOSET DOOR LEFT OPEN WITH the light on, the dust on the TV screen, the stainless steel silverware — always dried by hand because the saleswoman at Ashley's told her it would last longer that way — still sitting in the plastic utensil dryer, and the salt and pepper shakers off-centre on the kitchen table were enough to tell Jerome Dara hadn't been home for some time. But the morose lethargy of Bob, her Himalayan, the dirty litter box, and empty food and water bowls convinced him that the absence wasn't her doing. He even used to stop by the condo to look after Bob himself whenever Dara was gone for more than a day; when he wasn't available, she always hired a neighbourhood kid or got a friend to make sure the cat was comfortable.

He hadn't spoken or written to Dara since she visited him in the hospital. After he saw the blow-ups, he suspected that his attacker wasn't simply a self-righteous con enforcing the prison code. If that was so, the more distance Dara kept from him, the better. And Dara was enough of a professional not to question Jerome's warning that it was safer not to communicate until after his release, a task made easier by her distinct feeling, for once, that he would miss her. With the aura of just-sated lust lingering in the hospital room as she left, she took it home, letting it shelter her in that comfortable space where absence and silence were not the same.

Jerome arrived in Toronto on a sunny day in late July, barely taking the time to notice his freedom before he called her from a pay telephone at the bus station. But she wasn't home and he didn't leave a message. Anxious to preserve cash, he checked into an hourly-rated hostel in the city's east end while he looked for a place that was fairly central yet somewhat removed from downtown. But after three years in the joint, everything seemed to take forever. He wasn't in shape for the pace of the city — its bureaucratic rigidity combined with the uncertainty of real life exhausted him before each afternoon was out.

It was two weeks before he mustered the energy and luck to find a little furnished basement apartment nestled in a cul-de-sac off the Danforth, close to the subway but far enough from the trendy Greektown restaurants and bars. The space had its own bathroom, a laundry shared with the owners upstairs, a kitchenette combined with a small living area that boasted two above-ground windows and seemed almost cheerful, and twin beds in a windowless room just large enough to let two people move around.

Jerome gave the gay couple who owned the small, but immaculate and newly renovated mid-century two-storey home the phony ID — same first name, last name Masters — that the Mounties had provided. He was a just-separated freelance writer, he explained, who needed a place to live and work. Alana and Gert were quite happy to take Jerome on a month-to-month: they were renting for the first time only to help with the mortgage they had assumed to finance the renovations, and they didn't quite know what to expect from the arrangement.

"Do you have any idea how long you'll be with us?" Gert asked.

"Why don't we say three months? After two, we can decide whether we both want an extension. I can write up an agreement and pay the three months in advance, in cash."

"Are you OK with cats?" Alana asked, looking at Matilda, the Ragdoll who was eyeing Jerome from a safe distance. "She makes her way down here once in a while. She likes to nap on top of the washer and dryer when they're warm."

"No problem. My girlfriend had a cat." His use of the past tense didn't escape him.

He drafted the short agreement quickly and efficiently, and handed it to Alana.

She read it quickly. "Sure you're not a lawyer?" she asked, unaware that his draughtsmanship was calculated to impress his new landlords. They, like most people, shared the misplaced belief that competence, intelligence, and articulation, especially in combination, were compelling signs of character and integrity.

As Alana went upstairs to make a copy with her scanner and printer, Jerome took a stack of bills from his pocket and peeled off $1500 in $100s and $50s. That left him with about $6,000, literally in his pocket. At seven dollars a day plus the extra overtime George had worked in, he had earned more than $4,000 in jail, and saved two-thirds of it, spending the rest on the few amenities available at the weekly canteens and the monthly food drives the Warden allowed. And he hadn't touched the $5,000 Heidi had put in his account, without telling him, when she left Fairlawn for the first and last time.

"A friend of mine from out-of-town will be staying with me for a while, until he finds a place," Jerome said when Alana returned.

"That's OK. We're friends too," Gert replied, putting her arm around Alana.

After he rented the apartment, Jerome decided against a telephone line, which would have made it too easy to trace him, in favour of a pay-as-you-go cellphone. Still, he used it only when a payphone wasn't handy.

Jerome didn't tell Portland, his *de facto* parole officer — he checked in daily by leaving a message at a pre-arranged number — about the apartment or the cell, letting him believe that he was still staying in the flophouse, which had no switchboard or phones in the rooms. For a small weekly fee, much less than the cost of renting the room, the clerks were happy to tell callers and visitors that Jerome was still there but out, and pass messages on to him. The arrangement would work equally well when Dirk joined him and their expenses mounted.

After he arrived in Toronto, Jerome tried to reach Dara at least three times a day, though caution kept him from leaving voice mail. Finally, just after he rented the apartment, he tried e-mail from an Internet café, using an anonymous message service he had discovered on the Web, a revelation following his time in modem-less Lorimar. After a few more tries, he deleted his messages from the main server and sent a letter in the post.

A week later, when she didn't show up at Timothy's Coffees of the World in Eglinton Square, he tried calling one last time, then managed to rent a Neon cheaply from Rent-A-Wreck who, fortunately, took cash deposits in lieu of credit cards. He drove straight up the Don Valley Parkway and the 404 through Toronto's version of Silicon Valley — also a revelation — to Newmarket. The thriving bedroom town was no longer the hamlet he remembered from years gone by, when he and Heidi had passed through on their occasional antique forays after dropping Sarah off for her riding lessons on Davis Drive. Heidi hadn't wanted him to buy Sarah the horse, at first insisting that at ten years of age, she was too young to care for the animal properly and too young to appreciate the responsibility that came with gifts of that magnitude. But Jerome had prevailed after Pebbles's owner moved out of town and took Sarah's ride with her.

Daddy, do you know what horse I'll be riding now?

No.

I don't even know if I want to ride anymore. I miss Pebbles and it took me so long to get used to her.

Things will work out, honey.

You always say that.

Here they come.

He's beautiful. Look, he likes me. What's his name?

He doesn't have one.

Why?

Because he's yours. You'll have to name him.

After pulling into a gas station to compose himself, he filled the tank, then went inside and bought a street map. Without it, it would have been impossible to find Dara's place among the area's new sub-divisions, indistinguishable other than by the deft, superficial touch of their marketers.

Making an educated guess that Dara — a martial arts instructor in her spare time — hadn't installed an alarm, he bought a few tools at the hardware store in the mall across from the gas station where he found the map. With help from a trick or two that Fingers, a master cat burglar doing an easy trey for possession of stolen goods, had demonstrated at Lorimar as barter for Jerome's assistance with a steady stream of love poems to his girlfriend, he had little trouble breaking in through the side door.

Everything seemed fine in the downstairs study as he entered, but he felt uneasy when Bob didn't move as he came up the stairs, more so as he noticed the little things that made him realize he was closer to Dara than he had intended or understood. Everything was in order in the bedroom too, where the flowered pillows stood upright in front of the white ones on the neatly made-up bed. Whoever had come hadn't surprised her in her sleep: when she spent the night without Jerome, which was almost always, she made up the bed as soon she rose; and when they were together, making love on adulterers' time in mid-afternoon or the early evening, she invariably fixed up the sheets and pillows while he was showering.

Jerome was also sure that if they'd taken her from home, he'd have seen signs of a struggle. One dark night as they strolled in Montreal's Lafontaine Park before returning to their hotel after another pointless visit to the vicinity of Sarah's death, she had stared down a large knife-bearing thug who demanded their money and jewelery. Even as Jerome was advising her to give the thug what he wanted, she landed a hard kick to the man's groin and picked the knife up from the ground before anyone else could move. The thug disappeared at a remarkable if awkward pace considering the blow he had suffered, and she couldn't stop herself from laughing even as she wrapped herself around Jerome, who was trembling and trying to hide it on the park bench where he had stumbled to collect himself.

"That was the most romantic night we've ever had," she told Jerome a few days later.

After he cleaned out the litter and replenished Bob's food and water, which the cat took to immediately, it occurred to Jerome to check the garage. Accessing it from the study downstairs, he saw that it was empty and neat. He searched the built-in storage cabinet, and in a drawer found photocopies of ownership and insurance cards, both indicating that her Geo bore the licence number BASK-843.

Back in the basement, he looked around the study more closely. It was then he noticed the file folder on her desk, hidden from his first cursory review by the high-backed chair he'd bought for her lanky, five-foot-ten frame when she complained, though ever so slightly, of headaches and back pains while doing her paperwork.

"That's the problem with a body like mine," she laughed, tossing her long black hair by way of revealing her delight at his thoughtfulness when he brought the chair from Business Depot.

"Yeah, but it would be cheaper if you just wore a bra at home," he replied, even as he cupped her breasts from behind.

The rush of freedom had eluded him since his release. But now he wanted her. So he sat in her chair for a moment or two and lulled himself, rocking and swivelling in a soothing rhythm. It was then he noticed the loose wires on the desk: whoever took Dara had taken her computer too, though the monitor, printer, and scanner were still there. As he leaned over to open the file folder, a hushed sound behind and above, more frightening for its stillness, chilled him. He tried to swing around, but lost his balance as the chair moved forward even as a grip tightened on his shoulder. Panicked, he twisted the other way and kicked up, knocking the chair, whose tilt he had the store set for Dara's 130 pounds or so, over backwards. The screech from beneath him was deafening.

Bob, now between Jerome's back and the highback, was not

amused at the reception his renewed energy had engendered. Nor was Jerome, flat on his back and staring straight up at the ceiling. As he shifted to steady himself while Bob worked at extricating himself, Jerome brought one of the chair's legs, with most of his weight on it, down on his fingers.

"Fuuuck!" His scream terrified Bob even more when he grabbed one of the chair's casters, which had come loose, and threw it at the low drop ceiling where it pushed apart two of the tiles, then fell back down, narrowly missing both Jerome and the cat who, much like Jerome, couldn't seem to find safety anywhere.

"Come here, Bob," Jerome said, stretching out his aching hand to the cat, who responded, if somewhat tentatively, by curling up in his arms. As he stared straight up again, Jerome wondered at the force with which he had thrown the heavy caster from his unleveraged position. He stood up, put the cat gently on the Arborite desk, reached for the ceiling and discovered that the tiles had been manufactured in a series of sheets with lines etched in them to make them look like individual squares.

"That thing should have bounced right off," he thought out loud. Unwilling to trust the highback as a step-up, Jerome went upstairs for a kitchen chair. Standing on it now, his eyes crossed the plane of the displaced tiles. He saw the edge of an envelope.

Another noise startled him as he eased the envelope from its hiding place, and he almost fell again. Bob, perched squarely on the file folder, had jumped off the desk, the motion of his legs shifting the folder just enough to expose the edge of a photograph Jerome would never forget.

At the top of the police shot of Sarah dead on her bed was a message on a white label. "She's gone."

Underneath it was one of the enlargements of the third man at the police car.

"So forget about this."

And Dara's driver's licence.

"Or forget about her."

Shaken and breathing heavily, he put the driver's licence down and opened the envelope he had found in the ceiling. In it were log extracts from the morgue where Sarah's body had been transported. His legs trembled and went numb at the memory. He righted the chair; lacking the caster, it promptly fell over again, making a noise that sounded disproportionately in his head. Now his hands were trembling. He sat down, breathing deeply to calm himself. A few minutes passed before he could look at the documents again.

He and Dara had carefully checked these records many times, but found only the usual suspects among those who had inspected her body: the investigating officers from Metro, the pathologist, her assistant, one or two morgue attendants and of course, Jerome and Heidi, who had not confirmed their daughter's identity until a week after she died, having been notified only on returning to Whitehorse from their wilderness canoe trip.

The name Dara had underlined, in red, was not there to see Sarah at all; rather, its owner professed interest in the body of Erin Rice, the first corpse that appeared on the log. Erin Rice meant nothing to Jerome. But the name Pierre Lafond got his immediate attention, all the more so because Lafond had been accompanied by an unidentified person in authority whose signature was indecipherable.

Sarah had talked and written, though briefly, about the young man she met some months before her death. Pierre, a native Montrealer, was two years her senior and completing a chemistry major at Concordia University, the inner-city campus not far from her haunts at McGill. After a courtship of several months, she had planned to bring him home after finishing up the summer job she had taken at a French bookstore. But in mid-July, Sarah curtly announced that Pierre was history. Jerome and Heidi didn't pry, comfortable that if there was a story to tell, their daughter would tell it in her own good time.

A few weeks later, Sarah was dead and Lafond more or less forgotten. Later, Dara had contacted him, but he had little to say that was helpful. He seemed still genuinely fond of Sarah and shocked but not heartbroken at her death. Dara's intense investigation of Pierre's background, as well as a few days of surveillance, revealed no drug use or anything otherwise suspicious. He did seem a little easy with money and had a tendency to expensive clothes, but that was probably within normal limits for a kid who'd grown up in a piss-poor family and had earned his way through university on scholarships, bursaries, and part-time work.

"He told me the breakup was mutual," Dara informed Jerome. "But I didn't believe him. Jilted ex-boyfriends can be mean bastards."

"Speaking from experience?"

She cherished personal questions from Jerome, even the ones disguised as sarcasm.

"Wouldn't you like to know?"

"Seriously, Dara, do you think we should look into this kid further?"

"Not really, not for now at least. The police file said he was away when it happened."

■

To find Lafond, Jerome had to get his files from Heidi, because Dara's copies had disappeared with her. He called his old number, where a familiar voice answered.

"Willy?"

"Yes."

"It's Jerome."

"How you doing?"

"Nice of you to ask."

"Look, Jerome, I'm sorry I didn't visit. The one time I saw you in the bucket, I just couldn't stand it. Even today, I think of you every time I go there."

"You mean you can't imagine me out of jail? How's Libby?"

"We're . . . split."

"Really?"

"I live here now."

"With Heidi?"

"Yeah. Libby wanted to stay at our place with the kids, and Heidi and I thought it best that we stay in the house until things settle down. We'll probably sell when the market gets a little better."

"You fat fuck. You're selling squat. That's my house."

"Stop yelling at me, Jerome, please. Maybe you better speak to Heidi."

"Maybe."

He recognized her bare footsteps on the hardwood floor.

"Hello, Jerome. I should have told you."

"You don't owe me anything," he lied.

"Why don't we meet and talk?"

"Where? At his house? Or is it your house? Perhaps neutral ground, say Libby's place?"

"What do you want?"

"I want to know what you're doing with that asshole."

"He was your best friend, Jerome. He couldn't handle it when you went to jail. And he couldn't talk to anyone else about it."

"What about Libby? What does she think about all the talking now?"

"You know they were having their troubles."

"Why didn't you talk to me?"

"If you don't know, there's no point telling you again. Sarah's gone."

"Because someone killed her."

"What? You're crazy, Jerome. It's over. Try, for once, to act appropriately."

"Forget it, I need my files."

"Have you learned something new about Sarah?"

"What about my files, please?"

"Willy took them to his office."

"Oh, great. I'm not going over there."

"I'm sure he'll be glad to deliver them."

"Have him put them in a cab."

"Where do you live?"

"None of your business. I'll be waiting for the cab tomorrow morning at ten in front of the Holiday Inn by the courthouse. And I'll pay the cabbie."

"Is there anything else you want?"

"That was a more important question when I was in the joint. Send some casual clothes, a sports jacket, a tie, and a couple of pairs of shoes. Any other basics you can find, but not too much. I'll call when I'm ready for the rest."

"Please don't call any more if you're going to upset me."

"Why? The latest headlines from home are a little upsetting, to say the least. That makes my reaction appropriate, doesn't it?"

"I'm pregnant, Jerome."

He let it sink in. "Congratulations."

"I've already had one miscarriage. You wouldn't have another child with me. Fine. But I won't let you mess with this one. I'll make sure Willy sends your stuff. Bye."

■

All it took to find Lafond were a few telephone calls to the names on Dara's contact sheet. Lafond had moved to Toronto; there, it seemed, he had abandoned chemistry to write his chartered accountancy exams. But the relative isolation of Lafond's toney Caledon Hills address convinced Jerome that his current occupation involved a creative combination of chemistry and accounting.

So he rented the Neon again, this time for a month at a cut rate. Once he got off the 401 and past Brampton on Highway 10, the countryside turned beautiful. He couldn't help detouring past

Belfountain, then detouring again, against his better judgement, for a too pricey lunch at the Millcroft Inn, where he and Heidi had spent the night together just days after they met. He sat in the same bay window, by the waterfall, shedding the first tears he had allowed himself over her — over anyone but Sarah. When he returned to the car, Bob jumped into his lap. The cat's soft fur and warmth reminded him that Dara was gone too. He cried, without restraint, for all he'd lost.

■

It was late afternoon when he reached the country estate. An eight-foot-high stone fence surrounded it. The see-through wrought-iron gates were locked, which turned out to be a good thing when two Rottweilers objected as he got out of the car. Jerome could make out a Tudor-style mansion at the end of the long, treed driveway. He dialed the estate's phone number from his cell. The answering machine confirmed the place as Lafond's residence and the message suggested that he lived alone. That seemed a little odd considering the lace curtains on the windows, the carefully chosen mailbox in the shape of a lily by the gate, and the sign at the road that read, "Lafond du Coeur," which translated roughly as "bottom of the heart."

He got back in the Neon and drove west along the stone wall. Eventually, it reached a natural wood, and turned north. Jerome managed to edge the car into the trees, hiding it from sight unless somebody looked hard. He followed the wall for some distance until he arrived at another wrought-iron gate, secured by a remotely controlled locking system, like its counterpart at the front.

Jerome's amateurish performance at Dara's townhouse, which brought back the memories of his less than stellar macho debut at Lafontaine Park, reinforced his doubts about his suitability as a self-anointed private investigator. But preparation had been his strength as a lawyer, the weapon with which he beat off convictions that looked like sure things. As luck would have it, Fingers had told him where he could purchase anything he wanted if he found that he wasn't able to make a living through normal channels: tucked into the pouch slung over Jerome's shoulder along with the tools from the hardware store, a Swiss Army knife, and a new flashlight, were an electronic modulator, a loaded semi-automatic pistol with a silencer, and extra ammunition.

"How much?" he had asked the wizened dealer, whom he knew only as Roger.

"Usually $4,500. But I'll give it you for half, Fingers's price. He said his old lady wouldn't be around if it wasn't for you. That's good enough for me. So anything you want that you can't buy at Canadian Tire or Home Hardware, call me."

"Thank you."

"Don't thank me. Fingers said you'd be buying the booze when he got out."

The modulator did its job. The gate unlocked, but Jerome held on to it while he wondered what to do if the dogs, who were nowhere to be seen or heard, made an appearance. He noticed an old shed some 40 yards away, decided that if worse came to worse, he could shoot the Rottweilers. His pistol in hand, he raced for his bunker. The dogs were barking as he arrived at the door. A large padlock barred his entrance. He shot it off and entered the dark, windowless structure, then tripped and fell, whacking his head on a metal object. A bit sore, but unhurt, he rose to bolt the door. The dogs were quiet. He waited for a few minutes, and when he felt confident they weren't coming, he reached for the flashlight in his pouch. It didn't work. He had forgotten batteries.

Jerome felt around for the object on which he had fallen. It turned out to be a handle, maybe a door handle, with only a slight give to it when he pulled. After several attempts, he realized that his own weight was preventing him from opening whatever it was. He moved around carefully, tracing out the edge of a trap door that took up most of the shed's floor space. He managed to keep clear of the door and from a cramped position pulled on the handle. The door gave readily if somewhat awkwardly. But the smell when it opened made his eyes water. He used the Swiss Army knife to tear a strip off his sleeve, then ripped it into two smaller pieces. He wrapped one piece around his nose and used the other as a headband to control his profuse sweating. Breathing through his mouth, which was only marginally more pleasant, he lifted the door and leaned it against the wall. Then he worked his way back around the edge of the opening, reaching for a way down, and discovered a set of wooden stairs.

He backed down seven or eight stairs on his knees, until he touched ground. Still on his knees, he turned around and groped in the mud until he felt what was unmistakably flesh — hard flesh, flesh that had given up begging for air. He trembled slightly as his hand moved up a woman's body to her long hair, dirty and matted to the touch.

He moved away as far as he could, then composed himself before moving back. His hand brushed something soft. It felt like a purse. He reached in and found matches. Dara didn't smoke, but she always kept matches around, just in case giving someone a light helped her with an interview or an investigation. Using his fingers, he counted two matches left. He lit one near the woman's head, then ran the match slowly down her body. Her hair was black, its contours too familiar. He couldn't bear to turn her over and look at her face. Instead, as the match flickered precariously, he reached in her purse again and pulled out a wallet.

He had found Paula Maydek, the late John Felderhof's legal assistant.

CHAPTER
EIGHT

BY THE LIGHT OF JEROME'S LAST MATCH, THE INSCRIPTION ON the back of a photograph gave Maydek away as Felderhof's mistress. Another photograph showed the couple hugging on a tropical beach. Jerome put the photographs back in the wallet and the wallet back in her purse. He slung the purse on his shoulder and left as he had come, again unbothered by the dogs.

Wary of the front gate, he drove west to the first paved road he encountered, then turned south. He kept driving until he saw a diner with too many people in it. Hungry and unsettled, he stopped anyway, went in and ordered coffee, but then thought better of emptying the contents of a woman's muddied purse in the public eye when he looked and smelled like a convict who had escaped through the prison's sewer system. By then it was dark outside, and the burnt-out dome light in the Neon discouraged him from sorting the purse's disorganized contents in the car.

It was almost eleven when he stopped by the flophouse, where a message from George confirmed Dirk's arrival at the bus station at noon the next day.

"I need to register someone," Jerome told the clerk.

He filled out the form with Dirk's particulars.

"Will the arrangements we have be OK for this guy too?"

"Two for one?"

"No, no," Jerome laughed. "He'll pay the same as I do. Here's the first week's advance."

He gave the clerk a $20 bill.

"Tell your buddy on the day shift when you see him too. We'll stop by and pay him tomorrow or the day after."

"I can give him the money."

"I like the personal touch."

"Suit yourself."

Back in his basement apartment, Jerome sorted the contents of the purse. If Paula Maydek had killed Felderhof, there was nothing in the purse to give her away. In fact, an unopened bottle of Vioxx suggested she had been running an errand for *Brenda* Maydek when she was abducted; the prescription predated Felderhof's death by one day. The address on the tax receipt for the prescription, Jerome noticed, matched the address on Maydek's driver's licence. Maybe she lived with her mother or her sister.

Probably her mother. That drug's for arthritis, I think.

The telephone book listed "P. Maydek" and "B. Maydek" at the same address, but with different telephone numbers.

It was too late to call. But it had been a good day. He felt closer to Sarah than in a long time.

■

He slept well and rose just before eight. He called Paula's number and was surprised that the line was still in service, so he hung up as it started to ring. Ten minutes later, he dialed the other number.

"Hello, I'm looking for Mrs. Brenda Maydek?"

"Who is this?"

"My name is Jerome Masters."

"Yes."

Jerome recognized her tone, too defeated for curiosity or suspicion.

"I'm calling about your daughter."

"I've told you before, I have nothing to say to the newspapers."

"I'm not from the press, but I am investigating Paula's disappearance."

"Oh," with only a faint hint of interest. "Are you with the police?"

"No, I'm a freelance investigative journalist."

"Are you writing a book? Why? She didn't kill anyone. She's not dead."

He almost broke, almost told her the truth. Paula would never be dead to her, any more than Sarah was dead to Jerome. But Jerome had put his daughter to rest. He could do at least that much for Paula's mother. But if he did it now, he might never rest.

"I don't know if there's anything to write about, Mrs. Maydek. But I have information that may shed some light on your daughter's whereabouts."

"What do you mean?"

"I think it would be better if we could talk about it in person. Could we arrange to meet? I could come to your house, if that's convenient."

There was a long silence, then an audible sigh.

"Why are you interested in Paula, Mr. . . . ?"

"Masters. Jerome Masters. My daughter disappeared too. When I read the newspaper stories about Paula, I started looking around and asking questions."

"Come then, please. I'm in the Manulife building."

"At Bloor and Bay?"

"Yes."

"Do I need an access code?"

"No. The concierge will ring up."

"Is this morning all right?"

"Yes. I just need to get dressed and tidy up. When will you come by?"

"In about an hour, say at nine. I'll bring some coffee from Timothy's downstairs."

"That would be nice."

"How do you take it?"

"Just a small one, please, decaffeinated. Two milk, not cream. Two sugars."

"See you then, Mrs. Maydek. Goodbye."

■

Unless her mother had money, it was obvious that Paula Maydek had done well by her lover. Manulife was an upscale apartment block sitting over an equally upscale shopping, dining, and entertainment array on Toronto's equivalent of Madison Avenue, right across the street from Holt Renfrew's flagship store.

The concierge was expecting him and rang him up. The woman who opened the apartment door rather too quickly was in her mid-sixties. Her silky grey hair had never seen dye, and she was taller than her diminished presence suggested. But the hollowed lines on her face, worn without the relaxed folds that give wrinkles their beauty in women comfortable with themselves, hinted that her age had come upon her recently and accented the stiffness in her face, her body, and around her soft blue eyes that should have blinked more than they did.

"Thank you for the coffee," she said from her seat opposite Jerome on the large u-shaped leather couch in the modernistic living room that broadcast her daughter's taste. "Please tell me what you know. I've been waiting so long."

"Some of what I have to say is painful, Mrs. Maydek."

"Is my daughter alive?"

He hesitated, certain his discomfiture showed.

"I can't be sure. But I do know that John Felderhof was not merely your daughter's employer."

"That's very delicate, Mr. Masters. But it's not news to me. John was her life. But he was a respected and well-known man who had a wife and family. It took Paula a long time to realize he would never leave them."

"And did she?"

"Yes, that's why she quit. But she would never have done anything to hurt him. And I don't believe she would have left me without a word."

"Do the police know about their relationship?"

"No."

"You didn't tell them?"

"No, I thought it would only reinforce their suspicions about her — and destroy his family, for no good reason. There are young children involved, you know."

"But it might have given the police something to work with."

"Just more gossip, I'm afraid. She didn't kill him and the only thing she had to hide was the affair."

"Felderhof didn't fire her then."

"No. That's what he told his clients and his lawyer friends, the ones who spoke to the newspapers. She wasn't incompetent. He couldn't have run that office and all its complications without her, especially because he travelled so much. What are you getting at, Mr. Masters?"

"The complications. I believe Paula must have known something that could hurt Felderhof or the people with whom he was involved, or someone thought she did."

"Are you suggesting that John is responsible for her absence?"

"No, but people connected with him may be."

"What kind of people? What are you saying?"

"Felderhof had an international immigration practice. As you said, he travelled a lot, so his comings and goings wouldn't have attracted the attention of the authorities. Nor would the fact that a lot of money went through his trust account from all over the world."

"I don't understand."

"If someone wanted a legitimate front for illegal activities, Felderhof's office would have been an excellent choice."

"You mean like drugs."

"Drugs and money laundering."

"But do you have any proof?"

"I have proof of a link between Mr. Felderhof's office and a man who was likely involved in drug operations. Did Paula ever mention someone named Pierre Lafond?"

"No, not that I remember."

"Did she ever talk about the details of the 'complications'?"

Paula's mother thought for a while.

"From time to time, she complained that working for John was getting too complicated, that she didn't like some of the clients, one in particular that I can remember. But I thought a lot of that had to do with their relationship . . . with her unhappiness."

"Did she mention names or places?"

"No, she talked mostly about John, and her and John. Very little about her work."

"Is there anything she said that might identify the clients she disliked or the work she was doing for them?"

"No, she just said that he had a lot of files and that there was more pressure associated with those files than with all the rest of her work."

"I'm sorry I have to ask this, but is there any chance Paula was involved in anything behind John's back?"

"No," she replied with her first hint of anger.

She's not a witness. This isn't a courtroom.

"I'm sorry, Mrs. Maydek, I really don't mean to upset you."

She nodded. "John and her job meant everything to her. Her friends drifted away over the years. They had nothing to talk about. She wouldn't tell them anything and rarely went out with them. She spent every spare moment in the office, sometimes with him, sometimes without him, or else at home or going out with me. We've lived together since my husband died, just after Paula started work with John. Her relationship with him was hard on her sometimes, but we had a good life."

She looked down into her lap. He said nothing until she looked up at him and nodded so very slightly.

"Did Paula ever work at home?" He spoke more slowly and deliberately, trying to forestall the impression that he had the next question at hand even before she answered. She sensed the change, and relaxed.

"No," she said. "John's work was very sensitive. And besides, it was easier for them . . ."

"I understand." He waited.

"Did she leave any files here?"

"No, but . . ."

"Please, Mrs. Maydek."

"I'm sorry, but I still don't understand your interest in my daughter. And I'm sorry to bring this up, but how did you say your daughter died?"

"I didn't. I said she disappeared."

He had faltered just long enough for her to guess the truth about Sarah and tell her that Paula was gone too. She began to sob, uncontrollably, each sob framing an incomplete word. He moved next to her on the couch, his arm around her until she settled to a whisper.

"What was her name?"

"Sarah."

"How did she die?"

"Drugs."

She surprised him. "Was Pierre Lafond also involved?"

"I don't know. He was Sarah's boyfriend at the time."

Then, a quiet that the onset of words alone could not suspend. She got up. "Excuse me."

She walked slowly from the room. He could hear the sound of Kleenex leaving its box, then a drawer opening and her footsteps starting back, then waiting, long enough to let his thoughts wander and drown out her movements.

He had no idea how much time had passed before she returned. She was composed, but she didn't sit down.

"Here," she said, handing him a piece of plain white paper. "I found this after the police came. Paula had a spot where she hid her valuables, but they missed it. When I read it, I thought John just wanted her as far away as possible."

Jerome looked at the note:

Paula, My Love,
I miss you terribly. But it's not to be. I can't leave the children.
Please take the money and go far away, where it's safe. Take
your mom. And please don't call me again. It could hurt both
of us in ways you can't imagine.

John

"I didn't think much of it. I thought he was afraid that she'd cause trouble if she stayed in town. That's why he wouldn't give her any references. And he was always very generous, so even the money didn't seem strange."

"The money?"

"One hundred thousand dollars in cash. American dollars. I didn't know what to do with it, so I put it in my safety deposit box."

"Keep it, Mrs. Maydek, you deserve it. I'm sure Paula would have wanted you to have it."

"Can you bring something of her back to me?" she asked after a time."

"Mrs. Maydek, whatever I bring for me, I'll bring for you, I promise."

"Thank you."

He headed for the door, waiting as she took his jacket from the closet and handed it to him.

"One more thing, if you don't mind. Did John have other lawyers working with him?"

"No. Just he and Paula, and a receptionist."

"What about a bookkeeper?"

"That was part of Paula's job."

"Do you know what happened to his practice after he died?"

"His receptionist stayed on after his wife sold the practice. She used to call occasionally to ask after me, although I didn't know her well."

"His wife? Or the receptionist?"

"Both, actually. Please don't tell his wife. She's a good woman."

"I won't, Mrs. Maydek. I promise. Can you give me the receptionist's name?"

"Sally Clark. As far as I know, she's still working for the lawyer who bought the practice. They moved everything to his office."

"Where's that?"

"Not far. I met her downstairs for lunch one day. She said she walked over from work. I have her phone number. Would you like it?"

"Yes, very much. Was she Paula's friend?"

"I think so."

"Did she know about Paula and John?"

"We didn't talk about it. But I don't see how she couldn't. She worked for John for about three years, I think."

"I see. Did she say anything to the police about their affair?"

"No. She said all she knew was that Paula felt John had treated her unfairly. Just a moment, I'll get the number for you."

It took her just a minute to retrieve her address book. It took him much longer to leave her there by herself.

◼

The bus had arrived early, and Jerome was a little late. Deep in thought over his conversation with Maydek and how much to tell Dirk, he'd lost track of time at the café in the Indigo bookstore that spanned the west side of two floors in the Manulife.

The Colombian was waiting outside the station, his face to the midday sun. They hugged as he jumped into the passenger seat, tossing his one bag in the back.

"I feel like still in joint. Everything there late too," he laughed. "Nice car. Nice cat."

"It's good to see you, Dirk. Have you been waiting long?"

"Maybe 20 minutes. No problem. I call Juliana and Sonia, and my parole officer."

"How's the family?"

"Good. Happy we talk when we want."

"You look well too, Dirk."

"Not you. Maybe we go back to jail."

"I don't think so, Buga. We have work to do. But first, you need to show your face at our hotel."

"I have not much money. Think maybe we share room."

"We will. But not at the hotel."

Jerome explained their living arrangements on the way to the flophouse. He introduced Dirk to the day clerk, who gratefully accepted his increased stipend and gave them the key to the room allocated to Dirk for the benefit of inquirers.

"Make yourself familiar with the place. Your parole officer will be here to check out your living quarters at least once and then maybe once a month after that. He might even ask you for a description before he comes. He's probably had other clients in this dump."

"What I do when he visit?"

"The boys will let you set yourself up in the room the night before. Give them a couple of extra bucks. The chambermaid too, if she comes by."

"They have chambermaid here?"

"You bet. The clientele requires regular linen changes."

Dirk looked around the room.

"Jail look good again."

"The place I have is small, but it's clean, and in a nice area."

"And how everything else? Your parole officer is good guy, Jerome?"

"Girl. Shandy Wayne. Experienced. She doesn't bother me. I'm the least of her problems. How about you?"

"Don't know. Mike Brown his name. Sound nice on phone. I tell him you live here too?"

"Might as well. How often do you have to report?"

"Tomorrow, then to start every week, I think."

"Where's his office?"

"Downtown, he say," Dirk replied, producing a scrap of paper that he handed to Jerome.

"180 Dundas West. Right near the courthouse."

"Where your parole officer?"

Jerome, with Portland in mind, almost said "downtown," but caught himself.

"Near here. In the Scarborough Town Centre. They'll probably switch you over if you keep this address for a while."

"Maybe we get same parole officer."

"Let's get going."

■

"There's a problem," Jerome said as he navigated the traffic on the Danforth. "My contact's dead."

"You contact? I not know you have contact," Dirk replied, surprised at the abrupt remark that contrasted so starkly with Jerome's guarded ways at Lorimar. But then Jerome's offer of help had also come out of the blue. They were on one of their daily walks around the perimeter of the yard on the prison's running track, taking the exercise that had replaced racquetball after Jerome returned from the hospital.

"Help?" Dirk had replied.

"It's not hard to figure out, Dirk. You're not leaving the country for a while, maybe ever. What money you have is with Juliana or Ludwig. The Mounties may not know about Ludwig, but they do know there's no point in bringing your family to Canada unless you can provide for them. So you have to get the money into Canada, which fits nicely with tracing Ludwig's contact in Canada and maybe recovering what you lost. But they'll be watching you like a hawk if you make parole. Maybe that's even why you'll get out. On the other hand, I know my way around people who move money, and whatever anyone thinks about my having a stash, they certainly won't be watching for me to try to get it *into* the country."

"You smart man."

"Cut the bullshit, Dirk. For months now, you've been feeding me butter tarts, and not the kind that go so nicely with our evening tea."

"So why you help?"

"I'm glad you asked. I get one-third of what you recover from Ludwig or what you get into Canada with my help. Call it my fee for professional services."

"One-third?"

"Standard for contingency fees on high-risk cases. And if I wanted to spend my time nitpicking and negotiating, I'd still be practising law."

"Sound like you doing that still."

"Have we got a deal then?"

"I no understand. You take drug money after Sarah?"

"There's rough justice in taking it from the trade and using it to destroy the people who killed my daughter. And I won't help you unless you use what you know about drugs and drug people to help me find out what happened to her."

Dirk softened. "So this personal."

"Everything's personal."

"That what Juliana say when we start business together. I think."

Two days later, over their evening tea, Dirk agreed to Jerome's terms. "OK, my friend, how we start?" he asked.

"I start when I get out. We start when you get out. Until I get out, we don't talk about it and unless there's an emergency, we don't talk at all while you're still in jail." And they hadn't, except indirectly when George passed on the news of Dirk's release.

His contact, Jerome now explained — sticking closely to the version of events he had concocted for Dirk's ears — was John Felderhof, the lawyer who had helped him launder his own funds and who he thought might be able to help Dirk. Felderhof was dead, but he had discovered that a man named Pierre Lafond, who had coincidentally been Sarah's last boyfriend, was one of Felderhof's best clients.

"I found Maydek when I was snooping around Lafond's place," Jerome said.

"Lafond kill Maydek?"

"Must have."

"And Maydek kill Felderhof?"

"I don't think so. Maydek and Felderhof were lovers, and from what her mother said, she probably knew everything there was to know about his operation. I could see a crime of passion maybe, but not a cold-blooded killing with no clues. My guess is that once Maydek and Felderhof were on the outs, the situation became too unstable for Lafond, or someone connected to Lafond. So they killed Felderhof, then had Maydek disappear, making her the prime suspect."

"Very nice, but how it help us?"

"Felderhof's receptionist is still working for the immigration lawyer who bought the practice. She might know something, but first I want to see what I can find out about the lawyers and the files he took over from Felderhof. Any information we can get about Felderhof's partners or his clients or his activities could lead us to someone who can help you move your money. I mean, the channels are probably already set up, all we need to find is the front who replaced Felderhof or someone like him."

"The receptionist, she not recognize you?"

"I don't think so. She wasn't at Felderhof's when I was arrested. And, even though you haven't noticed, I've grown the moustache back since I got out."

"I come too?"

"No, I know more about the way law offices work. And if we need someone to go in a second time, it might be handy to have you tucked away. With that accent, you're a natural as an immigration client. And you can even tell them part of the truth: that you want to get your wife and kid out of Colombia."

"Thanks for you confidence. Maybe now we have party."

"OK, but I have to arrange an appointment at Galati's first. Then maybe a nice steak at the House of Chan."

"Steak in Chinese restaurant?"

"The world is full of surprises."

"No woman, Jerome?"

"No, not for me."

"Whisky, then."

"We'll stop at the LCBO. Lot cheaper that way."

"You drink with me?"

"One, Dirk, to our success."

But when Jerome put the scotch down in a single gulp, he was drinking to Dara.

CHAPTER NINE

JEROME HAD BEEN LYING. THE "CHAMBERMAID" GUNNAR HAD instructed Portland to put on Jerome's tail reported that Jerome hadn't slept in his room after his first two weeks of freedom. As a matter of fact, the ladies had started using it again. And even though Dirk had registered, there was no sign of him or his things. When Andrea asked the day clerk about them, he told her to mind her own business if she wanted to keep her new job.

"Don't worry. Is Wyndham still reporting in?" Yu said.

The reaction wasn't what Portland expected. Not that Portland knew what to expect. Yu had a habit of offering only the minimal response to the task at hand, as if every development, surprising or not, came with a "hold" flag pointing in someone else's direction. His style, Portland thought, shut him in and shut him out. Yu was either a man with no secrets or a man with a very big one.

"Yes," Portland replied. "But I won't be talking to him much until something happens. He says nothing's happened yet. I think we should arrest him, maybe offer him a deal if he helps us find Lewis and his stash, and agrees to help us get his own stash out of Provo. Why don't you buzz Gunnar?"

"I gave him a ride to the doctor to have his eyes checked. I don't know whether he's back."

Gunnar was in. Yu and Portland went to his office.

"Is Wyndham still in touch with the clerks at the hotel?" Gunnar asked.

"As far as I know," Portland replied.

"OK. Shake down the clerks. As long as he's in touch with them, we'll know he's not far away. I don't want you to let him know we're on to him. He's probably found a nice little piece of ass somewhere and prefers to keep it to himself. When the time's right, we'll put surveillance on him."

Portland persisted.

"This is a very clever man we're dealing with," he argued. "He's fooled everybody, and very elaborately. Me, the Crown, the accountants, his wife, his girlfriend, probably his lawyer, maybe even Lewis. If we leave him on the street, especially with Mueller and his international connections, we'll probably never see him again."

"What can he do?" Gunnar replied. "We know where his money is. His best bet is to co-operate with us and help us land the bigger fish in return for a share of the money."

"I don't know. It was his idea in the first place to go undercover."

"But he changed his mind," Gunnar said.

"No. We declined. He said 'No' only after we reopened it and tied it to Mueller, probably because it would have cramped his style to have Mueller around."

"I just don't think this guy wants to be a fugitive the rest of his life," Gunnar said. "Did you see the way he came after me over his daughter? He's not going anywhere until he finds out what happened to her."

Originally, Gunnar had been unenthusiastic about putting Jerome on Mueller. He didn't trust lawyers, he said, especially smart ones like Wyndham who, with the discovery of his stash, had now managed to make the force — meaning Portland — look like idiots. But he had to pass the information about the stash to his superiors, who checked out Dirk's file before making a decision. It turned out that, after calling Holland Drilling, Dirk had dialled a number they couldn't trace to confirm an appointment about "starting the transfer." That got the brass interested enough to alert CIMSC, the Criminal Intelligence Management Steering Committee that determined national intelligence priorities.

After the orders came down, Gunnar did an about-face, even suggesting that Jerome's cooperation be further secured by letting him keep some of the money.

"But tell him it was your idea, the only way you could convince me to go along with it," Gunnar had instructed Portland,

Maybe he didn't understand undercover operations well enough, but it seemed to Portland that Jerome had become a very bad risk. And why have Andrea keep an eye on him, only to get casual about arresting him when she discovered something amiss?

Then there was the phone call from Dara Addario's sister.

"I'm sorry to trouble you, Detective, but I remember Dara telling me what a kind man you were. You remember, you interviewed her when her boyfriend was arrested."

He remembered. And he remembered thinking it was the only time he'd disliked Jerome. Dara, he thought, was Jerome's victim as much as his wife was. But Heidi at least had the choice of loving him or leaving him. Dara never got to that point: Jerome cut her off before she even knew whether she wanted to choose. Heidi's despair, her losses, Portland thought, paled to Dara's sudden irrelevance — though Dara was certainly old enough and smart enough to know what she was getting herself into.

He'd seen Daras before, but very different versions. White-collar criminals invariably came with mistresses, who, unaccustomed to the tough times, stuck around much less frequently than the wives. This case was the exception: Dara's devotion rose above her obsession. But as far as he knew, Jerome hadn't seen her since before his arrest.

"Detective?"

"Yes, I'm sorry, I was just remembering."

Susan, who lived in Vancouver, hadn't heard from Dara in over a month. Neither had Leila, the youngest sister who was studying in the States. Or their father in Ottawa. They normally talked every week, sometimes by conference call.

"Have you called her place of work?"

"She worked as a claims investigator, on contract for insurance companies. I called two of the ones she mentioned. They told me she took a couple of months off."

"There you go."

But, Susan insisted, Dara wouldn't have taken off for so long without telling anybody, especially her Dad, who was worried sick.

"People do that sometimes. I imagine it's been a rough few years for her. Did you call any of her friends?"

"We don't know that many of them. But we did get in touch with Lucy Parrott — she's a doctor in Kingston — because we thought she might be staying there. She sees Dara more than she speaks to her."

But Lucy hadn't seen Dara for a few months, since Dara had stayed with her while visiting another friend who was in hospital.

"In the hospital in Kingston?" Portland asked.

"Yes, I think so."

"Who was in the hospital?"

"I don't know. Maybe Lucy does."

"Where can I reach her?"

He wrote the name and number down, advised her to call Missing Persons at Metro, and told her he'd do what he could and get back to her if he discovered anything.

"There's something else, Detective. She seemed so happy in the last little while. Lucy thought so too."

He reached Dr. Lucy Parrott at her office.

"Is there a problem, Sergeant Portland?"

"I'm looking into a missing persons report about Dara Addario."

"Her sister called me, they were worried about her."

"Yes, I understand you last saw her or spoke to her a few months ago."

"That's right. Let me check my computer. I had a note in my date book that she was coming . . .Yes, it was just about six months ago."

"Could you give me the exact date?"

He wrote it down.

"She arrived in the late afternoon, I remember."

"Susan said something about a visit to the hospital."

He could hear the first hesitation.

"Yes."

"Who did she visit?"

"She didn't tell me, just said it was a friend."

"Do you have any idea who it might have been?"

A second hesitation.

"How important is this, Sergeant?"

"It could be very important."

"Is Dara in danger?"

"I can't say. But what you have to say may help with the answer to your question."

"She was very coy, you know, in that happy way, when somebody's had a great night out, or met just the right person, or they're pregnant but can't tell you yet. But I'm pretty sure she visited Jerome Wyndham, her old boyfriend, in the hospital."

"Why do you say that?"

"I know he was in the hospital at the time."

"When did you discover that?"

"Before . . . I mean, after. Oh, geez, this could get me in a lot of trouble."

"I'll try to avoid that."

"Are you the policeman who investigated Wyndham?"

"Yes."

"Dara liked you."

Portland didn't break stride.

"Go on, please."

"A few weeks before she visited, she asked me to deliver something to Jerome without going through the formal channels, if you know what I mean."

"And what was that?"

"Believe it or not, just some papers."

"Did you know what they were?"

"No, she was very secretive."

"Did you look at them?"

"No, Detective, she's my friend."

"Did Wyndham say anything when you gave them to him?"

She smiled to herself.

"He didn't say anything. He was pretty sick. I was only in his room for about a minute."

"A minute can be a long time, Dr. Parrott."

"Not when the message is in your bra."

Portland laughed out loud. "I'm sorry. It's just that you were so serious."

"You make things serious, Detective. How serious are they?"

"I really don't know any more than you do. But I will stay in touch with Susan if there's new information. Thank you for your help."

A call to the hospital's forensic unit quickly revealed the date of Dara's visit, and surprisingly, the licence number of the car she was driving. On a cursory check, the car turned up on the RCMP's forfeited list, in the lot with other vehicles that were proceeds of crime.

His first instinct was to head to the lot and check the car out. His second instinct was to call Gunnar before he did that. The two clashed in his gut producing, oddly enough, a desire to talk to Jerome. That was wrong, but it felt right, a conflict Portland didn't come across very often.

Almost from the time his parents stopped making his choices for him, he had little trouble distinguishing right from wrong. He wasn't a moralist, an absolutist, a fundamentalist, or even a law-and-order guy in the political sense, though, to an onlooker, he may have looked and played the part.

Like most of his colleagues, Portland had an abiding respect for rules. Not because he believed the law or any particular law was right or wrong, but because he craved *terra firma*, a vantage point from which he could lead his life. And the law, at least in the democracy he firmly believed Canada to be — over the protestations of Patrick, his anti-corporate, anti-globalization, anti-free trade son who had stood out like a sore thumb during the three-year stint at Osgoode Hall School that preceded his current studies at the London School of Economics — was what maintained order between competing values, what allowed people to fight over right and wrong without killing each other.

So, in his days as a constable on the airport beat, Portland ticketed the drivers as soon as their meters expired, even as he saw them hurriedly approaching from the corner of his eye; on the drug squad, every joint merited a charge. Personally, Portland believed that the criminalization of marijuana was ridiculous long before departmental policy changed to formally allow the Mounties to ignore small cases of possession; but as long as it wasn't his decision to make, he wasn't going to make it. Both his heart and his head followed the rules, but only because they were rules; any doubts he had about their content, intellectual or emotional, remained theoretical, purely for discussion, until and if someone changed them.

At the other end of the spectrum, he escaped overzealousness by doing his job dispassionately no matter how much a crime revolted him. He had met few people he cared to characterize as pure evil, a reluctance he had absorbed during his stint in Kenora, in Northwestern Ontario. There, he discovered that the language and culture of Native Canadians didn't even allow for the notion of a "criminal," focusing on the sin rather than the sinner.

The distinction suited him perfectly: he could enforce the law without judging the gravity of the sin, and deal with the circumstances of the sinner when the question of punishment came up. Portland, unlike most of his colleagues, liked the broad sentencing options available to Canadian judges. They allowed him to enforce the letter of the law, but without a vengeance. A system of mandatory sentencing guidelines, like the ones in vogue in the U.S. federal system, might have disturbed the firmament of his dividing lines.

The commercial crime unit also satisfied the equation. Property offences rarely raised the passions and deep moral and societal questions that went with drug trafficking and crimes of violence. In fact, when financial institutions were the losers, an undercurrent of public loathing for the victims tended to obscure the very human face of the real losers, the mid-level managers who took the fall for the systemic negligence that allowed — perhaps encouraged — them to be duped, putting an end to their careers and more importantly, their self-esteem and trust in others.

Portland, however, didn't lose track of the people. He was as open to the humanity of the ones he arrested as he was to the plight of their victims, named and unnamed. The unnamed, in Jerome's case, included people like the branch manager at the trust company, Heidi, Dara, and all the other people who had believed in the lawyer.

In Wyndham, Portland saw the white-collar criminal whose greed was incomprehensible to most: a driven, successful man who craved both punishment and salvation for never overachieving quite enough. For Jerome, the punishment came with Sarah's death, granting him both guilt and the hopeless quest that eternalized it. By ruining his life over the loss of his daughter, he had ensured that he would never have to — and would never — overachieve; and if that wasn't quite enough punishment, he set himself the futile task of searching for Sarah's killers as his life's work.

None of it, in Portland's mind, mitigated Wyndham's greed. It wasn't just the money. Wyndham had ignored the law, annexed it to himself, put his grief above it and above the rights of others. Anyone who did that was greedy, and their reason for making the choice didn't make them any less greedy. Portland could be sympathetic to the reason, but he would never be sympathetic to the choice. If temptation had entered his own world, he hadn't noticed.

Ladner's revelations about Jerome's offshore account had excised Portland's sympathies. Because he believed that Jerome's crime was the man's way to freedom, to a life devoted to searching for Sarah, and because there wasn't a shred of evidence that Jerome had secreted any money, the stash came as a complete surprise.

Unless Jerome had cut a deal with Lewis. At the time of Jerome's arrest, it didn't make any sense: why would Jerome do time and let Lewis take off? Why not the other way around? And it didn't make any more sense just because it turned out there was a stash.

Or did it? Maybe he had been so taken with Jerome's contrition, his haste to get to jail, the salubrious effect of Jerome's co-operation on his career, or just the man's charm, that he had missed the obvious. Perhaps the quick plea bargain had been more than a way for Jerome to keep people off balance and himself in charge. If so, the plan was exquisite: three years in jail, nine on parole searching for Sarah, no wife or girlfriend to worry about, a life of leisure before he turned 55, enough money to continue his search for Sarah from wherever he was, and no one looking for him. Let Lewis be the fugitive. And if Wyndham's courtroom tactics were any indication, it all made sense. According to Ladner, the man specialized in blindsiding the opposition.

But why involve Dara? Unless she was involved already, unless their split had been carefully crafted. Is that why Dara disappeared? But why now, years before Jerome could leave the country? Unless an early exit was also part of his plan. But then he'd be a fugitive, without access to his money. Unless he had other accounts. *Didn't he say something about that?*

What was most puzzling, however, was finding Dara's car in the forfeiture compound, like it was the property of a drug dealer. Did she have a connection with Dirk? Was Jerome into drugs? Did Gunnar know about it? If he did, why hadn't he told him?

The last question stirred him at source. Gunnar was the boss. He made the rules. Maybe there was some bigger picture that made "need to know" the rule; maybe Gunnar was just leery of Portland's relationship with Jerome; or maybe, like most intelligence operatives, he habitually played his cards close to his vest.

Portland decided to report to Gunnar. After he checked out the car.

■

The compound operator wouldn't let him see Dara's vehicle, let alone touch it.

"It's off-limits until forensics takes it apart," he said.

"What for?"

"I have no idea. They don't tell us civilians these things."

"Can you tell me who brought it in?"

The operator scrolled down his computer screen.

"Says here it was in the City lot."

"Who authorized the seizure?"

"I don't get that information either."

"Well then, who did you notify, to say that it was here?"

"Nobody. I put it on the daily alert like I do with all the new arrivals."

"But you do know forensics wants it?"

"It's right here on the screen."

"Any idea who at forensics?"

"Beats me."

"Did we arrest the owner or question her?"

"How did you know it was a woman?"

"It's all that sensitivity training we've been getting."

"It says here we couldn't contact her."

"So when will forensics be finished with the car?"

"Who knows? They're always backed up."

"ok, thanks. Sorry to bother you. Do you need to log me in?"

"Didn't get in, did you?"

■

Gunnar knew nothing about the car. Neither did Yu.

"Who's Dara Addario?" Gunnar asked. The three men had met in his office at Portland's request.

"Wyndham's girlfriend at the time we arrested him. She's a private investigator," Portland replied. "I didn't know if it was important or not."

"Not unless they're up to something," Yu said.

"Her girlfriend says she delivered a message from Addario when he was in the hospital. Addario visited him later. She had some photographs with her."

"How many times?" Gunnar asked.

"Once. I checked the records."

"And after his release?"

"Andrea never mentioned any visitors."

"What about Missing Persons?" said Yu.

"The sister just reported it."

"So what do you want to do?" Gunnar asked.

"I think I should help out Missing Persons with whatever information we have on her, and do some checking around myself."

"Give the information to Tom. You concentrate on Wyndham."

"OK. Anything else?"

"Not unless we find out something you don't already know," Gunnar said.

CHAPTER TEN

THE INTERVIEW WITH GARY GALATI WENT SMOOTHLY ENOUGH. After Jerome explained that he needed a work permit for the writing job he'd been offered in California, the lawyer chatted perfunctorily, if politely, for about five minutes before he decided Jerome had only enough money to warrant the attention of his clerk.

Sheri Fitzjames was a pert, fortyish woman whose comfortable friendliness told Jerome that she had been around law offices long enough to lose her awe of lawyers but not long enough to loathe them. Her generous working space said she was a valuable employee, and the orderly arrangement of its contents told visitors she deserved the designation. Even the two dozen or so pictures she had on what could have been an overcrowded credenza behind her desk had a symmetry that spoke volumes about her personality.

"You like dogs," Jerome observed after glancing at the pictures. "Lots of ribbons there."

"I train them," she said. "It's a hobby."

"They're all different. Are any of them your own?" he asked, happy to ingratiate himself with the woman on a topic that was dear to his heart. Leaving Puffy behind when he went to prison was almost as difficult as leaving Heidi, if only for the dog's constancy: his relationship with the sheepdog was one of the few things that hadn't changed after Sarah died, and Jerome's arrest had made no impression on the animal whatsoever.

"No, too much trouble. I train them and leave them."

"Is it hard?"

"No. You don't have to be close to a dog to get him to trust you."

"I know what you mean. Getting close can blind you to a lot of things, whether it's people or dogs you're talking about."

"Will you be taking a dog with you to the States?" she asked.

"No, no. It's too hard to look after one when you're living alone."

"I see," she said and turned back to her notes. "You told Mr. Galati that you'd been a client of Mr. Felderhof."

"Yes. Did you know him?"

"Only by reputation. Mr. Galati is the only lawyer I've ever worked for. I used to be the only help he had, but now we have a receptionist who came from Mr. Felderhof's office. She was on her break when you came in. Did you know her . . . or Paula?"

"Not Sally. But when I retained Mr. Felderhof about five years ago to look into an American work permit for me, Paula was very helpful, very efficient."

"I can see that from the files. The whole business — you know, Mr. Felderhof's death and Paula being a suspect — is a tragedy."

"Yes, terrible."

"Well," she sighed, "it's probably best to move on. But if there's anything in your old files that might be helpful, we can get them from storage."

"I don't think so. It would probably be easier to give you the basics again. Do you charge for going to the warehouse?" he asked with a smile.

"The storage company does. We add it to your invoice as a disbursement."

"I see. Must be a problem when you take over a practice."

"Not really. We use the same system as Mr. Felderhof. We keep files on-site for two years after they're closed, so we rarely have to go to storage. For clients who have ongoing issues, we don't put individual matters in storage. Anyway, we should get on with your problem."

"Yes, I'm sorry. It's just that I used to do some legal writing and the workings of law offices have always fascinated me."

"Really?"

"Mostly from a business standpoint. I always wondered if it was worth it to buy a practice when so much of its value is in the selling lawyer's goodwill."

"We kept almost all of Mr. Felderhof's clients. Except for one large corporate client, but Mr. Galati says he took that into account in the selling price."

"That was good negotiating."

"More good luck really. The Law Society asked Mr. Galati to take over Mr. Felderhof's practice on an interim basis after Mr. Felderhof died, and almost immediately the client advised Mr. Galati that the files would be removed. I really shouldn't say anything more. Everything here is confidential, you know."

"Of course. What information do you need?"

"Your passport, birth certificate, driver's licence, and a careful family, educational and employment history. Some references — the more the better — and also anything you can tell me about your prospective employer and the job you've been offered."

"Would it be easier if I wrote it out?"

"Much easier."

"All right then. I'll bring my passport and other documents when I come back."

"Fine, I have sufficient particulars to open a file. We'll need a retainer of $1,000, Mr. Masters."

"Can I bring cash at our next appointment? I don't have any cheques on me."

"That's perfectly all right. Some lawyers take Interac and credit cards, but Mr. Galati feels it's not professional."

"He's right."

■

On his way out, Jerome allowed himself a long look at the receptionist. Sally Clark was a Rachel Hunter clone, maybe a little older but no less freshly encased in a batter of vulnerability and mischievousness. She wore a perfectly fitted dark suit — her skirt pulled up just short of Nirvana as she sat at the see-through glass table that was her desk. She saw him coming, nodded and pushed her shoulder-length blond hair back over her head, then reached for one of the lily-shaped drop earrings that enhanced her delicately formed, bite-size ears, massaging it slowly with her thumb and forefinger.

"Thanks for getting me an appointment so quickly," he whispered on his way out.

"Any friend of Paula's mother is a friend of mine. But feel free to return the favour, Mr. Masters."

Jerome was convinced that he never had what it took to make women come on to him. So they rarely did.

"I didn't mean to offend you, Mr. Masters," the receptionist said.

"No, I was . . . just surprised. When do you finish work?"

"Mr. Galati doesn't like us to date clients."

"You should have told me first."

"I mean, it wouldn't be right for us to meet here."

"Then how about a drink at the bar in the Four Seasons? The food's good at the hotel too."

"It's very expensive."

"Your company is worth it, Madame."

◼

The Four Seasons wasn't a good idea, although it was near Galati's office on Avenue Road in Toronto's Yorkville district. The area, a bohemian hangout in the sixties, had evolved lockstep with its denizens, who returned older, more prosperous, and more conservative to vent their nostalgia by transforming it into Canada's ritziest shopping and dining enclave.

Heidi liked to shop in the boutiques on Cumberland and Yorkville Avenues. Sarah not so much, though she could be lured, ostensibly by an invitation from her mother for an afternoon's shopping "on me," but really because she adored the lady in her mother and Yorkville was a great place to absorb it and show it off. Their forays usually ended with dinner at La Pêcherie, the Movenpick's downstairs seafood restaurant. There, even people distracted from their meals by mother and daughter laughing loudly over their futile attempts at cracking lobster claws, could tell they were the best of friends.

But Yorkville was also the kind of place, like the financial district, that diminished Jerome. The area had more than its share of lawyers, including high-priced criminal lawyers, and it drew a large after-work social crowd from all over the city. He dreaded running into old colleagues and friends, whose conversation tottered unsteadily on outdated assumptions; old acquaintances, forced to feign that familiarity, were worse. More than once since his release, Jerome had crossed the street to avoid the embarrassment of no longer being an equal.

He walked south along Avenue Road. Searching for distraction, he stopped at a payphone and dialed Dirk's newly acquired cell. He told him about his meeting with Galati and Sheri and his date with Sally.

"What have you been doing all afternoon, Dirk?"

"I read Sarah's files. Like you say."

"And?"

"Nothing yet. I read slow. But pictures more hard. I almost cry. Call Sonia."

"You're going to run out of money pretty soon if you call every day."

"Hey, we partners. You give me loan."

"Give me a break, Dirk. And don't fuck up."

"No worry."

It wasn't five yet. Unwilling to spend the price of liquor on a Diet Coke while he waited, he nestled into one of the wing chairs in the Four Seasons' lobby, securing his sense of safety by burying himself in the *Standard*. As usual, he scanned Ladner's column, out of the same crazy fear that his name would appear. It didn't, but that left him no more satisfied, and he quelled his anger by revelling in the monotony of the meetings City Hall reporters had to endure.

When Sally came around the corner by the elevators, he wished he had been in the bar: every eye in the place was on her, then on him, her choice, as they approached each other. Prompted by the watchers, they kissed hello lightly, then made across the lobby to a window seat in the far corner of the bar, which afforded seclusion from prying ears, but left him glancing outside nervously as she waited for her martini and he for his club soda.

"Are you expecting someone else?" Sally asked.

"No, just a rude habit."

"Maybe you should have ordered a drink."

"I'll be OK. I don't mean to get off on the wrong foot."

"You're not," she said, nuzzling his shoe with her toe.

"And you're not shy."

"I feel like I know you."

"I didn't really know Paula, but I knew her dad," Jerome explained. "I'm a writer. I have some police contacts. Brenda asked me to find out what I could about Paula before I left for the States."

"Oh, you're leaving?"

"Don't give me that. I'll bet you read my file or talked to Sheri before you came here."

She looked away. "Maybe."

"Look. I need you to help me. I think someone killed Paula, but I can't find out who it is unless I can see Felderhof's files."

"Ouch." But her eyes returned to his.

"Can you get in?"

"Yes, but the alarm system logs all the entries."

"Visually?"

"No, just the code."

Jerome thought for a moment.

"Couldn't you have forgotten something, a file?"

"We're not allowed to take files home."

Hypothetical objections, Jerome thought. "How about your purse or your glasses?

"I suppose. You talk like a lawyer."

A sudden fear of discovery irritated him.

"I thought you wanted to help Paula and Mrs. Maydek. Didn't you tell the police Felderhof mistreated her?"

"Yeah."

"Did you know about them?"

"I did, but I didn't, if you know what I mean."

"Did anyone else?"

"Mrs. Maydek. Otherwise, they were very discreet. It's not like there are a lot of people working in the office and we're not around a lot of lawyers."

"Are you going to help me?"

"How do you mean?"

"I need to get into Sheri's computer."

"Can't I just get the information you need?"

"I don't know what I need."

She rolled her eyes, but smiled. "That's a big help."

"Please."

"When?"

"As soon as it gets dark, after dinner."

"I was hoping to have some fun when it got dark."

"It'll still be dark when we finish."

Over dinner in the Studio Café, she told him that firewalls and Windows passwords on boot-up and for the screen savers were the only security on the office computers, which weren't networked. But when she started talking about being the odd girl out in Felderhof's three-person office, Paula came starkly alive for him, with Brenda Maydek, then Sarah, not far behind. It left him with insufficient energy to press Sally about Felderhof's clients. There would be plenty of time for those questions later. Instead he managed small talk, the kind in which lies serve as well as truths, usually better: his apartment, her apartment; his career, her career; his plans, her plans; all inter-spersed with the casual yet very personal asides that mark the onset of foreplay in the bar species and their social relatives.

At last it was time to go. He paid the bill. Unable to help himself, he left a big tip.

■

They crossed to the west side of Avenue Road, and walked back to Galati's past the fancy new condos, the precious boutiques and the discreet restaurants, their subtlety flawed by the limos parked nearby and the occasional "Free Valet Parking" sign, an expense the estab-lishments absorbed with the price of their most basic menu items.

He had moved to her right, to the outside as his mother had taught him. She tucked her arm in his weightlessly, foregoing the drag of intimacy. They walked in silence, his quiet a dilemma deeper than the crime he was about to commit, for even Sally's light touch dis-turbed the peaceful commitment that had lingered since Dara visited him in the hospital.

"Are you nervous, Sally?" he asked.

"Why? It's my office we're going to."

She didn't fumble for the swipe card in her purse, didn't push the door before she pulled, didn't seem surprised the lights were on. He couldn't help but wonder if she was as efficient in bed. She took her seat behind the glass desk, smiling as he averted his eyes from her legs.

"Nice shoes," he said.

"I think you're the one who's nervous," she said. "Just one second. I'm going to log on to my e-mail. It'll look better for me if anyone notices that I've been here after hours. They all know I can't go ten minutes without checking my inbox."

Her computer took less than a minute to boot up. He didn't hear the sound of the modem, then saw the always-on high-speed cable device behind her. Navigator's familiar ping told him that she had e-mail. She called it up, took a second to read something on the screen and typed what was likely a reply.

Sally got up and walked over to him, fingering the lapel of his sports jacket.

"Do I get a kiss for my trouble?" she asked.

"That and a lot more, but not now."

He had little trouble disabling the boot-up password on Sheri's computer: he'd spent hours learning the innards of Windows in the joint, even cracking the network code on George's computer on a dare from the teacher. He turned off the screen-saver passwords and called up Explorer.

"Who set up this file system?" he asked. "There isn't a separate directory for the data. It'll be a bitch to find anything."

"We all set up our own computers," Sally answered.

A quick foray into My Computer revealed that the six-gigabyte hard drive was 80 percent full. He scanned Explorer's hierarchy, looking for directories that would give him a clue to Felderhof's files. He found nothing. So he pressed the Windows key, held it down, and punched the "f," bringing up the "Find" function.

"What are you looking for?" Sally asked from her position behind him.

"I'm looking for a list of Felderhof's files, but nothing comes up under 'Felderhof.' How did you identify John's files?"

"They all ended with a 'j.'"

"How many of them were active?"

"I'm not sure."

"Was there a list?"

"I don't think so. Sheri gave each of his files a new file number, then entered the numbers on a database where she recorded the details."

"Where's the database?"

"In Access."

Jerome minimized the open windows on his screen, then clicked the Access icon on the desktop. Felderhof's files were in a database called "Client Information." Jerome sorted the database to provide a list of all files ending in "j." Fifteen hundred records came up. He opened the first, which duly recorded the client's name. Then he searched for "Lafond." Nothing came up.

"Who's Lafond?" Sally asked.

"Someone who was connected to Paula Maydek. What did you do when you closed a file?" he asked Sally.

"I really don't know. That's Sheri's job too."

But the records had a field called "Status." Some of the files were marked "O" and some were marked "C." Jerome sorted for the Cs, and a long list entitled "Closed Files" came up on the screen.

"Do you know anything about the files that Felderhof's clients took away from here? Would they be marked 'closed'?"

"I think so."

"Sheri said there was one guy who took a bunch of files with him. Did Felderhof have many clients with multiple files?"

"No, hardly any."

Jerome limited his search of the closed files to start with the date of Felderhof's death, then sorted the new list in ascending order of date. As he had suspected, only one date had multiple closures.

"This is what I need," he said, turning to look at Sally.

She was pointing a gun at him.

"I guess I'm just not destined for an uncomplicated lay."

"Sorry, but I need the information more than you do," Sally replied, "so take this disk and make a copy of those records."

He did as he was told.

"I don't understand," he said, as the computer made quick work of the process. "You could have gotten this list yourself anytime."

"The information I needed most was finding out what you needed to know. Get up."

"Where are we going?"

"You'll be joining Paula, I'm afraid. Get up, slowly." Now he was afraid, but only that he'd failed Sarah.

He rose and faced her. She pulled her hair over her head again. Her earrings glistened. He remembered the mailbox at Lafond's place.

"Where's Dara?"

"You're such a sweet man that I won't tell her you were planning to fuck me. Why make her miserable in her last hours?"

Jerome bristled.

"Easy, cowboy. I'm the one with the gun. Now move."

As they reached the door of Sheri's office, she pointed him past the reception area to a small hallway leading to the bathroom and an exit door just beyond it.

"Stop right here," she said as they reached the front of her desk. She stepped behind it and punched in a few words on the keyboard.

"Just using the wonders of wireless paging to keep my ride up-to-date," she said as she returned. "Turn around and keep walking."

"A driver, eh," he said. "Hookers use them all the time, but they probably can't take care of themselves as well as you can."

"Shut up," Sally replied.

She disengaged the alarm system on the rear exit door with her swipe card. They both stepped into the parking lot, shielded from Avenue Road by the building.

"Don't panic, the car will be here in a minute," she said.

He turned around again, waving off her gun as she raised it slightly.

"If I'm going to die, can you tell me what happened to my daughter?"

"I can tell you that if she wasn't as snoopy as you and your chum Dara —"

"Where's Dara?"

"Safe and sound at —"

"Put gun down," said a voice from behind her. She moved quickly, but her agility was no match for Dirk's semi-automatic, complete with silencer. He fired three times, hitting her twice. Her gun went off harmlessly as she fell; the bullet lodged in the motor of a car some-one had left in the lot.

Sally was flat on her back. Blood oozed freely from a gaping hole where her right eye had been. Jerome sickened as he bent over her, as much from the realization that death, which had haunted him, now inhabited him, taking him beyond revulsion at the merely physical. Sarah. Paula. Sally. His daughter's legacy had become his life. Something told him it wouldn't be long before he pulled the trigger himself.

"I thought you avoided violence, Dirk," Jerome said angrily as he rose.

"You lucky I practise just in case. Still, Juliana always shoot better. So I man, I practise more. Maybe you thank Juliana when you see her."

"Why did you bring the gun? I just asked you to keep watch on the front door for me."

"I careful person."

"I can see that. Sorry. Thanks for saving my life. I just wish I had a couple of minutes with her."

"Better she than me. You have information?"

"It's on a disk in her handbag. Let me get it. We've got to get out of here before her driver arrives."

"What you mean driver?" Dirk asked.

"He's got a wireless pager or something. She contacted him just before we left the office. Doesn't looking at her bother you, Dirk?"

"I no look. No think."

They heard the car turning into the driveway before he could retrieve the disk.

"Shit," said Jerome, grabbing Sally's shoulder bag and gun.

"I teach motherfucker lesson," Dirk said, aiming the pistol at the oncoming car.

"Shoot out the tires, we want him alive," Jerome said, even as the driver fired out the window of the car. Dirk dove to the ground just a second ahead of Jerome, returning the fire as he fell. The car squealed into reverse and backed recklessly out the driveway into the unsuspecting traffic, colliding with a southbound van. Dirk, now running down the driveway, had the good sense to stay in the shadows as the Geo pulled away.

Jerome, though out of breath, was right behind Dirk.

"I get licence number."

"Tell me, in case you forget."

"BASK 843."

It was Dara's car. "Did you get a look at the driver?"

"No."

"Was it a man or a woman?"

"I not see."

"OK. Let's get out of here before the cops show up. Where's our car?"

CHAPTER
ELEVEN

IF ANYONE HAD HEARD THE SHOTS, THEIR ATTENTION HAD BEEN diverted by the accident and the traffic melee that followed. Feigning interest in the chaos, Jerome and Dirk passed as latecomers to the action. There were few other pedestrians as they headed north on Davenport, to where Dirk had parked the Neon.

"You drive," Jerome said. "I want to check her bag."

Her address matched Lafond's; otherwise, the purse revealed nothing of interest apart from the disk. The Internet cafés Jerome had been using to surf the Web didn't have floppy drives or printers, but he had noticed that Kinko's, a 24-hour all-purpose copy shop, rented out computer time. There was one close by, near Spadina and Bloor, in the heart of the Annex just off the University of Toronto campus. Jerome didn't know whether the shop's computers could read Access-generated databases, but Kinko's was still their best bet.

Dirk stayed with the car in a no-stopping zone right in front of the shop. Students using Word occupied all the computers. To make matters worse, three people were ahead of Jerome in the computer line. He gave them $50 apiece to take their place, and explained that they would have to yield to his replacement as part of the bargain.

"What replacement?" asked the young woman who was at the head of the line.

"The person who's going to give up their computer to me, so they can get right back at it when I'm done."

"Who's going to hang around here when they've just lucked into 50 bucks?" she said, turning on her heel and leaving the store.

She was right. Even before he could settle in at the PC, the sweet young thing who gave it up was at the copy counter brandishing her $50 and offering her friends a free round of beers.

"There's a free drink for you too," she said as she left. "We'll be at the Brunswick."

"Thanks. That's very kind of you," said Jerome, who had discovered the Access icon in the Windows "Start" Menu.

He discovered little else. The records revealed that the mysterious client had operated a slew of numbered companies. Felderhof was the companies' sole officer and director. Though the records didn't give up the names of the shareholders, Jerome suspected that a search at the Ministry would just turn up more numbered companies. The companies listed had operated under a variety of random trade names, each probably set up for a specific transaction. As for contacting the client, the records uniformly bore the notation: "As directed by JF." But with Felderhof dead, Sheri would have had no authority to give the files to the man, likely Lafond, who proclaimed himself the "client." Sally must have vouched for him. Jerome could still smell her.

One hour later, all Jerome had were the same connections he had before: Sarah's death of a drug overdose was of some interest to the extra passenger in the police car; Sarah was also connected to Lafond, who had drug connections and was connected to Sally who worked with Maydek, the lover and confidante of Felderhof, who represented the mysterious client. Like pieces of a puzzle that were all the right colours but didn't fit.

If the third man was a cop, he could have been checking out Lafond or working with Lafond. Likely working with Lafond, if he was the person in authority who got Lafond into the morgue to do whatever it was he did there. But the evidence that the person who got Lafond into the morgue was the third man was entirely speculative. And after Lafond moved to Toronto, there was nothing to suggest that his relationship with Felderhof involved anyone other than Sally.

Frustrated, Jerome decided that the only thing he could do was print out every one of the records so that he and Dirk could take a closer, fresher look later. He removed his jacket and left it hanging over the back of his chair to discourage the curious while he made his way to the supply racks in search of something in which he could carry his material. Passing by the front window, Jerome couldn't see the Neon but gave it little thought, assuming that an overzealous cop had asked Dirk to move. He picked out a heavy-duty accordion file that came with flaps and elastic bands. After a long wait at the cash, he returned to the computer and spent the better part of an hour organizing and filing the pages as they came off the tray. The records were heavy and barely fit in the file, which only added to Jerome's discomfort when he left the print shop to discover that neither Dirk nor the car had returned.

They had agreed to leave their cells on whenever they were apart. But there was no answer when he called. Dirk had his car, his gun, and all his equipment. Jerome waited impatiently for 30 minutes, then decided there was nothing he could do but go home and regroup.

■

On the subway, he realized that home might not be the safest place. Still, most of his cash was hidden there, so he had little choice. Jerome wished he had his gun, then remembered Sally, and felt sick again.

The apartment was a brisk five-minute walk from Broadview station. It was a warm, moonlit night and he could see the Neon in front of the house as he rounded the corner. There was no parking on their street after midnight without a permit, and he had warned Dirk not to risk calling attention to their car by parking it illegally. He crouched by the front porch and peered down the alleyway leading to their door. The light over the entrance, which Dirk never bothered turning on even when he knew Jerome was coming home late, shone dimly. But darkness clouded the two windows into their kitchen area that ran along the front portion of the alleyway.

Hunched over awkwardly, still carrying the accordion file, Jerome moved around to the driver's side of the car, away from the house. Using the miniature flashlight he had put on his key chain a few days after finding Paula, Jerome spotted a dark object sticking out slightly from underneath the passenger's seat. It was Sally's gun. The semi-automatic might be under the driver's seat. He remembered telling Dirk to get it out of his waist in case the parking police or the regular cops got their noses out of joint at his cavalier use of the "no stopping" zone in front of Kinko's. Dirk had the only key Rent-A-Wreck provided. But Jerome, absent-minded since Sarah's death, had become a bit of an expert at opening car doors without a key.

Staying hunched over until he got to the corner about four houses down, he straightened at the intersection and ran two blocks to the dollar store on Broadview. The sales clerk forced him to purchase the entire set of a dozen wire hangers. Tossing the extras away as he ran, he returned to the car, where the remaining, bent hanger worked smoothly in his hands. Jerome leaned over, reached under the passenger seat and retrieved the weapon. He slipped it into the large, knee-level pocket of his cargo pants. The other gun was under the driver's seat and he tucked it into his waistband. He left the accordion files on the floor of the back seat and quietly shut the driver's door without locking it. Then he circled the house, making his way to the backyard from the alleyway on the other side of the building. Their apartment had no windows facing the backyard or the rear portion of their alleyway. He shuffled carefully to the door. It was locked. He turned his key slowly, then pushed the door open just wide enough to stick in his head. With the gun pointed straight down the circular stairway ahead of him, he hugged the inside wall and paused briefly on each of the ten stairs before stopping in front of the closed door to the laundry room.

No light came from under the door to their apartment, just a few feet in front of him. He put his ear to the door but heard nothing, then reached for his keys and the flashlight, but thought better of it.

With one high kick, he knocked the door off its hinges, then hugged the wall. Bob, terrified, ran out and up the stairs.

As he turned to watch the cat, a dim figure stepped halfway out of the laundry room.

"So much unnecessary violence," a man's voice said. "Drop the gun and turn around, or I will kill you."

Jerome hesitated.

"If you shoot me, Mr. Wyndham, you may never discover what happened to your daughter."

Jerome turned back to the apartment.

"Lafond?"

"Exactly. Put the gun down."

He bent to the floor and let the gun slip from his fingers.

"Go inside and turn on the light."

Dirk was lying by the far wall partitioning the living-kitchen area from their bedroom, beside one of the two white vinyl chairs arranged train style that comprised all of the seating in the room. He was still, a large bleeding welt on his left temple.

"If you don't mind, Mr. Wyndham, I'll sit in the chair so as not to dirty my suit. Step back to the doorway. No need to turn around."

He heard Lafond pick up the semi-automatic and settle into the chair.

"Now keep your hands in the air and sit down on the floor in front of your friend and across from me."

Jerome complied, his back still to Lafond.

"Good. Turn around, please, so that we can talk like gentlemen," Lafond said in the plainest of tones.

Jerome did, crossed his legs and looked at the man. Lafond had his own gun in his left hand and the semi-automatic in his right. He was dark, long-legged, fit, and Gallic, with curly black hair professionally trimmed to show off veiled grey eyes whose controlled stillness settled nicely in a soothing voice. The man's inflections, Jerome expected, distinguished little between love and hate.

"You and I, we have many things in common," Lafond said. "We've both lost loved ones and we both must know how and why. Unfortunately for me, you will soon die in peace while I will live on in sorrow. I would prefer that you not have that peace, but as you took Sally away from me, I must confirm what you have suspected for some time — I toast your persistence — I am responsible for your daughter's death."

He had been right all along. But where he expected sadness, there was relief; where he expected satisfaction, there was hate. Bound by his helplessness, the feelings fused. "You bastard."

"Yes, but necessarily so. Sarah became unhappy with — let's call them my 'unexplained absences.' She suspected I was cheating on her, which, incidentally, offended my sense of honour and decency. When we parted over these irreconcilable differences, amicably I must say, I forgot to take my apartment keys from her. A few weeks later, I stepped out for a few moments while writing up my business logs. Sarah unfortunately chose that time to recover some things from the apartment. She was gone before I returned, but she neglected to return my journal to the page on which I was working. I had no choice but to call my superior."

Jerome's pulse quickened. "And who was that?"

"Please do not interrupt, Mr. Wyndham. All in good time."

Lafond's affected politesse energized Jerome's hatred. He had never felt so strong, so sure, so focused. Sarah was near. But when Lafond began to speak again, it was her absence that was closer than ever.

"We felt it necessary to visit her. As soon as I arrived, she began berating my profession somewhat viciously. I was surprised, believing that she would be overjoyed at the realization that I'd been faithful to her — rather more devotion than you were prepared to show to Ms. Addario, I expect. I find the remaining details gruesome and leave them to your imagination."

"You also hid drugs in her apartment and just enough money to make the police suspicious that Sarah might have been dealing as well."

Lafond didn't respond.

"And the morgue. Why did you go to the morgue?" As subtly as he could, he took a few deep breaths.

"Ah, I see you are a thorough man. Of course, or you would not have had your friend backing you up when you were with Sally. But we will talk about that presently. What were we saying? The morgue, yes, the morgue."

His senses back in focus, Jerome thought he saw Dirk stir. But his eyes remained closed and his body limp.

"Later that same day, it occurred to me that Sarah had not returned my keys, probably forgetting about them in the excitement of seeing my private records. We had not searched her person, out of respect, you understand. So my superior arranged a visit to the morgue. The keys were in her pocket."

"Why don't you just tell me your friend's name?"

"To ensure that you remain interested in what I have to say. Sally was very dear to me. She worked for almost four years as a hand-maiden to that slothful lawyer, while we waited to enjoy the things we had earned. After his death and that of his paramour, which were necessary because their situation had become alarmingly unstable, your indiscreet persistence caused Sally to stay on at Galati's longer than we had planned, and now you are responsible for her death. I ask you, how do you suggest I find my own peace?"

What did Sarah ever see in this pompous jerk? "Turn yourself in, you motherfucker."

Lafond stood up, pointed the gun at Jerome, and kicked him in the face. Jerome's head exploded, then exploded again as it hit the floor. But he was conscious, and as he struggled to get up, he could see Dirk's eyes open briefly, then close again.

"There is no point in talking to you. Get undressed."

"What?"

"To those who care, you will both have died in your sleep."

"What about Dara? Where is she?"

"Your treacherous arrangement with the authorities is directly responsible for any harm that comes to her."

Lafond motioned with the gun. Jerome removed his jacket and bent down to untie his shoes. He took off his pants and leaned over to put them on the floor near Dirk's face. His friend's eyes were open. Jerome tapped the left knee pocket gently with his forefinger. Dirk's eyes closed.

"Leave your underclothes on and lie down on the bed."

As he turned away toward the bedroom, Jerome couldn't help glancing at Dirk. The Colombian was motionless, his eyes still shut.

"Don't worry about your friend, Mr. Wyndham. His end will be no more painful than yours."

Jerome walked into the bedroom. He lay down on the bed, closed his eyes, and prayed for the loudest gunshot he had ever heard. He had always believed that he could die happily if he understood Sarah's death. Now he did. But he wanted to live. His fantasies of a satisfied death, he realized, were what had allowed him to host pain, even welcome it, for so long.

When he heard the shot, it was loud and clear and welcome and bold. Not like the lethal thump of a muted pistol. Lafond was still standing, gun in hand, when Jerome opened his eyes. Dirk, on the floor in the doorway between the two rooms, shot him again and he fell.

Jerome jumped off the bed, grabbing Lafond by the head.

"For God's sake, Lafond, give yourself a chance to get out of hell. Where's Dara? Tell me, where's Dara?"

With his last breath, Lafond spit a mouthful of blood into Jerome's face.

Wiping his cheek with his hand, Jerome heard hurried footsteps in the main floor dining room above them. He looked at Dirk, still groggy and struggling to get to his feet; he almost made it, but fell over backwards just as their landlords appeared on the staircase. Gert, with Bob in her arms, led the way, her square-set body weighing on each stair with more determination than concern; Alana followed much more tentatively, without her usual litheness.

"What the hell is going on here?" Gert said. "Are you guys drunk? Why is the door broken?"

Moving up beside Gert, Alana saw Lafond's body first.

"Is he dead? Is he dead?"

Dirk had managed to stand up.

"My God, Dirk, what happened to your face?" Alana said, still shouting.

"You don't look so good either, Jerome. I'm going to call the police," Gert said.

"I'm sorry. You can't," said Jerome, who had picked up the semi-automatic that lay in front of Lafond. He felt ridiculous in his underwear.

Alana began to whimper. "He's going to kill us, Gert. He's going to kill us," she said, moving closer to her lover.

"Nobody's going to hurt you," Jerome said. "This was an accident. I was trying to help Dirk. That man wanted to kill him."

"Why didn't you just call the police?" Gert asked defiantly.

"I'm sorry. The police are out of the question. Dirk, are you well enough to take them to the attic and tie them up?"

"Yeah, I think so. Yeah. First I take towel for head."

"Do you know how to tie proper knots?"

"Hey, I show you pictures of sailboat, no?"

"Get the girls to give you an envelope. Mark it 'mailman.'"

"Women to you," Gert interrupted.

"Shut up, you're going to get us killed," Alana said. "This is already all your fault."

"It's OK, Alana," said Jerome.

"What about body?" Dirk asked.

"See, they're going to kill us." Alana started crying.

"He means the body in the bedroom. I think we should leave it here, with his gun. His prints are on it, so at least we'll have some corroboration if we ever have to tell our stories. Now take Alana and Gert upstairs. Make sure you don't hurt them when you tie them up. I'll get our stuff. Have you got anything hidden away I don't know about?"

"No."

"Good."

"What about cat?"

"Bob belongs to Dara. We'll take him with us," Jerome said.

"Matilda doesn't like him anyway. Now I know why," Gert said.

The threesome started up the stairs. Dirk asked Gert for a towel. She stepped into the bathroom, grabbed one and threw it at him. Dirk put it to his temple, motioned to the women and started up the stairs behind them.

"Just a minute," Jerome said. Forgetting for a moment he wasn't wearing pants, he tried to stick the gun into his waist.

Dirk laughed. So did Gert.

"I hope this isn't your full-time job," she said.

"If it was, you probably wouldn't be alive," Jerome shot back, evoking the first fear he had seen in her eyes.

"I'm sorry," he said, looking away.

With the gun still in hand, he went into the bedroom, stepped over Lafond's body to the bed farthest from the door, put the gun down, and reached under the mattress for the cash he had hidden. He counted ten $100 bills as he walked back.

"Here," he said to Gert. "This should help with the damage."

"I don't want your dirty money," Gert said.

"I do," Alana said, grabbing it from Jerome so aggressively that Dirk raised his gun. "We need it, Gert."

Gert didn't object a second time.

"Good. Make sure you gag them, Dirk."

"I not child." *That's what Heidi used to say to me.*

Jerome listened to their footsteps until he could no longer hear them.

He gathered his few effects, then Dirk's gear, leaving whatever had been splattered with blood. Most of their things were in the bedroom, an area so small he couldn't avoid Lafond, stepping over him again and again. His foot brushed the body and he thought it stirred. Startled, he stumbled and tripped. He caught himself before landing beside the corpse, but as he straightened up, came face-to-face with Sarah's killer. *When did you do it? What did she say? Was she asleep? Did she die peacefully or look into your eyes? Are you the one who held her down? Did you chloroform her? Was it you who put the needle in her arm? Did you watch her die? Why? Why do I have to know everything, every last detail?*

"Tell me, you son of a bitch, tell me!" He grabbed the corpse by the throat and squeezed as hard as he could. "Tell me." He was pounding on Lafond's chest with both fists when Dirk came down, envelope and Scotch Tape in hand.

"Easy, my friend, easy," Dirk said. In a few moments, Jerome's heaving slowed. He turned to face Dirk.

"I thought it would be over when I knew," he said quietly.

"It never over, but soon be easier, not right away," Dirk said. "Now you know how she go, she really gone. Like she die again. Need time."

With the back of his hand, Jerome wiped the tears from his eyes, the drip from his nose, the sweat from his brow and hairline.

"Let's go."

"Where?"

"I need to think about that."

Dirk was holding the towel to his head.

"How are you feeling?" Jerome asked.

"Be OK. While you think, I put up note. Then I take shower and change clothes. They in bag?"

"Yes, that's a good idea. So will I."

Jerome washed his face quickly while Dirk went upstairs. He was staring at himself in the mirror, his mind blank, when Dirk returned. His friend went to the bedroom, kicked the corpse, and sat on Jerome's bed. Jerome followed him as far as the doorway, not quite sure what to do. Dirk undressed quickly, throwing his clothes on the other bed. His pants hit the wall, making a metallic noise as they slipped onto the sheets.

"My key chain. Have car key." Dirk started back over the corpse somewhat distastefully and hampered in his balance by the towel he was still holding to his head.

"Go on. I'm used to it. I'll grab the keys while you shower," Jerome said.

Dirk headed for the bathroom, taking Sally's gun with him.

"You don't look so great stark naked with a towel to your head and a gun in your hand," Jerome said. "Make sure not to take the damn thing in the shower."

"Funny man," Dirk retorted. "Maybe better if you being careful too."

Jerome had to climb back on the bed to get Dirk's pants, badly stained with wet blood. He felt queasy on what moments earlier had been his deathbed. He backed off gingerly, pants in hand. Moving into the kitchen, he felt the keys in Dirk's right pocket; he fumbled briefly, then impatiently pulled the pocket inside out. The key chain fell to the floor. So did a folded piece of paper. Jerome put the keys in his pocket and unfolded the paper. The local telephone number typed on it was vaguely familiar. He picked up a pen, pulled the notepad he had taken to carrying around with him out of his back pocket, and copied the number. Then he put the keys and the paper back in Dirk's pants before tossing them on the bed. When he heard Dirk turn the shower off, Jerome dressed hurriedly and looked around for their bags.

Jerome had fit his things in a purple duffel bag, a going-away present from George, to whom he'd mentioned that purple had been Sarah's favourite colour. Dirk's bag was prison issue, smaller, more like a gym bag. But there was plenty of room in it for his meagre possessions and the few things he'd bought after his release. Jerome grabbed both bags and put them on one of the vinyl chairs.

Dirk came out of the bathroom, gun still in hand and the towel still to his temple. He put the weapon beside the bag and using his free hand, rifled through his clothes until he came up with a grey Ocean Pacific T-shirt and navy sweatpants, which he also laid on the chair. He reached for the towel and tied it around his head before he put his clothes on. He returned to the bathroom and came back wearing his running shoes, the fresh bloodstains lost in their grime.

"Ready?" Dirk asked.

"Yeah, but take a look around to see if I missed anything. Oh, the car key's still in your pants."

"Too much blood for you?"

"Let's just say I've had all I can take for one day."

"You not kidding," said Dirk. "We go?"

"After I shower. I stink."

"Something stink, for sure. Sit down, please, Jerome."

"Excuse me?" Jerome turned around. Dirk had the gun in his hand, shaking it nervously but firmly enough to establish its purpose.

"What's going on, Dirk?"

"Please sit, Jerome," Dirk said, motioning to the empty vinyl chair.

"I'm fucking tired of people with guns telling me what to do all day."

"I talk with you. Maybe everything be ok."

"And if not?"

"We talk for now."

CHAPTER TWELVE

JEROME HUNCHED FORWARD, HIS ELBOWS ON HIS KNEES, HIS eyes on the floor between his legs, his hands alternately holding and rubbing the top of his head. He glanced up at Dirk, who was leaning back against the widest part of the kitchen counter, his legs crossed. His arms were on the counter, the gun in his hand behind him. Dirk was strangely calm, surrealistically so, like someone who had no doubt about what he knew and where he stood. Jerome couldn't hold his friend's gaze. Neither man said anything.

Jerome wondered how long Dirk had known about his deal with the Mounties. *Lafond must have told him, and if Lafond told him, then whoever ordered Sarah's murder is a cop for sure.* Still, Dirk could have killed him many times over, but didn't. Jerome waited.

Finally, the Colombian spoke. "Good sign for you, Jerome."

"What?"

"You quiet. Man who lie always speak first."

"What do you want, Dirk?"

"I want know who is Dara?"

"What?"

"Dara. Three times you say her. Before Sally die, when Lafond die, when we take cat. Not Sarah. Dara. Why?"

The question took Jerome by surprise. So did his answer.

"She's my girlfriend. She's missing, but she might still be alive. Sarah was dead. Nothing I can do about that."

"Why missing?"

Jerome was about to tell the truth when he remembered his uneasy feeling over the telephone number in Dirk's pocket.

"She went missing after I found Paula Maydek. Somebody didn't like me snooping around and decided to take her as insurance."

"How you know this?"

"They left a note," Jerome lied.

"Why no tell?"

"When Dara got into the mix, I was worried that you might think this was all about me and Sarah — especially after I found out Felderhof was dead."

"Felderhof's files best way to find someone else, no?"

"Yes, but I didn't know I could convince you of that. It's too bad you're such a good shot."

"Maybe. But no need convince me. You friend, you say, I believe. I friend, I say, you believe. Also Lafond tell he know me."

"What?"

"He say he know me."

"What did he mean?"

Dirk took his palms off the counter, turned them up, gun in hand, and shrugged. Both men went silent again.

"Maybe you ought to take a look at those records," Jerome said finally.

"Why?"

"If Lafond says he knew you, maybe there's something in there that you can recognize."

"Maybe. But first other thing, more important."

Jerome's stomach turned.

"Why Lafond say what you arrange with authorities hurt Dara? What you arrange?"

So Lafond didn't tell him. Or maybe he did. It hadn't occurred to him that Dirk was conscious enough to make sense of anything while he and Lafond were talking.

"I made a deal with Portland, the cop who arrested me."

"You deal me?"

"Don't be stupid, Dirk. I wanted to be sure the cops wouldn't be on my back all the time. So I promised that if Sarah's death was tied to drug trading, I'd let them know."

Dirk wasn't convinced.

"How Lafond know?"

"He's a big time drug dealer. Maybe he had some Mountie on the take."

"Make sense in my country. Now I tell something."

He reached in his pocket and appeared confused for a moment.

"Where dirty pants?"

Jerome motioned to the bedroom.

"Please get," Dirk said.

Jerome did and handed them to Dirk, who had moved away from the counter, leaving the gun there. He reached into one front pocket, then the other, retrieved the keys and the paper Jerome had found, and handed the paper to Jerome.

"You know number?"

"No."

"Sure?"

Jerome thought again.

"I don't know the number, but I do know the exchange. It's the one on my contact number for the cops." That much was true.

"What happen when you call?"

"I haven't called."

"I call, to see what is, but only get machine. When I leave Lorimar, I find number and letter in papers. Letter say you work with police against me and if I help police, they help me."

"And you didn't tell me, right?"

"I be careful."

"Me too, you should be able to understand that."

"First I think is trick from police, even after I hear Dara. Then too much coincidence when I hear what Lafond say."

"Well, I can't help you anymore," Jerome said. "You either believe me or you don't."

What Dirk said next would determine whether Jerome jumped him.

"You alive only because you see I leave gun there and you do nothing."

As he spoke, Dirk pulled the semi-automatic from behind him and pointed it at Jerome. "But I still not sure. Where records?"

"In the car."

"Good. Where we go?"

"To Lafond's place." Where, it occurred to Jerome, nobody was home.

Jerome picked up their bags and started up the stairs. There wasn't much point covering their tracks: Gert and Alana knew his alias and Dirk by his first name. The police would have an APB, a nationwide warrant, and an Interpol alert out on them by noon tomorrow. It would describe them as "armed and dangerous."

■

Bob sat contentedly in the front passenger seat. Dirk was in the back going through the records, using the flashlight Jerome had retrieved from the trunk and for which he had purchased batteries. Jerome took a left at Broadview and drove towards the nearest exit to the Don Valley Parkway. It was almost midnight when they turned onto the highway, but a steady stream of traffic flowed north towards Toronto's bedroom communities until the never-ending construction on the Parkway slowed things down near Lawrence Avenue, about halfway to the city limits at Steeles. From time to time, Jerome feigned a mirror check to glance at Dirk. His friend's face was intense but impassive. He worked slowly, turning the pages and moving them to and from the accordion files to produce the only sound inside the car apart from the occasional ticking of the turn signal. It took them almost an hour to reach the 401 from Lawrence, a ten-minute drive by distance alone. Jerome turned west on the 16-lane artery that skirted the city's north end. Traffic slowed again due to an accident near the airport exit, turning the 15- or 20-minute ride to Highway 10, which would lead them north to Caledon and Lafond's estate, into a 45-minute ordeal.

When they cleared the arteries around Brampton, the lights disappeared and the traffic dissipated. Dirk was still at work, wearing the same unchanging expression, as if he had no inclination to breathe. The darkness made it hard to see him in the rear-view mirror, and soon Jerome found himself lost in thought, driving by rote, one hand gently stroking Bob's back.

Somehow, Jerome had expected that when he finally laid Sarah to rest, truth would no longer elude him. It was as if Sarah's death had eliminated truth as a way of life. He had lied to everyone: Heidi, his friends, his clients, judges, his colleagues, Dirk, Portland, he could go on forever. He had even lied to Dara, weaving emotional silkscreens that let only the facsimiles of his feelings emerge. But now that he knew that his daughter was who he believed her to be — not a druggie, not unhappy, not suicidal — he wished Heidi were around. He wanted to tell her that she was right: they had been good parents, they hadn't failed Sarah, and they hadn't failed themselves. He also wanted to tell her that he missed her, but settled for silently wishing her happiness with Willy and their new baby.

For a moment, he was himself content. Yet just as quickly, he knew he would continue to lie to Dirk and to Portland and to whomever else it took. He would lie because he had, yet again, lied to himself: he had promised himself that knowing how Sarah died would bring him peace, but that was a lie too. Knowing was not enough: it was just that without it, he could not have imagined revenge. Now that Sarah's end was real, now that he knew he wasn't crazy, he would find and kill the man who had ordered her murder. If Dirk didn't kill him first.

"Where we are?" came Dirk's voice from the stillness of the rear seat.

"A few miles from Lafond's house. We turn left at the next corner, about four miles down the road."

"Then stop car," Dirk said.

They were on a lonely gravel road defined by a ditch on both sides that left just enough room for two cars to pass each other.

"Here?"

"Yes, stop now."

Jerome pulled the car over as best he could, which left almost half its width on the road. He turned on the four-ways. Dirk chuckled.

"Now you careful. But nobody here."

"Actually, that's too bad."

"Depend for who."

Jerome's mind raced for a response that would buy him time. Dirk got out of the car and moved quickly around the back to the driver's side, the semi-automatic in his hand. Staying clear of the driver's door, Dirk motioned Jerome to get out and waved him to the rear of the car near the ditch. Clouds obscured the moon and in the darkness, the barrel of Dirk's gun reflected the rhythm of the four-ways.

Flickering my life away.

Dirk raised his arm. Then he reached for the gun with his other hand, held it by the barrel, turned it around, and handed it to Jerome — who almost dropped it.

"I sorry, my friend. I wrong about you," he said, embracing Jerome in a tight bear hug.

Jerome stepped back to balance himself against the trunk of the car, breaking Dirk's grip.

"Jesus," he said. "What the hell did you find in those records?"

"I find Holland Drilling."

"Holland Drilling?"

"Yes. You know where database say 'Trade Names.' I find Holland Drilling."

Jerome had no idea what Dirk was talking about.

"Holland Drilling is name of company where I ship cocaine. Company close so they arrest me. Records show Lafond make Holland. He man responsible for my jail, my wife and daughter —

and me — alone so long. If Holland Drilling in lawyer's records, Felderhof is Canadian contact for Ludwig. So we on right track. If I not find money, I find someone to kill."

Jerome finally let out his breath.

"Do you think the police know about the connection between Felderhof and Ludwig?" he asked.

"I not know name of contact. But maybe police trace company to Felderhof."

"What did you say on the telephone at the airport?"

"Nothing. I give code name."

"What was that?"

"I no remember."

"And?"

"Woman ask me questions about shipment. Stupid questions. Address. Where come from. Where stay. I angry. I want speak to Ludwig's friend about transfer my money."

"You mentioned transferring money?"

"Yes. I say 'Ludwig's friend, lawyer.' She tell me go to hotel and wait for telephone next morning. I hang up, turn around, maybe ten police around me. What you think?"

"I'm thinking we should get back in the car and go to Lafond's place. Maybe we'll find some more pieces of the puzzle. I hope Dara's alive."

Jerome drove. He'd had quite enough of driving, but he didn't want to talk, and driving allowed him to get away with silence. Besides, he had no truth to add to their conversation.

Not that the truth was obvious, even with the new information from Dirk. To be sure, Gunnar and his crew had been straight with him about Dirk's intentions in Canada, though they didn't know that Dirk was looking to recover money as well as launder it; in any case, tracking Dirk would lead them to a bigger catch. But either the horsemen didn't trust Jerome or one or more of them wanted to derail the investigation. There could be no other explanation for trying to turn

Dirk into an informer too. Even Portland's offer to let Jerome keep some of his stash — not to mention the beating he got at Lorimar — could have been a subtle message to go easy with the informer stuff. Still, if the Mounties wanted him off the case, why hang the stash over his head in the first place?

Dara's abduction could also support the derailment theory, except that nothing her kidnappers did suggested they were concerned with Dirk or anything but putting an end to Jerome's investigation of Sarah's death. The only link — and a tenuous link it was — between Dirk's activities and Sarah's death was Lafond's involvement with drugs and laundering. But even that could have been coincidence: Dara's interview with Lafond after Sarah died would have made it clear to him that Jerome wasn't buying the official version of Sarah's death. It made sense for Lafond to keep an eye on him. And Jerome's call to Sally arranging the appointment at Galati's likely put Lafond on high alert: he had made a mistake mentioning Brenda Maydek's name. The other explanation was that a cop had betrayed Jerome to Lafond. But a connection between Lafond and the police was even more tenuous, based solely on the photograph of the "third man" entering the police car at the scene of Sarah's death, and Lafond's reference to a "superior." The "third man," who may or may not have been a policeman, and may or may not have been Lafond's "superior," could easily have been a well-connected member of the drug under-world whose strategically dispensed dollars bought access to the morgue.

"You not say we turn left when is next corner?" Dirk asked.

"Yes, have we passed it?"

"Yes, maybe one minute. You sleep?"

"No, just thinking."

"Think what?"

"Probably the same things you're thinking," Jerome said, as he swung the car wide to the right and initiated a U-turn that he completed in two passes. "Actually, I'm very worried about Dara."

"You love her?"

"I'm worried about her. It's my fault she's in danger."

"When you don't worry, you love her?"

"I don't remember."

"You still big talker, my friend."

"Go easy, Buga, we're getting close."

Jerome slowed down as they drove along the wall. Wary of rousing the dogs, he slowed further as they passed the gate. He parked the car in the woods again.

"Did you bring the other gun with you from the apartment?" Jerome asked as he opened the trunk.

"Yes," said Dirk, reaching behind him for Sally's weapon.

"Then let's go."

"First better you put bullets in gun," Dirk said. He returned Sally's weapon to his belt.

Jerome pulled the semi-automatic from his waist. The magazine was gone. Dirk took it from his pocket and gave it to Jerome, who shoved it into the pistol.

"Better to be sure. Back on road I no sure. Now I sure."

Either way, you're a liability now. Apart from providing backup, Dirk's usefulness had expired. He had no other information that could help Jerome find Dara or Sarah's remaining killer. And as soon as the police interviewed Gert and Alana and discovered Lafond's body, Jerome's role as an informer was no longer an advantage.

"Put your hands up, Dirk," Jerome said, pointing the gun at the Colombian.

Dirk raised his arms slowly. "You have to kill me, my friend. I no go back to jail. Even if nothing else sure, that sure."

Lucky for you that you love your daughter and she loves you. "Kidding, Dirk. I just wanted to see how someone else looked down the barrel of a loaded gun."

Unbelieving, Dirk left his hands up.

"Come on, Buga, have a hug. I'm sorry."

The men embraced. Jerome thought he felt Dirk wipe away a tear. "Let's go," he said.

The full moon was still behind the clouds. Jerome took the flashlight from Dirk and started toward the rear gate.

"Stay back and cover me," he said.

The modulator worked perfectly again. Jerome opened the gate slightly and stepped into the yard.

Viciousness alone couldn't explain how quickly and effectively they attacked. They had been trained to kill without quarter, an instinct refined perhaps by hunger, perhaps because they had been waiting too long for their masters.

The larger of the two Rottweilers bounded to Jerome's throat in a single, soundless leap. The second snarled as it bit into his calf. The gun flew from Jerome's right hand, the flashlight from his left to the ground behind him, its still-shining light pointed uselessly away from the fray. He staggered sideways and went down just outside the gate, both dogs on top of him.

Without his own light in the blackened countryside, Dirk was afraid to shoot. He wasn't even sure how many dogs there were. Or whether there was anyone following them. He fired once in the air, as close to the confusion as he dared to. The dogs were undeterred. He fired again, into the ground near the outline of the writhing bodies. This time, the smaller of the Rottweilers took umbrage and came at him. The dog was in mid-air when Dirk shot him, yet the animal's momentum bowled him over. He was unhurt, and rose. He could hear the fatally wounded dog on the ground near him, breathing heavily. But it was strangely quiet otherwise, and suddenly very bright. The dogs had knocked the gate wide open, triggering a series of lights on top of the wall and another set along the ground illuminating a pathway to the house.

A low growl reoriented Dirk. He stared in the direction of Jerome, who lay still. The remaining Rottweiler stood beside his body, poised to take on Dirk. The dog moved toward him. Dirk raised his gun and fired. He barely heard the click of an empty chamber, a sound far deadlier to a shooter than a gunshot, before the leaping dog obliterated his senses. He landed on the ground with the dog on top of him, seeking his throat. Dirk flailed at the animal, who bit into his left palm for his trouble, then continued his pursuit of his victim's larynx. Through the pain, Dirk pushed at the animal's chest and managed to move him slightly upwards, raising his front paws and keeping his teeth from inflicting a fatal wound. The dog retaliated by tearing at his arms, and it wasn't long before he could no longer maintain his hold.

"Enough!" The dog froze in response to the voice — a woman's voice — from the shadows by the wall. Sheri Fitzjames stepped into the light and hand-signalled the dog over with her right hand, then moved it back to the shotgun she was supporting in her left.

"Thank you, madam," said Dirk disingenuously, holding his bleeding palm face-up.

"You two must be the reason Pierre and Sally didn't come back or answer their cells," she said. "I guess you're a little smarter than they gave you credit for. Sometimes it doesn't pay to be too smart. Where are they?"

"I not know what you mean."

She eyed the dog, who was still at attention. "Brutus here can do the job quickly or he can do it slowly," she said. "You might not get off as easy as your friend."

Jerome was still lifeless on the ground.

"I not understand."

"You understand very well. So do I. Sally told me what Masters — excuse me, Wyndham — was up to after he left the office. Now, who are you?"

"I friend for Jerome. Help to look for Dara."

"And what else?"

"He tell nothing."

She glanced at the dog. "I'm not going to ask any more questions. Either you tell me the whole story while you still have all your body parts or you tell it to me when you're a little more fragmented."

"Frag — ? "

"Missing pieces."

Dirk jumped at the sound of a gun discharging. Brutus, momentarily stiller and more menacing than he was before, fell to the ground, blood oozing from under one ear.

"I'm afraid you're the one who will have to tell us the whole story, Sheri," Jerome said. "Throw your weapon over near Dirk."

She did, then dropped to the ground beside Brutus and took the dog's bleeding head in her arms.

"You shoot good too. I think you dead. Now we almost even," Dirk said, picking up Sheri's pistol, then hurrying to take the semiautomatic from an ashen Jerome, who was still on the ground propping himself up on his elbows. His jacket, shirt, and pant leg were torn, and he was bleeding from a large gash on the side of his face and wounds to his left shoulder and thigh. Jerome collapsed his elbows and shuffled his weight onto his right shoulder. Dirk, behind his friend so he could face Sheri, picked up Jerome's pistol, put it in his belt, and reached for Jerome.

"Not yet," Jerome said. "I need to rest."

Sheri hadn't moved from beside the dog.

"I thought you trained them and left them," Jerome said weakly.

She began to blubber, her bravado stripped by her dog's death. "I just wanted my own dogs. Sally said if I helped them, I could make enough money to do that. Mr. Galati signed whatever I put in front of him. After you left, they told me you would get us all arrested. So I agreed to watch Addario. I didn't know this would happen."

"You mean you happier if you still have gun and dog still alive," said Dirk, who had moved a few steps toward the gate to retrieve the flashlight.

"Just a minute, Dirk," said Jerome. "Where's Dara now?"

"I don't know. They took her about an hour before you came."

"Who took her?"

"I don't know. Pierre called me earlier and said a man would be coming. He said to leave the door open after the man identified himself on the intercom, then make myself scarce and stay in the den until after he left."

"How did he identify himself?"

The bullet from behind her went though her throat before she could answer. Dirk, lying near the gate, had sufficient presence of mind to pull it shut. The lights went out. All was still save for those sounds of a country night that attain significance only when frightened people listen for them. After a few minutes, they heard soft steps moving away from them, then a vehicle starting up and leaving.

"Dirk," Jerome whispered. "Open the gate and trigger the lights, but be ready to close it."

The lights came on, transforming the night's sounds to a background hum again. They waited. Nothing disturbed the sudden transparency.

But for Jerome, the respite was brief. He saw Sarah, then Dara, before his own darkness took the light from him again.

■

When he awoke, he was laid out in the back of the Neon with Bob sitting contentedly on his stomach. Dirk was driving along a paved, dark road with no traffic in sight.

"How you are, my friend?" Dirk said.

"Weak. What happened?"

"You faint. I carry you to car."

"Where are we?"

"I go north. Too many police in city. We stop at pharmacy in morning. Get something for bites, me and you. Meantime you sleep, but first I show you."

"What?"

Dirk pulled the car over to the narrow shoulder. He reached for the dashboard and picked up several pieces of paper. Then he leaned forward, and from the floor in front of him, he retrieved their flashlight. He turned around and held up three documents of varying sizes. "This under wiper."

Jerome squinted to focus his vision. Dirk handed Jerome his glasses and shone the light on the first document. It was Dara's social insurance card, with the word "insurance" circled boldly in black ink; the second was an airline itinerary for passengers Lafond and Clark, bound from Toronto to Provo through Miami on the following Thursday; the third was a piece of stationery bearing the Island Trust logo and the words "Sunday, 9 a.m." printed across the middle.

"What day is it?" Jerome asked wearily.

"Tuesday morning, almost."

"We've got five days to get to the Turks and Caicos. Call Roger. He'll pick us up and get us a doctor. I'm sure we can stay with him. Maybe he can help us figure a way out of the country."

PART

THREE

CHAPTER THIRTEEN

"WHO'D HAVE BELIEVED WYNDHAM WAS A KILLER? IT'S A HELL of a ride," Buddy said, not without relish as he picked over his mid-afternoon muffin at the Second Cup on Queen's Quay. "How can you be sure?"

Portland had told him early on that Jerome had admitted to hiding money away. Buddy agreed to keep the information confidential until the "continuing investigation" was over. But when Wyndham's involvement in the Clark and Lafond shootings surfaced, Portland, after talking it over with Gunnar, decided the prudent course — given his promise to keep Buddy up-to-date — would be to call the reporter before the reporter called him.

"He and Mueller were living at the apartment where Lafond was shot. The landladies eyeballed both of them. Besides, Wyndham was using an alias we knew about and Mueller was using his own name."

"The landladies?"

"Yeah, they heard the shots and came downstairs. Wyndham and Mueller tied them up overnight and left a note for the mailman."

"Very considerate."

"Also very indiscreet. If this was murder, why leave witnesses?"

"Anybody else involved?"

"Just a cat."

"A cat?"

"Yeah. Wyndham brought it to the apartment soon after he rented it and took it with him after the shooting. Turns out it was Dara Addario's cat."

"Wyndham's girlfriend — but I thought they split when he was arrested."

"She visited him in prison. Now we know he's been in touch with her since his release. Do you know about the shooting at the lawyer's office in Yorkville last night?"

"Gary Galati's office, wasn't it?" said Buddy, who rarely skipped a news item involving lawyers or the law. His interest in the legal profession had, if anything, heightened since he changed beats. The *Standard* had never got around to canceling his subscription to *Law Times*, the weekly that catered to the Ontario bar, and he read it assiduously. Still, while he saw the occasional lawyer at City Hall, he missed his everyday dealings with them — the passion, competitiveness, wit, and capacity for hard work that imbued their daily lives. The combination showed well in proximity, he thought, but at a distance and in the glare of the headlines that always accompanied lawyers' misdeeds, gave rise to a collective public persona of arrogance, shrewdness, and greed.

"Wyndham may be involved in that too," Portland said, as Buddy reached into his knapsack for his steno pad. "But the information isn't for attribution or for print — that goes for anything I say today — unless I tell you otherwise."

Buddy nodded.

"A witness heard shots from behind Galati's building. Then a car pulled out of the driveway and rammed a southbound van on Avenue Road. The car took off, but the witness got the plate number. It's registered to Addario."

"Did anybody get a look at the people in the car?"

"Witnesses say the driver was the only occupant, but nobody got a good look at him . . . actually, we don't even know if it was a man or a woman."

Portland's voice trailed off. He'd carefully thought out what he would tell Ladner, but the reporter's conversational tone had imparted an intimacy to the narrative that made it hard for him to be selective.

"Holding out on me, Adam?"

Portland shook his head. "It turns out that wasn't the first we'd heard of Addario or her car. A few weeks ago, Tracey Young, she's with narcotics, got an anonymous tip that the car was an abandoned drug transport. Sure enough, it came up as unclaimed on the City's tow sheet. She couldn't find Addario — she didn't know anything about her connection to Wyndham, of course — so she got a warrant to haul the car in to our compound. But when forensics checked out the car, it was clean. So is Addario: former cop, PI licence, no arrests, no shady connections — except maybe Wyndham — and a good reputation with the insurance companies who use her. Young was about to send the car back when she got a call from a woman named Sheri Fitzjames who said she worked for — get this — Galati & Associates. She said the firm represented Addario and demanded the immediate return of the car or else there would be a lawsuit. Her client, she said, was too upset to pick up the car herself, so could she get it? Young says OK. She shows up at the compound, produces the car registration and ID, and away she goes. Next thing we know the car's speeding away from Galati's office."

"So Addario's at one shooting and Wyndham's at another. You think the car's enough to get Wyndham convicted of both murders?"

Portland couldn't tell whether the reporter was skeptical or not.

"We've got more. Clark was living with Lafond. And one of the landlords at Wyndham's place said she saw two guns. She doesn't know anything about guns, but from the way she described them, one could have been a .38 and the other a semi-automatic. A .38 calibre killed Lafond and a semi-automatic killed Clark. We also found a .38 calibre bullet lodged in a car in the parking lot where she was shot. When we hear from ballistics, we'll know whether the .38s match."

"When will that be?"

"Soon, hopefully."

"What I don't understand is why Wyndham would want to kill these people," Buddy said.

Portland took a sip of his decaf latte. "The killings may not have been planned. The bullet we found in the parking lot could have come from a weapon Clark was carrying, which suggests a gunfight of some kind. And in Lafond's case, Wyndham must have known there was a good chance the landlords would be home that time of night. Also, the way the landlady described the semi-automatic suggests it had a silencer. If this was planned, why use the .38 and broadcast the killing?"

Portland's cell rang. He took it from his inside breast pocket, answered it, held up a finger, stepped outside, and walked towards the lake. His absence let Buddy reflect on his enthusiasm for the news he had just heard.

He wanted Wyndham to be a killer. He knew that. The bigger this story got, the better it got. Violence — especially serial violence — from the upper classes or the professions, even more than violence against them, moved crime stories and reporters above the fold to front page space usually reserved for wars and budgets, from local headlines to national and even international headlines. Getting a tip about a stash was one thing; getting a tip about a stash that led an ex-lawyer to kill randomly was quite another; and being the reporter who got the tip was best of all — the definitive professional tribute. If Wyndham wasn't a killer, the accolades wouldn't be quite as boisterous.

Buddy had little sympathy for Wyndham, a by-product of his years watching, interviewing, and analyzing criminal lawyers and defending their peculiar set of moral priorities to his readers and friends. To be sure, when criminal lawyers did their jobs well and the system worked as intended, and whether or not he agreed with the outcome of a particular case, Buddy's respect for a job well done ruled him; but when lawyers screwed up or went bad, he couldn't help but feel that they had been tarred with the constant exposure to their clients' brush — dulled, as it were, to moral sensibility.

So despite Portland's assurances to the contrary and despite his visceral need to rub against the grain, Buddy could never separate Wyndham from Lewis when it came to the missing funds. He just couldn't suspend his disbelief that a lawyer who had crossed the dividing line — especially a professional as accomplished as Wyndham was — could resist all the benefits on the other side. And resistance was what it was about. As keepers of the public trust, professionals were subject to temptation. There were those who succumbed, and those who didn't. Those who succumbed were no different than their clients, just better-placed until they were caught.

Portland returned with more news.

"That was Gunnar. They found Sheri Fitzjames's body at Lafond's place. Someone shot her from behind, likely with a rifle. They also found two dead Rottweilers and an empty .38 pistol. The .38 killed one dog and a semi-automatic the other. And . . ." Portland's voice trailed off. "Addario's car was in the garage."

"What's wrong, Adam?"

"Nothing."

"Come on. You've been talking a mile a minute, and all the time you look like your head's still way ahead of your mouth. What's up?"

Uncharacteristically, Portland averted his eyes, letting them wander around the coffee shop without taking anything in. He didn't blink until just before he looked at Buddy with the unpractised gaze that, both direct and yielding, had disarmed so many suspects and calmed so many victims.

"Wyndham was supposed to be working for us."

"Say what?"

"We suspected that Mueller, who was his pal in prison and doing 18 for importing cocaine, was laundering in a big way into Canada. So we used the information you gave us as a hook to turn Wyndham into an informer. The press is going to have a field day when they find out we arranged parole for both these guys, practically married them. Got any suggestions?"

Buddy couldn't believe his ears.

"Take early retirement. Does this have anything to do with the money in Provo?"

"It might. Sally Clark used to work for John Felderhof, the lawyer who was shot at the TD Centre last year. Metro believes that a former employee, Paula Maydek, was responsible. But she disappeared and it's still unsolved. After Felderhof died, Galati took over Felderhof's clients and Clark moved to his office."

"Who's got the case at Metro?" Buddy asked.

"The Felderhof murder?"

"That too."

"I don't know who's in charge of the Felderhof investigation. But Shane Whiteside got the Clark shooting, and because of the connection, he got the Lafond murder too. We're working together. Gunnar's leading our side."

"That's always fun. Who's got jurisdiction?"

"Hasn't come up specifically yet."

"It will. Do you remember the brouhaha between Einarson and Whiteside a few years ago after a botched drug sting ended up with three people dead, including a civilian? That was good copy."

"Wasn't fun for us, I imagine."

"Do they get along better now?"

"Between you and me? No. By the way, Whiteside asked if you'd been in touch with me recently."

"I told him I was going to call you about Wyndham, but I didn't tell him why. Tell me more."

"Felderhof's been murdered and Maydek's nowhere to be found. Clark, who worked with Felderhof and Maydek, is dead. Lafond, Clark's common-law, is also dead, and so is Fitzjames, who we're told worked closely with Clark. Wyndham is implicated in both murders that occurred after his release. His girlfriend, who may have drug connections Wyndham does or doesn't know about, is also a suspect. Wyndham was in prison when Felderhof was murdered and Maydek disappeared, but Addario was alive and well in Toronto and not too long after, she visited Wyndham. The wild card is that Wyndham's daughter died of a drug overdose. To my mind, all that information is a route map — however convoluted — from Wyndham to Felderhof, but the road signs are disappearing and Wyndham is taking them down. Why? All I can think of is that somehow Felderhof and the people around him are linked to Wyndham's and maybe Lewis's offshore accounts. With or without Lewis's input, they decide that they're better off with Wyndham serving his entire sentence. They tip you off to the account. But he gets out. When he does, he decides he's not going to tolerate any more surprises, so with Mueller's help, he takes things into his own hands. They make a few visits. Things get messy. Whiteside says both killings smack of drug deals gone bad, which is where we come in. There's also our connection to Wyndham and Mueller."

Portland paused.

"You're right. I am running at the mouth. What do you make of all of this, Buddy?"

"Nothing right off the bat. Why do you ask?"

"I was hoping you'd have some new ideas about who tipped you off to the account."

"I wish I did. To my mind, Lewis is the only one who'd want to keep Wyndham in jail, especially if they had a deal to split the money when Wyndham got out. So Lewis sets up an account in Wyndham's name, puts some money in it, and then leaves me an anonymous note. Slick. Have you discovered how much money is in that account, Adam?"

Portland shook his head. Without a formal application to the Turks and Caicos courts, it was virtually impossible to find out anything about Island Trust. Gunnar's prediction that the higher-ups at Justice Canada would take months to approve the application had proven accurate. Gunnar didn't seem concerned, saying that Wyndham's "confession" was enough evidence for the time being.

"I can believe Wyndham tucked some money away," Portland said.

"But I can't believe he made a deal with Lewis. He distrusted him. Loathed him. He told me he wasn't particularly fond of him even when they were just playing squash."

"And that leaves the crew around Felderhof as the most logical candidates to have planted the note."

"Except that there's no evidence Felderhof was doing anything shady. And apart from these two killings, there's nothing to suggest that Wyndham even knew these people before he was arrested."

"They're killing each other."

Portland shrugged. He finished his cold coffee and stood up to go. "Let me know if you get any more notes on your desk," he said.

"Naturally. Thanks for the information. I appreciate it. By the way, Helen and I are having dinner at Sood's next week. He always asks about you."

"Is he still doing that computer stuff on the side?"

"Yeah. Making quite a reputation for himself. Glad he's with the good guys."

"No kidding. We could use his talents on the force. Technology's everything these days."

"I'll tell him. See you, Adam."

■

From the slew of reports on his desk, Portland discerned that Whiteside and his team had been working with their usual dispatch. They had found Paula's body in the shed, where the lock had been shot off the door; a single set of man-sized footprints, a few days old and roughly matching a partial footprint found outside Jerome's apartment, led up the stairs, but there were no matching footprints indicating a corresponding entry. The bullet that killed Maydek came from the gun discovered beside Lafond's body in the basement bedroom. Only Lafond's prints were on that gun. The .38 calibre bullet that turned up in the parking lot and the shots that killed Lafond also came from one gun, though not the one that killed Maydek. Lafond's prints were all over the Geo, as were Fitzjames's; Dara's prints — on record in her PI licence application file — were there too, though only a partial print appeared on the steering wheel. Other prints belonging to her, Lafond, Clark, and Fitzjames turned up in a large storage area in the basement of Lafond's home. Among the stored items, more or less what one would expect to find in the basement or garage of an upper-class home, the police discovered a cot, recently used, partly covered by a thin blue acrylic bedspread and a mattress that wasn't much thicker; they'd sent it to forensics, hoping it would give them some clue as to who was in it. Whiteside's squad also found a tray, a plate with remnants of food still on it, a fork, and a used plastic cup. In the corner lay an enamel bowl half-full of water; beside it, a small bar of soap that had "POLICE #3" etched into it, likely with the fork. Dara's prints were on the fork.

An urgent message to call Whiteside was in Portland's voice mail.

"I think you should give Brenda Maydek the bad news about her daughter," Whiteside said. "She's not comfortable with us because Paula was our prime suspect in Felderhof's killing. She's been saying all along that we had it wrong. Since somebody's got to tell her, it might as well be you. Nobody working for me has what it takes to finesse this."

Portland agreed, though he wasn't happy about it. Finesse wasn't his strong point. It wasn't Whiteside's either, he suspected, albeit for different reasons. The people who had that talent, Portland thought, were either afraid to or didn't want to tell it as it was, or they were afraid that the people they were talking to didn't want to hear it as it was — as if they could somehow discern the emotional agendas of those to whom they were unable to speak frankly. But in either case, self-interest, which was a way of trying to ensure where the chips would fall, governed their conduct. And self-interest, from Portland's perspective, was what distinguished finesse from tact and forthcoming from blunt.

Wishing to have as little time elapse between his initial contact and his visit, he called Paula's mother from a payphone in the Manulife's concourse after parking his car in the underground lot; if she wasn't home, he'd get a coffee and wait it out, maybe buy Bonnie a treat from the Swiss chocolatier on the second floor and check out the newest stereo components at Bay Bloor Radio. Listening to Bocelli and Battle on his old system, which had come with a turntable, didn't do them justice, nor did what passed for a stereo system in his Escort.

But Maydek was in when he called, and when he stepped off the elevator just after five o'clock, she was waiting in the doorway of her apartment, looking as she did when Jerome left, wrapped in the same moment of time that made the future irrelevant.

"I know why you're here, Sergeant," she said with unexpected calm. "I've known ever since Mr. Masters — I guess his real name is Wyndham — came to see me."

Portland, surprised, hesitated at the door.

"Do come in," she smiled. "I've put coffee on."

"Thank you, I can use some," Portland said, as she sat down on the couch and motioned him to the chair Jerome had occupied.

"I'm very sorry about your daughter," Portland said.

"I have little grieving left in me now that I know I can bury Paula. Do you know how she died?"

"She was shot. We found her on a property north of Toronto."

"Did she suffer?"

"We don't think so. She seems to have died quickly, without pain before or at the time she died."

"Who killed her?"

"We don't know yet."

"I turned on the news and saw you were looking for Mr. Wyndham. His picture was on all the stations."

"He's a suspect."

There was a long silence. Maydek cleared her throat and covered her mouth.

"Did you know that Mr. Wyndham's daughter had died too?"

"I did," Portland replied.

"I saw his face when he talked about it. He couldn't have killed my daughter, then come to our house and looked me straight in the eye."

"He thought Paula was dead?"

"He didn't say so explicitly, but we both assumed it."

"Do you feel up to talking about his visit?" Portland asked.

"You didn't know about it?"

"Does that make a difference?"

"Of course not," Maydek said, sounding rather as if she welcomed the topic.

Jerome had given her some closure, she said. He seemed to know a fair bit about Paula. He was aware that Paula and Felderhof were lovers and that Paula wasn't fired but had quit. She had shown him the note from Felderhof and told him about the $100,000 in her safety deposit box.

"Why did you tell Jerome these things when you withheld them from the police?" Portland asked.

"He was on my side," she said. "He believed that John used his immigration practice to launder money. He also said that John knew a man named Pierre Lafond, who had something to do with drug trafficking. Lafond was the boyfriend of Mr. Wyndham's daughter when she died of a drug overdose. We both lost a child. That's why he contacted me."

Portland fought off the urge to interrupt her so he could make sense of it all. "Did he tell you anything else about Lafond?"

"He thought Lafond was involved in Paula's death too."

"How?"

"He didn't say."

"What about Felderhof?"

"No. He seemed to know almost nothing about John or his office."

"Did he mention Sally Clark, by any chance?"

"I did. I told him we'd stayed in touch. I gave him her number."

"Did he say why he wanted it?"

"Not specifically. But I got the impression he was trying to find out more about Mr. Felderhof's files."

"And was he in touch with you again?"

"No, but he promised to bring whatever he could of Paula back to me. He's done that, hasn't he?"

"I suppose so."

"Thank him then, please, if you see him. Now, if there's nothing else I can help with, could you let me know when I might see my daughter?"

"I can take you there now."

They drove to the morgue in silence. After Portland arranged for her admittance and she identified the body, she told him she wanted time with Paula by herself. She would take a cab home. A man with more finesse might have tried to talk her out of returning to her apartment alone.

But it was almost as hard for him to leave her as it had been for Jerome.

■

Portland called Gunnar as soon as he had his four-year-old sedan out on the road. Gunnar didn't answer, so Portland called Marta, who said her husband was locked up with the brass and she didn't know when he'd be home. Portland left urgent messages with dispatch and on Gunnar's voice mail.

If Lafond was Sarah's boyfriend and had drug connections, the investigation took on a new perspective. But it was after eleven now, and Portland had worked through the last two days with little sleep. He was too tired to figure out whether things added up. He'd give it another shot during his three-mile run at sunrise, then trade thoughts with Gunnar and Yu first thing in the morning. Right now he was hungry, not having thought about food since he grabbed a sandwich in the police cafeteria early that afternoon.

He took the old highway home to Whitby, avoiding the 401 which, depending on the traffic, went by too fast or too slowly to let him think. True, there wasn't much farmland on the old road anymore; in its place were strip malls, family restaurants, and other commercial developments that served the bedroom region's booming population. But this late on Tuesday night, the four-lane thoroughfare that had replaced the old two-lane blacktop was mostly at rest, the business lights dimmed, the drivers in no particular hurry; and from time to time, the road still skirted unobstructed stretches of Lake Ontario's shore, where Portland invariably opened the windows, even in winter, to soothe himself with the sounds of things that didn't change. He'd stop at Jade's 24-hour diner, where nobody knew he was a cop and nobody would ask, for a vegetable burrito or the occasional home-made pie and hot chocolate, and play at travelling salesman with Angie, the same waitress who'd served him at the window table since he first found the place almost ten years ago. By the time he cuddled up to Bonnie, asleep on his side of the bed, he'd be at peace, ready to rest and grateful for the ease with which he could put his day behind him.

But there was a note on the ensuite bathroom mirror. "Call this number. Urgent. Doesn't matter what time." He took the bedroom portable into the bathroom. No answer. He hung up, put the telephone on the large vanity safely away from the sink, removed his Suit People jacket and tie and his Stedman's undershirt, hung them temporarily over the hook on the back of the door, turned on the water, felt the urge, and was sitting on the toilet seat wondering what the message was all about when the phone rang.

"Adam," Jerome said after hearing Portland's hello. "I need to see you."

Portland stayed on the toilet, trying to collect his thoughts. "I've never had a suspect leave a message with my wife before," he said.

"I'm not going to stay on this line long, Adam. Listen to me. You can't tell anyone that we're meeting. If you do, they'll kill me and they'll probably kill you too."

"Who?"

"Gunnar for sure."

"All right. Where?"

"I'll let you know."

Portland was dialing Gunnar even as the line clicked dead on Jerome's end.

Bonnie stirred. "What's going on, love?" she murmured from the bedroom.

"Go to sleep, sweetheart," Portland said as he hung up. "I'm just going downstairs to make a call."

The walk down the hall and the stairs to the den on the first floor of the two-storey builder's model that he and Bonnie had almost paid off might have afforded some men the pause the strange telephone call surely deserved. But not Portland. He was a cop. Gunnar was his boss. Jerome was an outlaw and from all appearances, a dangerous one. He'd deal with his doubts after he did his job.

Gunnar was calm when he heard the news. "He's a very clever man, pitting us against each other. There's nothing else we can do until we hear from him again. Let's meet at seven in my office."

"We should bring Whiteside to the meeting," Portland said.

"No. I want to get to Wyndham before Metro does. The suits want to keep as much of a lid as possible on this. Now get some sleep."

Two hours later, lying beside Bonnie, Portland decided he'd best put it all in writing before the meeting. He got up, put on one of his two track suits, and went for his run. When he returned, he took fresh clothes from the bedroom, showered in the bathroom off the hall, made coffee, then went back upstairs to leave a note for Bonnie and kiss her goodbye. Coffee mug in hand, he took the 401 to the office.

■

The message light on his desk phone was blinking. Reception had a package for him. He called down for it. A nervous young constable

brought up the plain white envelope. The handwritten note, in red, was in block letters: "1:30. RADIO SHACK. EATON CENTRE."

He wrote his report from the notes he made of his conversations with Maydek and Jerome, then, to keep himself awake, climbed the stairs to Gunnar's office one floor up and left the material on his assistant's desk. It was just before six. He went back the same way and started a fresh pot of decaf in the lunchroom before returning to his office. There, waiting for Gunnar and Yu to arrive, he took off his shoes, leaned back in his chair, and put his feet on his desk. He got as far as wondering whether there was anything to Jerome's warning of danger, but the answers he got from his dreams, all played out in swatches of red, weren't convincing enough to rouse him.

■

He woke with a start, barely able to remember where he was. His phone was ringing, his dollar store desk clock said it was seven twenty. His voice mail picked up the call before he could, but he gathered the presence of mind to hit the "Link" button and tap into the message the caller was leaving.

"Where the hell are you?" Gunnar was saying. "I saw your car in the garage."

"I'm here," Portland said. "I fell asleep. Just give me a minute."

He retrieved the travel toothbrush and the small tube of toothpaste he always carried with him from his briefcase and freshened up in the men's bathroom. He took the elevator up and went straight to Gunnar's office. All this he did with the unhurried dispatch that was his trademark.

Gunnar was at his desk on the telephone, fingering his tie pin. Yu was sitting in front of him. There was something different, almost ungainly, about Yu today — even from behind. As Portland knocked on the open door, Yu turned and Portland could see why: the Asian stillness that so became him was gone, replaced by a stiffness that occupied more space than a man at ease would demand. Portland shut the door behind him and seated himself in the simply upholstered straight-back chair that matched the one Yu was in.

Gunnar got off the phone. "That was my wife. Calling about my health. She's not too happy about the hours the last couple of days."

"Sorry I'm late. I nodded off at my desk." Portland said. The fact that he had come in early to prepare a report would speak for itself.

"No problem," Gunnar said. "We had lots to talk about before Marta called."

"Have you both had a chance to read my report?" Portland asked.

"I haven't," Gunnar said, a little self-consciously. "Tom took it off my desk before I got in. He's been briefing me."

"I've got it here," Yu said, reaching into a file he took off the small glass table that separated him from Portland. "I came over here to see you guys. No one was here, but I saw your report on Jen's desk. I thought I should read it."

Portland, who hadn't shot so much as a quizzical look at Yu, found his defensiveness puzzling.

"So Wyndham doesn't trust me," Gunnar said, his eyes on the report Yu had passed to him. "That's a big surprise. But he trusts you. Another surprise. What do you make of these accusations, Adam?"

"They're inventive. Like you said, he's an expert at getting people on his side."

"You ought to know, Adam. What a mess," Yu said.

Portland let it go. He had set out his reluctance to employ Wyndham as an informer in a memorandum he wrote to Gunnar when the idea resurfaced after Ladner discovered the hidden money: *The existence of the offshore account indicates clearly that Wyndham has little remorse for his crimes. More telling, however, is his ability to convince everyone connected with the case otherwise. His irrational pursuit of the cause of his daughter's death indicates that he is a man who will be difficult to control. It also suggests a certain instability. Complicating the case is Mueller's character. He is a known drug dealer on an international scale who refused to co-operate in any way with authorities on arrest. Both before and during his imprisonment, he refused several reasonable offers to reduce his time in prison in return for his co-operation. Both these men have funds available elsewhere, which makes the prospect of their flight significant.*

He wrote another note after confronting Jerome with the account: *I had the sense that Wyndham took a certain delight in our discovery of his further crime. He showed no remorse when he was presented with the evidence. His concerns focused on the way in which we discovered the account and on the consequences for him. My sense is that he will agree to this only if there is some hidden advantage for him, additional to avoiding further jail time and being allowed to keep some of his money. He remains more independent, more capable, more of an unknown quantity, and more elusive than the average informer. His relentless pursuit of the reasons for his daughter's death continues as a destabilizing element in this case.*

With deep thought as their cover, the three policemen stared grimly at nothing in particular. Gunnar was the first to speak.

"He's pretty smart, arranging a meeting at the food court. A perfect place for two cons running around with guns they enjoy using. They know we won't be taking chances with heavy artillery in that crowd, especially since they've already got four dead bodies, not including the dogs, that establish their respect for life."

"Sir," Portland said, "if Brenda Maydek's information is correct, we may be dealing with cases of justifiable homicide."

"Two of them?" asked Yu.

Portland explained the conclusions he'd drawn in fits and starts overnight.

"From Brenda Maydek's account, Wyndham knew that Paula was dead before he called her mother. Someone gained forced entry to her body. The footsteps forensics found went up the stairs, but not down, indicating that the intruder may have fallen."

Yu interrupted. "What the hell was Wyndham doing at Lafond's place if he wasn't involved in something?"

"Let me finish, Tom," Portland said, his impatience surprising him as much as it did the others.

"Lafond was Sarah's boyfriend around the time of her death. For some reason, maybe because of something Mueller told him, Wyndham became suspicious and went out to Lafond's place. He's been clutching at straws for the better part of ten years now, so how could he resist? He discovered Maydek. From that point on, either Clark and Lafond were out to get him, or he was out to get them."

"Or they're all fighting about drugs and offshore money, which makes more sense and doesn't involve a bunch of coincidences," Gunnar said.

"What does it matter?" Yu said. "He and Mueller are fugitives, one way or the other."

"True," said Gunnar.

"Being fugitives doesn't make them murderers. It's possible that they were defending themselves both times," Portland said.

"Then why run?" Yu asked.

"Maybe that's why Wyndham wants to see me," Portland said.

"Adam, he suckered you once and you sound like you want to be suckered again," Gunnar said. "Have you stopped to consider whether you're also on a mission?"

"What kind of mission, sir?"

"To vindicate your first mistake."

"I don't think so, sir. I'm fully aware that Wyndham successfully lied to me about his assets and got an early parole recommendation in the bargain. That doesn't make him or Mueller cold-blooded killers. We also have a situation here where the public is at risk, and the way we handle it should depend on whom we're dealing with. I think it's important to establish whether Lafond was involved in illegal activities."

"Whiteside tried the usual searches. Nothing. I also ordered a search of our own records and sources. Nothing again. The only thing I didn't check was the undercover database."

"And I've sent queries to all major forces across the country, asking for a first priority search," Yu said. "Twyman's on it. I told him to interrupt us if he heard anything. If he doesn't, I say we're wasting our time."

Yu was out of character again, Portland observed. Normally, he avoided the risks of initiative or the crapshoot of opinion, invited or uninvited. He had risen through the ranks by dint of Gunnar's stewardship and a polished bureaucracy that passed for administrative efficiency in an organization that had never escaped its historic obsession with ritual. It occurred to Portland, briefly but forcefully, that his own devotion to the law of the land and the chain of command was but a myopic step removed from his observations about Yu.

"I don't have the last word on this," Gunnar said. "But I'm going to recommend we go with our team, including snipers."

"Shoot to kill? At the Eaton Centre?" Portland was incredulous.

"Of course not. I'm counting on you to lure him to where we can get a clear shot or make an arrest without a lot of civilians around." Gunnar said. "We'll embed a GPS tracking device in the heel of your shoe and sew a wireless microphone chip into your lapel. Are you up for it?"

"Yes, sir. I suppose Metro will have to be involved."

"That's my call. Let's get going. I'll make the arrangements and then decide what to tell Whiteside."

CHAPTER

FOURTEEN

PORTLAND HAD NEVER HEARD A SENIOR OFFICER MENTION THE undercover database before. Few in the force could verify its existence, even fewer knew what it contained. Lore had it that only a handful of senior officers in CID were privy to the passwords. There were good reasons for the secrecy: with crime assuming increasingly global proportions, the international web of informants was so large that some central authority was needed to ensure order in the secretive world in which informants and their handlers operated. Handlers had long kept their own files on their informants, but domestic criminal activity, which had become incrementally mobile and multi-jurisdictional, required a cohesive overview to prevent the various forces, officers, and informants at the federal, provincial, and municipal levels from tripping all over each other and more importantly, endangering the lives of informants.

Because of the database's sensitivity, special software limited access: using artificial intelligence techniques, the software flagged conflicts among informants, sending a message to the handlers involved when problems arose. Each system query was automatically logged and every officer accessing the database had to justify it to a three-member panel of his peers, all officers who also had access privileges.

Gunnar certainly had access. All the more reason, Portland thought, for him to adhere to the unwritten rule that said no one ever talked about it. Unless he suspected, or knew, that Lafond was a high-level informant, in which case his comment may have been consciously or subconsciously intended to squelch any suspicion Portland or even Yu — who may or may not have had access — might have had about

Lafond's status. And if Gunnar were that concerned about Lafond and the force's relationship with him, he would have little hesitation in sacrificing Jerome or Dirk. With Gunnar behind them, and one or two parolees on a killing spree in their sights, the SWAT team wouldn't need much encouragement to shoot first and ask questions later. Especially because Jerome, alone, desperate, and believing he was close to solving the mystery of Sarah's death, was unlikely to come along quietly.

It shouldn't have mattered to Portland: Gunnar was his superior and he gave the orders, which in this case complied with the rules — even Gunnar's reluctance to include Whiteside might stem from Lafond's activities as an informant.

It shouldn't have mattered, but it did: his conversation with Brenda Maydek had revived Jerome's lingering enigma. And never before had Portland's deference to authority and the rule of law run smack into the possibility that someone might die as a result. To be sure, he'd had doubts about the legal guilt of the odd suspect, but he contented himself with telling it as he saw it, avoiding judgements, and letting the judge or jury decide; as for moral guilt, that hardly entered into it, except as a consideration for the sentencing judge. If the truth were told, the cases he had investigated over the years — driving offences, drug offences, regulatory charges, and commercial fraud — were rarely of the order of life and death. Perhaps, he thought, everything must bend to life, even the rules.

That was certainly Buddy's view. He and the reporter had been something more than acquaintances, something less than friends, since they worked on Wyndham's case. They met haphazardly, always for lunch on a working day, never for drinks or dinner or in the company of their spouses or others, and usually on Buddy's initiative, though Portland would make the call when guilt overtook him every so often. On one of the rare occasions when they seriously discussed something other than the law, lawyers, the criminal justice system, or police politics, Buddy had described their relationship as a "situational friendship." Portland, uncomfortable with the discussion to begin with, didn't like the combination of words, though he didn't say so. To him, "situational" and "friendship" were antithetical: loyalty, trust, love, and devotion, could never be short-term or compartmentalized if they were to mean anything. Simply liking or admiring someone, enjoying their company or their conversation, and partaking of it when circumstances gave rise to the opportunity, hardly qualified people as friends. If Portland was to expend energy on intensity, he preferred the long, slow burn to the explosion, the embers to the flames. Always appealing to the opposite sex, he had never picked up a woman or had a one-night stand. Bonnie was much the same, and they lived a quiet life in which their everyday routines were also their diversions, which left them mildly shocked by their son's proclivity to rabble-rousing in his self-anointed role as social activist law student, a quirk which made them no less proud of Patrick's academic achievements.

In some ways, his son reminded him of Buddy. Neither seemed fulfilled unless he was agitated — not necessarily upset, angry, hurried, or brooding, just on to the next thing whether he could see it coming or not. That trait probably explained why Helen had become Buddy's third wife before he turned 35. They had been married for a decade and, as far as Portland could tell without having met Helen, seemed happy enough; for one thing, Buddy, in his agitated way, was forever babbling about the kids, usually by way of unrelated asides to the main thrust of their conversation. His previous marriages lasted a total of 28 months: the first was an unlikely union with an aspiring model and actress who was a full six inches taller and never had a thought that didn't come out of her mouth, followed quickly by equally incomprehensible nuptials with a dour academic ten years his senior who had fallen in love with the notion that a man married to a bimbo would have her as a mistress.

Portland and Ladner also approached their professions differently. Ladner did whatever it took to get his stories, unless it met two conditions: it was clearly wrong *and* it could get him into career-threatening trouble; Portland rarely gave his career or anything else he considered extraneous much thought when he made decisions. The Mountie, who read the newspapers avidly, took occasional exception to the way Buddy obtained information, but he never shared these thoughts with the reporter, who had always dealt with him fairly.

Still, both men were deeply committed to excellence, both treated their occupation as their vocation, and both brought their own brand of passion to the things they believed in, truth most of all. However it was labelled, this was what drew them to each other.

It was almost eight. Only five and a half hours until the meeting with Wyndham. Two calls in a row from Portland. Buddy would be surprised.

On the pretext of going out for a decent cup of coffee and a touch of breakfast, he left the building and used a payphone to reach Buddy at home. For a guy who loved being in the thick of it, the reporter was unexpectedly hesitant. He was sure, he told Portland, that he could convince Sood to help out, especially with Portland behind the plan. But he was reluctant to do so: Sood had built the life he wanted to for himself, finally out of the spotlight and the tumult after he had unmasked Lewis and Wyndham, and endured the battle of attrition Terra Nova had waged in the courts.

"Ali grew up in Kashmir," Buddy said. "His grandfather, two of his brothers, and a sister died in the violence. He came to Canada for a quieter life, 'smaller but fuller,' he once told me. He doesn't even go to the movies. Cracking into an RCMP database won't be his idea of fun."

It hadn't occurred to Portland that Buddy might harbour affection for Sood. But he was sure there was more to the reporter's reluctance, a hint of disappointment at this turn of events. Portland didn't try to figure it out: in his mind, complications invariably attended subterfuge and deceit. If he didn't believe lives were at stake here, he'd have let it go.

"That's why I called you, Buddy. He owes you."

"I don't think of it that way."

"Think of it as the biggest story of your life," Portland said, but in disbelief at his words.

"We must be friends. You know me too well. But obviously I don't know as much about you as I think I do."

Portland flushed. Buddy picked up on the pause.

"Don't worry, Adam. I'm looking forward to getting to know you better. I'll get Ali down here as quickly as I can."

When Portland put the phone down, he still wasn't sure he'd go through with it.

■

With lots of work on his desk and not much will to do it, Portland was glad when Sandra, his assistant, appeared at his door.

"There's a lady waiting for you at reception downstairs, Adam. She has no appointment and she won't give security her name. What do you want me to do?"

He was thankful for the distraction. "I'll go downstairs."

"She's pregnant," Sandra said, unable to suppress a smile.

Portland shot her a dirty look, smiled back artificially and put on his jacket. "Don't tell reception I'm coming."

He didn't recognize her immediately. She was one of those sexy women whom men, even Portland, found hard to imagine as pregnant. But this too she wore in perfect proportion.

She seemed surprised when she saw him. She walked towards him purposefully, as if she was intent on getting as far away as she could from the officers at reception.

"Hello, Sergeant Portland," she said, speaking barely above a whisper.

"That's very formal. Wasn't it Adam when we last met?"

There had always been something between them. Something

acknowledged but not quite shared that surpassed respect but fell short of attachment or attraction. More than once, throughout the ordeal of Jerome's arrest and sentencing, they had bonded without a word, each acknowledging that what the other was doing had to be done, nothing more, nothing less.

Her voice, still hushed, brought Portland back.

"I was afraid someone might recognize my name. With Jerome all over the news, I didn't want to embarrass you. I was about to leave. They didn't tell me you were coming down."

"I thought it best to have a look before meeting someone who wouldn't identify herself."

"Do you like what you see?"

"To be honest, I didn't expect it."

"I have a new life, Adam. But I'm here about Jerome."

"Let's get a coffee across the street." He could feel the eyes of the young officers on them as they left.

He was sorry he had chosen the diner. It was a place that attracted him only when proximity mattered. Josef, the longtime owner, had a way of intruding even when he was cooking silently over the grill at the far end. He managed to distract Heidi without ever looking directly at her.

"Would you like coffee?" Portland asked.

"No, if you don't mind, I'll just have some pop."

They picked up their orders at the counter and sat at a window table opposite each other.

"I imagine Jerome would have come here, or to a place like this, when he was practising," she said.

"Why do you say that?"

"I don't know. It was always important to him that his clients be comfortable."

"It's a little too close to the cop shop, as the clients would call it," Portland said with a smile.

"But he often saw his clients at the police station after they were arrested. Wouldn't he arrange for their release?"

"It's not that simple. If Jerome came down here, his clients would have been facing serious charges. And we likely wouldn't release them without a judge's order."

"I see. Sometimes I wish I knew more — cared more — about what he did." She took a sip of her pop. "Does the fact that I'm here about Jerome surprise you?" she asked.

It had. "Yes."

"I had the feeling, right from the first time we met, that you thought I didn't care about Jerome very much."

"I respected you for your dignity."

"You mean my detachment."

"That's your word."

"Did you respect me for leaving him when he was in jail?"

"That's not for me to judge."

"But did you judge me?"

"No."

"You stayed a friend to him, didn't you?"

"I suppose."

"What's going on, Adam?"

"I'm not free to tell you more than what you can get from the news."

"He's not a killer. You know that, don't you?"

You didn't know he was a thief and an adulterer either.

She read his thoughts. "The difference, Adam, is that when I found out what he'd done and that he cheated on me, I didn't want to believe it, but I could. He could never think straight after Sarah died. But even if you caught him and convicted him, I could never believe that he'd killed anyone in cold blood."

"What makes you so sure of that?"

"I could say that I lived with him, laughed with him, slept with him for a long time. That I knew what was in his heart even if I didn't always understand or agree with what was in his mind. But most of all, I know this: after Sarah died, life became more precious to him than ever."

"You know he believes that someone killed Sarah?"

"I know. Boy, do I know."

"Do you think he could kill Sarah's killer?"

"What are you saying, Adam? That someone killed Sarah? That Adam's been right all along?"

She broke down and cried the tears she wasn't able to cry with her husband. From the counter, Josef took it in. Adam shot him a dirty look and he went out the door by the grill to the supply room. Heidi took another sip of soda.

"I'm not sure he was right about Sarah," Portland said. "But everyone has their breaking-point, and no matter how close we are to them, we don't always know what that breaking-point is."

She sat still for a long time before she spoke again.

"Do you remember when we walked out of the courtroom after Adam was sentenced? You said everything had gone as it should, by the book. That his arrest and the plea bargain and the sentence were good examples of how justice should work."

"I remember."

"I agreed with you then. It only occurred to me long afterward that Sarah dying wasn't by the book. There wasn't any justice in her death, for her or for me, or especially for Jerome. You know what, Adam?"

"What?"

"Sometimes there's a bigger book."

"I've been thinking about that."

"That's all I wanted to hear."

■

He had arranged to meet Buddy and Ali at the coffee shop on the north side of Adelaide between Toronto Street and Church. Buddy knew the place from his police beat days when he'd pump information from the cops who worked at the Bail Reporting Office nearby. It was just after nine, and few of the morning crowd still lingered. Buddy had reached Ali at his office on Cherry Street near the Lakeshore — fortunately a lot closer to downtown than his Markham home was — where he had arrived promptly at seven. Portland hadn't been looking forward to the meeting, and he'd arranged with Buddy to give them a few minutes alone before he joined them.

They were in a booth at the back. Buddy was leaning forward, his elbows on the table, occupying a disproportionate amount of space; he looked uncharacteristically grim. Sood, apparently seeking breathing room, sat precariously close to the edge of the bench, almost diagonally across from Buddy. He looked as Portland remembered him, a slight, self-contained man, dark from his jet-black hair to his complexion to his alert eyes to his choice of suit and tie, his socks and his shoes, all offset by a pristine white dress shirt, seemingly starched to the limit of its endurance. Portland recalled Sood's deferential, precise manner when he had first questioned him about Wyndham. His scrupulous regard for detail and tendency to answer only the questions asked, which had frustrated Buddy, made him an excellent witness: his words were precise, he bore no judgements, took no pleasure from his discoveries beyond a job well done, had nothing to hide, and lacked the frailty of ego defence lawyers preyed on in cross-examination. Not a man who would be comfortable in a covert let alone illegal operation.

"Ali's agreed to help," Buddy said with no apparent satisfaction as Portland extended his hand.

"Good to see you, Mr. Sood. Thank you."

"Ali is fine, Sergeant Portland."

Buddy moved into the corner of the booth and Portland squeezed in next to him. Buddy motioned for the waitress, but Portland waved her off.

"I've told Ali what you want, and that you need to do it in the next few hours."

Ali nodded. "It is impossible to access a highly secure police network in such a short time. However, I understand that you may have access to the computer of the person who has a password to the database."

Portland hadn't thought about it. "Yes."

"I will return to my office and send to you a file by e-mail. You must transfer the file to a floppy disk. Then you must access the computer of the man who has the password. Once you have done so, you must copy the file to the 'System' folder on his computer. The file is self-executing and will capture all the keystrokes entered into the computer. Are your computers online constantly?"

"The network is. The individual computers go on-line as they're turned on."

"Once the program has captured the keystrokes, it will send them to a disguised address without leaving an electronic trail, or at least not an electronic trail that is easily detected."

"What you're saying is if Gunnar punches in the password, your program will send it to us," Buddy said.

"Exactly."

"Will that allow you to access the database from your computer?" Portland asked.

"Yes, but then you must provide me with the password you use personally to access the police network from a mobile location."

"So the problem is getting your file onto Gunnar's computer and getting Gunnar to access the database with the password," Buddy said.

"There is another problem. It will be difficult, perhaps impossible, for anyone to trace the destination of the e-mail containing the password. But I am certain that the network has logs recording all entries. At the point where it is discovered that there has been an unauthorized intrusion to the database, it may be possible to trace that intrusion to Sergeant Portland's network password."

"That should put all of us on a first-name basis pretty quickly," Buddy quipped. "How often do they check for unauthorized access, Adam?"

"I have no idea. Ali, if you gave me the password after you got it, could I access the database directly from an authorized computer?"

"Most likely only from the computer of the person whose password we have."

"How are you going to be sure Gunnar stays away from his office when it suits you?" Buddy asked.

"You're pretty close with Whiteside, aren't you?" Portland said.

"I think you're starting to enjoy this."

■

Soon after Portland got back to his office, the file arrived. As Portland had suspected, Gunnar was out finalizing the details of the stakeout. He loosened the video cable on the back of his own processor and had Sandra call the IT department for help. Then he took the elevator to Gunnar's office.

"Jen, is the boss here?" he asked, knowing the answer full well.

"No."

"I'll have to leave him a note. Can I use his computer for a minute? Mine's down and I'm in a rush on this."

"Use mine. I was just going to the ladies' room."

"The note's very confidential. I don't want to do it out here in the open."

"OK. But make it quick, Adam. The boss doesn't like anyone, including me, on his computer. And I don't want him taking it out on me. His temper's been a little short lately."

"Then we don't have to tell him. No harm done."

"Perfect."

"Can I print the note?"

"I can't see why not."

"Great. I'll leave it in your top desk drawer if you're not back when I'm done."

It took him no more than three minutes to call up Explorer, open the floppy, transfer Ali's file to the "System" folder, and double click on the file. If anything happened, he couldn't see it on the screen. Just as well, he thought. Though a little concerned that he hadn't installed Ali's program properly, he was unwilling to repeat the procedure for fear of mucking things up. He called up Word, opened a blank document, and typed a note to Gunnar: *It occurred to me that we should check to see whether Lafond, Clark, Maydek, Felderhof, Galati, or Addario are in any of our classified databases. Could you let me know ASAP? It might be useful information should Wyndham happen to mention them at the meet.*

He printed the note and put it in an envelope Jen had thoughtfully left on her desk. The whole thing was so risky: he had no idea when Gunnar would return and no idea whether Gunnar would search the undercover database.

Back in his office, he tried to call Bonnie, but call waiting interrupted him before her office answered. "What's this about classified databases? Say what you mean," Gunnar boomed. "What makes you think any of these people are informants?"

"Just a hunch."

"That isn't a good enough reason to check out all these names. Meet me in my office at 11:30. The SWAT team's set and I've arranged for the installation of the tracker and the microphone. We can go over the details of the meet again."

Portland's heart sank. He'd have to decide what to do about Wyndham in a vacuum. It wasn't his way. Not averse to going with his gut, he preferred to have it full up with information before acting on it. He was tiring again. A glass of water would help him think. On the way to the kitchenette, he saw the note from Wyndham in a plastic bag on Sandra's desk. Forensics hadn't collected it yet. Something about it — something familiar that he couldn't put his finger on, like a lost word on the tip of his tongue — drew him closer to Jerome. Even as the feeling washed over him, he remembered Gunnar's caustic remarks that morning. Maybe Gunnar was right, maybe his objectivity had disappeared in his desire to be vindicated.

But he'd been fighting off his suspicions ever since he saw the photograph of Dara's etching on the soap bar, and he couldn't help but stare at the note on the desk. Sandra noticed.

"Forensics say they're on the way," she said.

"They always say that," he laughed.

The cold spring water from the cooler refreshed him. He drank a second cup, then a third and returned to his office. The phone rang. He was disinclined to answer it, but he did.

"We've got it," Buddy said. "Got a pen?"

"What are you talking about?"

"He accessed the database. Whiteside's already called him to a meeting. You better get to his office soon."

Buddy read out the password, an eight-character combination of numbers and letters, twice. Portland repeated it back to him.

"Good luck," Buddy said. "Do we need Ali anymore?"

"Just make sure you can reach him if we do."

He didn't relish the thought of getting past Jen again. She had been with Gunnar for a long time and was intensely loyal to him when it mattered; if she had even an inkling of what Portland was doing, she'd let her boss know.

Without a plan, he took the stairs to give himself as much rehearsal time as he could get. When he reached Gunnar's landing, he paused at the exit door, then started back down just as slowly. By the time he exited the stairwell, he was moving decisively. He went to his office, got a large envelope and filled it with blank paper and a note to Buddy. Then he buzzed Sandra, who came into his office.

"Sandra, have you finished updating that material on the Wyndham case for Gunnar?" he asked.

"No, but Jen called to tell me you're meeting him at 11:30. I'll have it ready in half an hour, by eleven."

"I have something more important for you to do," he said. "Please take this over to Buddy Ladner at the *Standard*. Here's a taxi chit. It's very sensitive and I promised it to him right away, so I don't want to trust it to a courier."

"Should I give it to him personally?" Sandra asked.

"Absolutely."

"What if he's not there?"

"Wait as long as you have to and give it to him yourself."

"What about the stuff for your meeting?"

"Where is it?"

"Spread all over my desk. I'm working on the index."

"See if Jen can finish it for you."

Sandra hesitated. "It'll be hard for her to move all that stuff and still get it done on time."

"She can work at your desk while you're gone. Here. Use my phone. Tell her she can forward Gunnar's calls here."

Sandra called Jen, and very deferentially asked for help. Portland could tell from her expression that Jen had agreed.

As soon as she left, Portland called Buddy and explained his plan.

"Make yourself scarce until 11:30," he said.

He passed Jen on the way to the elevator.

"Going somewhere?" she asked.

"I've got a meeting. Can you meet me upstairs when you're done?"

"OK. Sandra said it wouldn't take more than half an hour."

"Great."

The elevator came quickly. When he was sure no one could see him, Portland went into Gunnar's office and shut the door behind him. At the computer, he called up the password dialogue box and typed in the code Buddy had given him. The screen responded quickly, but only a "Search Database" dialog box appeared. He typed in "Lafond," and "Search Term Unknown" came up. In succession, he keyed in "Wyndham," "Mueller," and "Clark" and each time got the same response. He was beginning to doubt he was in the right database, and could see no "Help" menu item to assist him. He looked at his watch. It was 10:50. He had neglected to take Ali's number and

Buddy, on his instructions, wouldn't be at the paper. He took his Palm from his pocket and found the reporter's cell number. He'd have to use Gunnar's phone. The Hawk answered.

"Where can I reach Ali?"

"I can get him on a three-way. Hold on."

Portland heard a couple of clicks before Ali came on the line. Portland explained the situation.

"Try 'informant,'" Ali said.

"Don't hang up," Portland responded.

Using his shoulder to hold the phone to his ear, he typed the word into the dialogue box. A second search box came up. It gave him the choice of sorting by name, region, or handler. Portland chose "Name," and typed in "Lafond."

"Not found," the screen read.

"Felderhof," "Clark," "Fitzjames," and "Galati" yielded similar results.

"Something's got to be in here," Portland muttered under his breath.

Buddy's voice came over the receiver. "What's going on?"

"Hold on," Portland said.

He entered Dara's surname. Nothing came up. He returned to the menu and typed in "Target." The search box appeared. He sorted by name and entered "Addario" again. This time Dara's profile materialized on the screen. Portland clicked on "Handler" and got "CID, Toronto." *The "anonymous" tip off about her car came to Young from another cop.*

He clicked on "Contacts," then typed in "Mueller." Dirk's particulars and a new menu came up on the monitor. He clicked "Status" and got "Uncertain;" then he clicked on "Handler," and got "CID, Toronto Region;" finally, he clicked on "Target" again and got "Wyndham, Jerome."

"Portland?" Buddy asked again.

"I'm in. No time to chat."

Portland hung up and returned to the Informant database. He keyed in "Wyndham." A new dialog box came on screen, offering him the choice of typing in a first name or selecting "All."

He selected "All" and had only enough time to see Sarah Wyndham's name underneath Jerome's before the office door opened behind him.

CHAPTER FIFTEEN

"SORRY I DIDN'T KNOCK," YU SAID. "I SAW THE LIGHT ON JEN'S phone go off and thought Gunnar was free."

As casually as he could, Portland exited the database and turned the swivel chair around.

"Hey, did you put your file on a floppy?" Yu said. "You know you can't save to Gunnar's hard drive without his password."

"Yeah."

"Don't forget the disk," Yu said.

"Thanks," Portland said, even as he bent from the waist to feign retrieving the non-existent floppy from the drive on the mini-tower that sat on the floor, aware all the while that the familiar sound accompanying the disk's ejection was missing. Still bent over and hoping that the sound had become so ubiquitous that no one noticed its absence anymore, he feigned tucking something into his pants pocket.

"You look good in Gunnar's chair, Adam," Yu said. If he noticed that his colleague, who rarely perspired, was sweating through his shirt, he didn't let on.

"It's like a simulated spacewalk, as close to the experience of command as I'll probably ever get," Portland said, coming around the desk just as Jen entered.

"Here's the stuff, guys," she said. "Gunnar's left his meeting with Inspector Whiteside. He should be here soon."

"Great," Portland said.

"You both look tired. Want some coffee?" Jen asked.

"No, I'll get it myself," Portland said. "I can use the walk. Want one, Tom?"

"No, thank you. I'll wait here," Yu said, as he seated himself in his usual spot. "I better read this stuff."

He thought better of leaving Yu alone with Jen while the image of Portland at Gunnar's computer was still fresh in his colleague's mind.

"Me too, come to think of it. I would appreciate that coffee after all."

"No problem."

Jen had three sets of materials. She gave them each one set and left the other on Gunnar's desk. Both men started reading.

"Are you nervous about this meet?" Yu asked.

"Not really. I'll have the microphones, the tracker, and the SWAT team covering me. I feel as safe as a hard drive at the Bank of Canada."

"Hard drives crash on their own, Adam."

"What do you mean?"

"Only that you should be careful around Wyndham. You've been unusually tight with him."

"I know. I'll be careful. Thanks."

Gunnar came into the room.

"Gentleman, Metro will give us support, but it will be our operation. Adam, they're ready to fit you downstairs. When you're done, come back up and we'll go over the final details again."

Portland wished he knew what Buddy had told Whiteside to get him to call Gunnar away.

"Have you guys been using my phone?" Gunnar asked. He was staring at the LCD display on his phone through the magnifying glass he kept handy.

"Adam was on before I came in," Tom said.

"Good, it always makes me nervous when I see a caller or a redial number I don't recognize."

"I better go now," Portland said.

He had no way of reaching Jerome before the meet. Even then, the sophisticated technology he'd be wearing would pick up his every word.

■

Portland still hadn't figured it out two hours later. He looked like the other casual shoppers in the crowded aisles of the Radio Shack located on the bottom floor of the cavernous mall, but he was oblivious to the display items he was examining. On the way in, he couldn't help but marvel how well the snipers had hidden themselves. And he couldn't even tell which of the faceless passersby were the cops stationed in and around the store.

A shrill voice came from the front desk. "Excuse me, is there a Mr. Portland in the store?"

He walked over to the cash. The clerk was holding a telephone.

"I'm Adam Portland."

"There's a call for you. Please be brief."

"Adam, what did you think of the note I sent you?" There was nothing tentative in Jerome's voice.

Portland breathed a sigh of relief. He moved away from the cash. "It convinced me."

"All right, there's a Dairy Queen on the northwest corner of Broadview at Pottery Road. You'll find picnic tables in behind overlooking the Don Valley Parkway. Be there no later than 9:00 p.m. Don't leave, no matter how long you have to wait."

The microphone recorded everything.

"What if I get hungry? Can I pop in for a hamburger?"

"What?"

"Can I get something if the wait's too long? Those Brazier Burgers aren't bad at all."

"I know. They must use good beef."

"Probably."

"Goodbye, Adam. Be on time."

Disoriented, he left the store slowly and got only as far as the top of the escalator before Gunnar and Yu confronted him.

"Bit of a waste of time talking about hamburgers," Yu complained.

"I was just keeping him loose. He's too smart to answer questions or stay on the line. Let's concentrate on getting ready for tonight."

■

The stakeout lasted for two hours, until 11:00. Jerome didn't show up. Whiteside didn't show up either, sending a subordinate in his place. Gunnar, visibly upset, suggested they reconvene in the morning.

"You want something to eat before this place closes?" Gunnar asked.

"Sure," Portland replied.

"My treat," Gunnar said.

They settled down inside over a banana split for Gunnar that dwarfed Portland's small cup of soft ice cream.

"Should I call Tom?" Portland asked,

"No point," Gunnar said, "I sent him to the lab. He'll be in touch when he has an update, probably around midnight. Let's meet in my office at 9:30. I'll let Whiteside know."

Portland rang Bonnie on his cell.

"I'm ok," he told her.

"I knew Jerome wouldn't hurt you," she said.

"He didn't show."

She couldn't tell whether her husband was disappointed or angry or relieved.

"Oh. What are you going to do?"

"I'm coming home."

"Going to play travelling salesman first?" she asked good-naturedly. She knew that he didn't like to bring his job home, and appreciated it, but once in a while wished he'd let her in a little closer: he always told her about his days and his feelings, but by the time he got home they'd been cleansed, and sometimes his even narrative was an unsatisfying proxy for the outpouring she craved. Most of the time, it worked for them, because a cleansed Adam wasn't all that different from an uncleansed Adam: whenever his emotions threatened to run away with him, he rooted himself in that place where he knew he belonged and stood firm, like a man who believed he could fend off the wind by wrapping his arms around himself.

She hadn't seen him much in the past week, but he called her frequently at the hospital, as was his habit. And if she wasn't in the OR administering anesthetics, her assistant always put his calls through. Thinking about it while she waited up for him, she realized that their regular contact, however brief, helped him shed his day without bringing it home all at once, and that what she missed wasn't so much the tide as the torrent.

When he talked about Jerome, though, the intensity was always there, as close to excess as her husband drew. But the intensity came in a vacuum. Something about the lawyer made him sad, he told her, and he identified with the sadness, although he didn't know why. Bonnie thought she understood: Jerome, the wanderer, could never stray far from his fixation on Sarah, while Adam, his life entrenched, could never stray far from the values that kept him there. Adam, perhaps, had got to the age when he realized that neither man was free: how he lived with that, Bonnie thought, would shape the continuity of their happiness.

■

Too exhausted to fight his habits, Portland turned into Jade's lot, then parked his car where he could see it. He took his usual seat and looked around for Angie. She was carrying someone's order, but came straight toward him.

"It's OK, Angie. I can wait."

"It's for you. A vegetarian burrito and a salad. But you'll have to eat it back there with your friend," she said.

Portland turned around. Jerome waved to him from a booth in the corner of the restaurant farthest away from the windows.

"Surprise!" Angie giggled, misunderstanding Portland's stunned demeanour. "What's the occasion?"

"I'm not sure, but I'll let you know," he said.

"An old friend?"

"You could say that."

He followed Angie to Jerome's table and sat down opposite him without a word.

"Don't you guys have anything to say to each other? How about a hug or something?" Angie said.

"Some things take time, don't they, Adam?" Jerome said.

"Do you want to order for yourself?" Angie asked Jerome.

"The largest, juiciest, all-beef hamburger you have," Jerome said. "Rare."

"I see you got the message," Portland said.

"Yeah, I remembered when you interviewed me at the cop shop just after the arrest. You wouldn't touch the hamburgers they brought to us halfway through the night. Didn't Gunnar know you were a vegetarian?"

"I don't think so. He doesn't make a point of eating with me. How did you know I'd be here?"

"You told me about this place that night. You said you'd get one of these veggie burritos on the way home. I was hoping you'd do the same tonight."

"Don't you ever forget anything?"

"Just who I am sometimes. I'm glad you understood my message, too. Would you have believed me otherwise?"

"I think so." Portland thought better of mentioning his chat with Heidi. "I managed to get some information on my own. But it was a nice touch anyway."

"What kind of information?"

It wasn't the time to tell him about Sarah and the database either. "I found out that CID probably had a hand in Dara's disappearance."

"Why do you say that?"

"Her car got hauled into the compound on a tip. The tip came from CID. Do you have any idea where she is?"

"Provo."

"Provo?"

"Whoever took her told us."

"Us?"

"Me and Dirk. Whoever shot Fitzjames at Lafond's place made it pretty clear that if I didn't get down there, Dara was dead."

"Speaking of Dirk, where is he?"

"Right behind, officer. Please not move." Dirk came into view, his right hand holding the gun in his pocket. He was pointing it at a distinctly unhappy Shane Whiteside, who was standing directly in front of him, right beside Buddy Ladner.

"I guess we've got a lot to talk about," Portland said to no one in particular.

"What's up, Dirk?" Jerome said.

"These men come park car soon after you friend. They sit. I wonder. I look inside and see microphone. Police car."

"That's not very nice, Adam," said Jerome, obviously angry.

"He didn't know I was tailing him," Whiteside said.

"Very nice story," said Dirk.

"He's right," Portland said. "What are you doing here, Shane?"

"You know this man?" Dirk asked.

"Yes, he's with Metro. Buddy there is a reporter. What's going on?"

"Excuse me, gentlemen," Angie interrupted. "Do you need a bigger table?" She winked at Portland. "We don't usually get groups this time of night. Must be some occasion."

"It is."

Dirk, who was still holding the gun but no longer pointing it, nodded at a round table in the middle of the room. "We sit there."

"I'll get it ready," Angie said.

"I no want trouble," Dirk said to Whiteside. "But have insurance."

He motioned to Roger, sitting a few tables away. "He have your gun, Inspector."

Roger waved. "Evening, Inspector," he grinned. "Fine piece of equipment. I suppose you'll want it back. Shame."

"Kiss my ass, Roger."

"Then I'll just borrow it for now."

Roger went back to his meal. Angie signalled, and they all went to the round table, the two suspects a few steps behind the others. Dirk, his chair slightly back so he could access his weapon, sat between Jerome on his right and Portland on his left. Across from them were Whiteside and Ladner, with empty seats where the table's semicircles met.

"Gentlemen, would you like to see the menus?" Angie asked.

"Vegetable burritos all around," Jerome said. "And Coke for everyone."

Buddy was the first to speak after Angie left. "Perhaps more formal introductions are in order."

"Leave your notebook where it is," Jerome said, with satisfaction. "I think we all know each other well enough. So what's going — "

"I'll tell you what's going on," Whiteside said. "First Buddy comes to me with this story that Gunnar's holding out on me about a meet. So I get together with Gunnar, get in on the meet, but I still have the feeling that I'm not getting the whole story. Then Gunnar's secretary sends me a transcript of the telephone call at Radio Shack. I happen to remember Hawk telling me once that we should both become vegetarians and then we'd look as good as Portland here. I got the distinct feeling that you, Mr. Wyndham, weren't going to show up at the Dairy Queen."

"Shane threatened to tell Gunnar that I was the one who informed him about the meet," Buddy said. "I was afraid that might establish a suspicious connection between me and Adam, so I told him everything I knew. Sorry, Adam."

"Everything he knew still didn't make a lot of sense," Whiteside said, speaking directly to Portland. "I put a tail on you, but you didn't leave your office. So I put Jardine on the night meet and kept out of sight. When Wyndham here didn't show up, I stayed with you."

"Dirk," Jerome said. "Keep an eye on the press while I have a private conversation with Adam and Inspector Whiteside."

"You want gun?"

"No, Roger can cover me."

The three men went back to the booth at the back of the restaurant. The police officers sat together on one side of the table.

"I'm prepared to clear everything up to your satisfaction, Inspector," Jerome said, "but only if you arrange safe passage to Provo, no later than Saturday."

CHAPTER SIXTEEN

LOOKING DOWN FROM HIS WINDOW SEAT OVER THE ARCHIPELAGOS
covering less than 200 square miles and located some 575 miles southeast of Miami, it wasn't hard for Jerome to see why the Turks and
Caicos economy depended so heavily on tourism, fishing, and offshore
financial services. The Columbus passage, a 22-mile channel that connected the Atlantic to the Caribbean, separated the Caicos to the north
and the Turks to the south. Seven thousand feet deep, the Channel
featured a profusion of marine life that gathered along one of the
longest coral reefs in the world around the 250 miles of coastline, some
90 percent of it sandy beaches that attracted about 100,000 tourists
annually, more than half of them from North America.

To the windward side of the low-lying islands — the Blue Hills
on Provo, the country's highest point, was barely 100 feet above sea
level — Jerome could see limestone cliffs and sand dunes. The leeward
sides had some vegetation, mostly scrub and cactus, he imagined. The
brochure Jerome was reading said that Salt Cay and South Caicos were
the driest islands of the lot, their trees felled by salt rakers long ago to
discourage rain. Soil was almost non-existent, and no more than two
percent of the land could be farmed: there were no permanent crops,
no permanent pastures, and no forest or woodland. That left mostly
sand to the eye, low, flat limestone punctuated by extensive marshes
and mangrove swamps, all infrequently interrupted by the country's
paltry 70 miles of roads, barely 20 percent of them paved.

Travel agents were fond of calling Provo the cosmopolitan centre
of this tiny land, home to three-quarters of its inhabitants, though the
capital was Cockburn Town on Grand Turk. "Cosmopolitan" in this

case meant a golf club, a casino, two marinas, and according to the tourist material, "a number of bars and excellent restaurants." But Provo's 38 square miles were a water lovers' paradise, particularly a 12-mile stretch of beach on Grace Bay sheltered from the sea by a protective barrier reef.

With 30 years' experience that included a three-year secondment at Interpol, Whiteside had little trouble making the arrangements. His superiors didn't question him — they'd long given up asking for details — when he told them where he was going with only the briefest of explanations.

"The Department will pay for my ticket, but you two have to pay your own way and Portland's," Whiteside said to Dirk and Jerome. Jerome handed over the cash. Then Whiteside drove back to Toronto with Buddy, who agreed to hold his questions and his story for 48 hours, when he would get an exclusive.

"Just tell me this, who's the bad guy?" Buddy asked as he got out of the car.

Whiteside smiled. "Who do *you* want it to be?"

"It's a great story either way," Buddy shrugged.

"But only Wyndham is *your* story, right?"

Whiteside had instructed Portland to drive Jerome and Dirk to Roger's place, while Roger drove home on his own. Portland had barely pulled out of Jade's when he turned into a strip mall, got out, and telephoned Bonnie. He told her as much as he could under the pressure of time.

"Will you be safe, Adam?" she asked.

He was going to answer that he'd never had to unholster his gun on duty and probably wouldn't this time. But he didn't believe it.

"I'm sure I will be," he said, sorry that he hadn't been to the shooting range recently. "Call Sandra tomorrow morning and tell her I've come down with the flu."

Roger, already flattered to have the objects of a nationwide man-hunt as his house guests, was equally delighted to have an RCMP officer enjoying his hospitality. A broker by nature, he had become a respected intermediary between the cops and the underworld, a trusted untouchable to both sides. Keenly aware just how far he could push his protected status, he carried on his thriving business with little interference from the police. It was rare that he got as close to the action as he had by taking in Jerome and Dirk. But Fingers, who had given him his start in the business, told him that Jerome was "big stuff," a potential connection to the global dealings to which Roger aspired.

Jerome, Dirk, Bob, and now Portland fit in nicely as visitors to his spacious new four-bedroom home, decorated in aging but eager bachelor and man-about-town, on the old racetrack grounds at Queen and Woodbine. Portland slept better and longer than he had in some time. Dirk stayed up late, spending a long time on the phone in the privacy of his bedroom. Jerome tossed fitfully at first, unable to tolerate the interruption so close to the end of his journey and wondering whether losing Dara would be the price for finding Sarah. It was one of the rare times he'd questioned his course. But the inquiry exhausted him and he fell asleep.

■

Roger had a hearty campfire breakfast ready for the group when Whiteside called at about eight. Afterward, he checked out the fugitives' vital statistics, left the house, and returned an hour and a half later with sports jackets, pants, cotton shirts, dress socks, and oxfords. His guests had passed the time watching NewsWorld and City TV to discover that there had been no further developments in the Wyndham case and that the police still had no idea about the whereabouts of Jerome and Dirk. But Buddy, who had missed his print deadline, turned up as a guest on a mid-morning talk show to discuss "The Ongoing Mystery of Jerome Wyndham," where he exuded a confident prescience that all might not be as it seemed.

"Whiteside will have a shit fit over this," Jerome said.

"I'm not feeling so good about it myself," said Portland.

Just before noon, Roger drove them to Pearson International Airport, an uneventful 40-minute ride during which there was little chit-chat. As they turned off the 409, Portland directed Roger to the Administration Building. There, they all thanked Roger — Dirk was particularly profuse — then bid him goodbye.

"Jerome, I need to ask you something about Bob," Roger called from inside the car just before they stepped into the revolving door.

Jerome walked back and lowered his head to the open passenger window.

"I thought you should know that Dirk spent a lot of time on the phone last night."

"He's always calling his wife and kid. Didn't he leave a 50 with you?"

"That's not the point. The calls weren't to Colombia. They were to Provo. What do you make of that?"

"I don't know. Do you have the number?"

"Yes. I wrote it down for you." He produced a slip of paper that Jerome put in his pocket. "Thanks, Roger. Give my best to Bob."

"You'll be seeing him again soon, don't worry. But be careful, real careful, anyway."

"What that about?" Dirk asked, when Jerome returned.

"I gave him the name of a vet in case the cat gets sick."

■

Whiteside met them in a back office that housed the revenue people. At one o'clock, a U.S. immigration officer arrived and escorted them through customs and security to the boarding area. The Air Canada agent who took them on board was clearly expecting them. Apart from their carefree pace, having arrived just seconds before the plane's door shut, they fit in easily with the other passengers.

"First class, is good," Dirk said delightedly as they took their seats.

"It's business class and it's good for you because it's my money," Jerome complained good-naturedly.

They had two pairs of seats, separated by the aisle. Jerome and Portland watched Whiteside motion Dirk to a window seat and sit down beside him. Much more tactfully, Portland told Jerome he'd prefer an aisle seat.

"That Whiteside is a piece of work," Jerome whispered to Portland when they were seated. "He's got a lot of nerve considering we're going to make his career."

"Like you made mine?" Portland asked.

"I've thought that once or twice."

"That's not why I'm here."

"Why are you here? Why did you visit me in the joint?"

"I don't really know. I'd never seen anyone ruin his life so needlessly. It's always intrigued me, especially after my wife remarked that in some ways you and I come to the same place from opposite directions."

"You haven't ruined your life," Jerome said.

"No, not at all, but we're both . . . stuck, I guess."

"It's been worth every ugly minute."

Portland waited until the thrust of the plane's engines as it taxied down the runway drowned out his whisper.

"Sarah was on the informants' list in our undercover database," he whispered.

"What?"

"Sarah was an RCMP informant. I don't know what she did, who she worked for, nothing. Just that she's listed as an informant in our database."

It was information Jerome didn't need. Without a word, he turned and looked out the window. Portland was sure he could see his temple throbbing. Jerome held his silence all the way to Miami.

■

A U.S. marshal put them up in Miami airport's security office, where they waited for 90 minutes. He escorted them to the boarding gate just before the plane left.

Two hours later, the jet made its final approach to Providenciales Airport, located in the middle of the island, just a short drive from the collection of disjointed mini-plazas and two-storey commercial buildings that made up downtown. Accompanied by a uniformed policeman who had been waiting for them on the tarmac, they passed undisturbed through customs and immigration. As they left the small terminal, the officer handed Whiteside a briefcase. Whiteside motioned Portland over.

"I thirsty." Dirk pointed to a local standing under an umbrella behind a wooden stand of dubious permanence. On the stand was a large tub of melting ice intended to cool a mishmash of canned juices and pop.

"What you drink?" Dirk said.

"Ginger ale, if he has it. Otherwise, doesn't matter. Better get two extra."

"Now we serve cops. Very nice. Maybe we buy dinner tonight, what you think?"

Jerome grinned and looked over at Whiteside and Portland, who were questioning the local policeman intently.

"Do you know where I can get a newspaper?" Jerome asked the pop man.

The vendor leaned over behind the stand, picked the remains of a newspaper from the ground and shook it free of sand before presenting it to Jerome with a self-satisfied grin. Thin as it was, it was a mess, with the obituaries and legal notices staring up at Jerome in the place of the front page.

"Is this for sale?"

"Everything is for sale."

"Is this the whole paper? Where's the front page?"

"Inside. Everything is there."

"How much?"

"My only one. Very valuable. All island papers is sold by now."

"How much?"

"Five dollars, U.S."

Jerome reached for his wallet.

"Now you rich?" Dirk said. "Not enough Whiteside take your money?"

Jerome shrugged. "What's the difference?"

"Four dollars, U.S.," Dirk said. He turned to the vendor. "I give you one dollar."

"One dollar is no profit. Cost me one dollar."

"One dollar new. Now worth nothing."

"Worth something to your friend," said the vendor, nodding at Jerome who was already leafing through the pages.

"One dollar," Dirk repeated.

"Give him the five," Jerome said, without taking his eyes from the paper.

"You give five. I give one."

"Why don't you just do what I ask you for once?" Jerome said. He pulled a Canadian ten-dollar bill out of his wallet and handed it to the bemused local. "Keep the change."

"What so important about paper?"

"Nothing." Jerome folded the paper and tucked it under his arm. Best not to let on that the murder victim on the paper's front page was Scott Lewis.

■

Lewis, identified as Paul Kelly, had been shot at his upscale home on the beach sometime the previous evening. There were no signs of forced entry but there had been a struggle in his study. The police discovered documents in the safe indicating that Lewis, described as "secretive," had connections to several financial institutions on the island. Detectives were hoping that the dead man's business associates would come forward to shed more light on the case. Police were also looking for a woman seen getting into a small car down the road by two of Lewis' employees who happened to be looking out the windows of the servants' quarters. The woman's description — 30s, tall, dark-skinned, long hair — was all too familiar to Jerome.

■

"Let's get a car," Whiteside said. They turned toward a makeshift booth that advertised itself as a car rental service. An ancient Cavalier wagon was the only vehicle available.

"Got money?" Whiteside said to Jerome.

"We require a credit card, sir," the man at the booth said politely.

"You're kidding, right?" Whiteside said.

"No, sir, we also offer insurance," the man said, proudly producing a form and a manual credit card device.

"You're out of luck this time, Inspector," Jerome laughed.

"Not really. Departmental expense," said Whiteside, reaching for his wallet.

"How many drivers would you like on the contract?" the attendant asked.

"Just me . . . and Mr. Portland here," Whiteside said.

Jerome shook his head at Dirk.

Portland was looking at a map of the island.

"Where we stay?" Dirk asked, a bit anxiously, Jerome thought.

"We'll sleep in the van in shifts while we stake out Island Trust," Whiteside said.

"I prefer Sheraton, it have casino," Dirk said, taking a look at the map.

"Forget it, Mueller. If it's any easier on you, you can have your choice of me or Portland as your sleeping partner."

"Not get excited, Inspector. You not sure choice," Dirk replied.

By the time they got to the wagon, Jerome and Whiteside were sweating profusely in the 90-degree heat. It was mid-August, just after the Islands' temperatures began their three-month retreat from the pleasant under-80 highs that persisted from December to July. Whiteside and Jerome removed their jackets before they got into the front of the Cavalier. Dirk and Portland removed theirs as well, but much more casually and only, it seemed, in solidarity with their company. The Cavalier had no air conditioning, but the owner had tinted the windows heavily enough so that no one could see inside.

"No gun, Inspector?" Dirk said, after Whiteside had started the vehicle. "You more trust than I think."

"That's none of your affair," Whiteside said.

"Inspector, I'm not going anywhere on this island without a weapon," Jerome said. "Adam, what have you got in that briefcase?"

"Guns, but they're not for you," Whiteside said.

"Let me get something very clear," Jerome said, "I didn't come this far to be a chump. I mean it. Either Dirk and I get weapons, or we go our separate ways."

Whiteside pulled the Cavalier to the side of the road.

"Are you threatening me?" he said.

"Not at all. We could have done that at any time. Dirk."

Velcro crackled as Dirk ripped away the shoulder pad from the jacket he was carrying on his lap and pulled out a Walther PPK semi-automatic, James Bond's favourite; Roger's tailor had had little trouble concealing the small pistol — six inches long, four inches high, an inch wide, and weighing less than a pound — in the material and padding it with foam. Although it would have been a problem had they encountered metal detectors, Jerome had been willing to take the risk, and the guns easily passed the frisk Whiteside had insisted on in Toronto.

Dirk pulled four extra magazines from the other shoulder pad.

"Airport security good idea," he said, as he snapped a magazine into the gun and pointed it at Whiteside, removing the briefcase from Portland's lap as he did so.

"It's OK, Adam," Jerome said. "Look, Inspector, either we're in this together or we're not. I think Dirk and I have learned how to use guns in the last couple of weeks. Think about it. We could have blown you away at our leisure. So how about it?"

Whiteside turned awkwardly to Portland, sitting behind him. Portland nodded.

"All right. We're a team, but I'm in charge. Got that straight?"

"Fine with me," Jerome said. "Dirk?"

"OK with you, OK with me, my friend."

"Then let's get on with it and check out that Island Trust office," Whiteside said.

The little they saw of the island was unremarkable. The homes and small resorts were typically Caribbean, with private cisterns for collecting rainwater attached to most dwellings. Everywhere, even on the routes that passed for main thoroughfares, pedestrians easily outnumbered vehicles, sidewalks were non-existent, and walkers mingled benignly with automobiles despite a dearth of traffic signs or, it seemed, rules of the road.

They parked opposite two small buildings on an unpaved, but fairly wide street. Looking in the wagon's side mirror, Jerome noticed a small garage and gas pumps about 75 feet behind them; otherwise, there was nothing on their side of the road as far as they could see in either direction. A large sign directly beside them announced that the land was "approved for development" and was for sale.

Across the street was a free-standing convenience store, built entirely of wood. To its right was a two-storey structure housing Dinmore, Feltz & Chudley, Barristers & Solicitors, and a real estate office on the ground floor. Both businesses had their curtains drawn and "Closed" signs on the doors. Between the two offices was an open entrance that revealed stairs leading to the second floor. Opaque curtains matching the ones on the ground floor framed the large upper-storey windows. Whiteside made a wide U-turn that revealed equally large windows on both floors on the side of the building nearest them; he moved their vehicle forward and they saw the same configuration on the other side.

"Island Trust must be upstairs," Whiteside said. "It's going to be hell to get near that building in daylight, maybe even at night, without being seen. Let's check out the back."

As he spoke, a black woman walked from the entrance to the stairs, closed the door behind her and locked it, checked the door again before she walked towards them and got into a beat-up car parked in front of the real estate agent's office.

"Does anybody know her?" Whiteside asked, but got no answer. Apart from the Honda Civic that followed her down the road, the street was quiet.

"Wyndham, keep the people in the convenience store busy for about five minutes while I look around the building," he said. "Adam and Mueller can cover us."

"Is big honour," Dirk said. Portland moved to the front passenger seat.

Whiteside waited until Jerome made his way into the store before he got out. He walked casually away from their wagon, paused in front of the door from which the woman had come, then disappeared around the side of the building. He was back in short order.

"What you see?" Dirk asked.

"Let's wait until your friend gets back and then I'll only have to tell the story once," Whiteside said.

Soon, Jerome returned with several large bottles of spring water.

"Good thing they take Canadian dollars," he said. "The exchange isn't bad either."

"Listen up," Whiteside said as he started the wagon. "As far as I can tell, Island Trust is the only business upstairs. But it looks like everything in the building is closed on Sunday. There are windows all around and there doesn't seem to be any way up from the back or the side. There might be a staircase from the interior on the first floor. But I doubt it."

"Maybe we should break in and wait inside," Portland said.

"There's a private security label on the front of the building. We'll set an alarm off," Whiteside said.

"Don't trouble yourself, Inspector," Jerome said. "I'm going in first through the front door and up the stairs, by myself. That's the way they're expecting me and that's what's most likely to keep Dara alive. From there, we'll have to improvise."

"They be watching for me too maybe," said Dirk.

"That's true. We'll both go. But after we're in, they won't be watching for anyone else. Then maybe you and Adam can make your move, Inspector."

"The deal was I was in charge," Whiteside said.

"You have a better idea?"

"I'll tell you if I think of something overnight. And Wyndham, call me Shane, that's my name."

■

They drove straight down the road for a half-mile, where they arrived at a small plaza boasting what would have been a neighbourhood restaurant had there been a neighbourhood in sight. But four middle-class whites away from the beaches and the hotels caused nary a stir in a setting where race and class issues had long given way to the real-ities of economic survival: anyone ready to spend was welcome to mix, and the further they cast from their usual tourist haunts the more welcome they were.

Jerome, Dirk, and Whiteside opted for a cold chicken sandwich and pop served with obvious relish by a proprietor flattered by the for-eign visitors seated at one of the half-dozen unmatched institutional tables in the place. Portland took to the grocery store two stores down where he would assemble his meal from the fresh fruits, vegetables, and nuts available, and stock the wagon with supplies for the long night ahead.

"So how's business?" Whiteside asked the hovering restaurateur.

"Welcome. My name is Gregory." The restaurateur extended his hand and Whiteside took it.

"I'm Shane. My friends are Jerome and Dirk. So how is business?"

"Always slow in the heat. But thank God the murder didn't happen in the tourist season."

"What murder?" Whiteside looked at Dirk, who shrugged, and at Jerome, who did the same.

"You have newspaper?" Dirk asked.

"No, I threw it away. Nothing worth reading," Jerome said.

"But the murder was on the front page," the proprietor said.

"I didn't notice. The paper was a mess."

"Who was murdered?" Whiteside said. "A tourist?"

"No, a businessman who lived on the island. But he was a white man, and this is never good."

"Are there any suspects?"

"A white woman."

"Who?"

"You have newspaper?" Dirk asked.

"No. I see it on TV."

"I look for newspaper." Dirk pushed his chair away from the table without finishing his sandwich.

"What's eating him?" Whiteside asked Jerome.

"No idea."

"I don't believe you, but I'll let it go for now."

■

Portland, half-leaning, half-sitting on the hood of the wagon, was finishing his meal when Dirk came out.

"You see telephone?" he asked Portland.

"No, what's up?"

"Give me car keys. I call home. Maybe last time I speak to family."

"OK. But don't be long."

Bonnie and Patrick flashed through Portland's mind. He lost his appetite and seeking diversion, went inside.

■

The restaurateur was only too happy to chat and serve them bad coffee — "on the house" — until it became dark enough to go. But Dirk hadn't returned.

"Maybe he's waiting outside," Portland said.

"Go ahead. I'll pay the bill," Jerome said.

"Generous. Planning to get rich?" Whiteside said, but with a smile.

Jerome caught himself smiling back. "I'll be out in a minute. I've got to go to the john too."

When the officers disappeared from view, Jerome picked up the bill from the table, took out his wallet, and signalled Gregory.

"Do you take Canadian dollars?" he asked.

"Two for one, not including tip."

That'll cover the on-the-house coffee. He put the money on the table.

"Do you have a telephone here?"

"Yes. In the kitchen. At the back."

"Do you mind if I make a short call?"

"Local call?"

"Yes."

"Go ahead."

The kitchen was sparkling clean. Jerome dialed the number Roger had given him. He hung up when the hotel answered.

■

Dirk and Whiteside were talking animatedly as Jerome approached the truck.

"I tell you I go for phone. I call wife and daughter."

"While we're standing around in the middle of nowhere?" Whiteside said.

"Is dark now only."

"That's not the point. You don't take off without checking with me."

"OK. OK. I sorry."

"All right. Get in the van. I'll be out in a minute."

Whiteside wheeled around and walked into the restaurant.

"What's with him?" Jerome said.

"Maybe he pee when he hot," Dirk said.

"Get off it, will you?" Jerome said. He took the hotel parking sticker from under the wiper on the passenger side before anyone else noticed it.

Whiteside was in the restaurant far too long.

CHAPTER SEVENTEEN

WHITESIDE PARKED THE VAN OFF THE ROAD ABOUT A QUARTER mile from Island Trust. He opened the briefcase the local cop had given him and pulled out two guns and four small black devices, no larger than the palm of his hand.

"Those things look like toys," Jerome said.

"They're two-way communicators. Half-mile range," Whiteside replied.

"How often will we switch off?" Jerome asked.

"At one and at five. We don't want anyone moving around in day-light. We'll take the last hour together."

"I wouldn't mind the second shift," Jerome said.

"OK. You and Adam move the van back in behind those construction sheds on the other side of the road. We'll do the changeover one at a time, so the place is always covered, front and back. Whenever you're moving, stay out-of-sight, in the shadows."

"What's the plan when Dara arrives?"

"She may be there already. But we'll wait until nine in either case," Whiteside said.

Jerome started to say something.

"I know it won't be easy for you if she gets there early," Whiteside said. "But remember, she's a hostage and we don't want any surprises."

"You're right."

"At 4:30, I'll replace you. Dirk will wait for you in the car. Adam will stay where he is, behind the building. At 8:30, Dirk will drive to the restaurant — "

"I no break law again," Dirk said.

"What are you talking about?" Jerome said.

"No have driver's licence. No have name on contract," he said with a straight face.

"What's the matter with you?" Jerome said. "This isn't a joke. When are you going to stop kidding around? If you haven't noticed, this is very serious, for me if not for you. I don't even know if Dara is alive. You've been on a kick for days now. Get off it."

Even at Lorimar, Jerome had noticed that when Dirk had something on his mind that he couldn't or wouldn't talk about, the inappropriate humour escalated.

"What's bugging you, Dirk?" Jerome said.

"Nothing. I sorry."

"As I was saying," Whiteside continued, "Dirk will drive you to the restaurant where we ate. A taxi should be waiting there. I gave the restaurant owner a few bucks and told him there would be more for him and the taxi driver if he's there on time. Both of you wear your jackets. Put the walkie-talkies where Roger put your guns. Take your guns too. The taxi will take you to Island Trust. Give yourself five minutes so you arrive just before nine. Pay the cabbie before you leave. If the door's open, go up the stairs carefully. If it's not, ring the bell. If nobody answers, kick it in."

"What about the alarm?" Jerome asked.

"It won't be on. Whoever's expecting you doesn't want the attention," Whiteside said. "Dirk will cover you, Jerome, but be ready to use your gun, just in case the idea is to kill you off the bat."

Jerome noticed himself unable to stand still, instead shunting back and forth rhythmically without moving his feet, like a devout worshipper in a place of prayer.

"What happens after I get upstairs?" Jerome asked.

"Leave the walkie-talkie on. What we do depends on what we hear. Stay by a window. See if you can lure whoever's there over near you. Rub your nose with your right hand if you want us to move in. Any questions?"

Jerome shook his head.

"That's it, then," Whiteside said. "We'll see you guys at one. Don't oversleep."

■

Jerome hadn't expected to sleep, but he did. Sleep was his favourite diversion — angst-free denial of both risk and reality — from Sarah's death, Dara's fate, and the prospect of his own death in just a few hours. It was the purest form of escape for a man with hopes but no dreams.

Portland had to rouse him. He looked at his watch. It was just after eleven.

"Did you sleep?" Jerome asked, instantly alert.

"A bit. Whiteside just called in. A truck's come by the building a couple of times. He thought it might not be a bad idea for you to get over there in case you could recognize anyone in it. Got your gun?"

"In my pants pocket."

"The communicator?"

"In the other pocket."

All was quiet in the vicinity of the building. Using the communicators, Whiteside guided him through the shadows to their hiding place behind the gas station.

"Get down," Whiteside said.

As he spoke, they could hear a motor in the distance.

"It looks like the same truck," Whiteside whispered as the ten-foot cube van approached. The truck slowed as it neared the building, then reversed and backed towards the entrance to the staircase, blocking their view of it. Two figures jumped out of the cab and went behind the truck. One seemed to be standing guard as they heard the other, now out of sight, raise the door to the cube. They heard a man's voice bark an order, then the sound of footsteps, more than one pair. The man guarding the truck got back into the driver's seat, started the engine, and left.

"Adam, there's a light truck leaving the building," Whiteside reported. "Follow it. Grab the driver and make him tell you what's going on. Then stash him somewhere close in case we need him again. Dirk, do you copy?"

"Roger," Dirk said. "I stay behind house."

"I'm on my way," said Portland.

The wagon went by just as the lights went on upstairs, but the shades had been drawn and they could see nothing more — except that the door to the stairs was now wide open.

■

Jerome kept watch with Whiteside, his eyes darting between the open door and the upstairs windows, closing them only to concentrate on the faint sounds of the faraway engines he hoped signalled Portland's return. Concentrating on hope had become habit for him, but he wasn't quite as good at it as he had been before getting on the plane. Hope and immediacy were mismatched partners: when they touched, hope became apprehension and immediacy became fear. Roger's warning at the airport, the news about Sarah, Dirk's temporary disappearance, and Whiteside's lengthy return to the restaurant whirled Jerome's mind without resolution beyond the realization that Portland was gone and those who remained all had agendas as veiled as they were different.

If Whiteside was concerned that their plans had gone awry, he was keeping it to himself. The conversation he shared with Jerome was limited to questions about Dara, her reaction to their rescue attempt, and her ability to help in a shootout. Just before light, he muted his communicator and motioned for Jerome to do the same.

"What's the deal with Dirk?"

"What do you mean?"

"I mean is he getting part of the stash?"

"What stash?"

"Get off it, Jerome. I treat you with respect. Do the same for me. Dirk doesn't look, smell, or feel like the Salvation Army. He's in this for something."

"What the hell are you talking about?"

"Everything OK?" Dirk's voice came over the communicator.

"Roger," Whiteside responded.

"Everything OK?" Dirk repeated.

"Shit," Whiteside said, releasing the mute button. "Yes, Dirk, everything's fine."

"Roger."

Whiteside waited for a while before muting the communicator again.

"You know, I always believed defence lawyers underrated cops. Treated everyone with a badge like the universal soldier."

"I don't think so."

"So why are you shoving a lead pipe up my ass and hoping I won't notice? You make excuses to get on the telephone. Dirk develops a sudden interest in the local affairs of the Turks and Caicos. He disappears without an explanation and comes back without a newspaper. Cleaning up after Scott Lewis maybe?"

Jerome's hopes sank with the weight of the gun in his pocket. Just then, a small black car pulled up at the convenience store. A tall, well-groomed Hispanic woman dressed in jeans and a white shirt got out. She opened the trunk, removed a medium-sized cloth bag, went to the front door, took something from her purse, entered, and disappeared without removing the "Closed" sign from the window.

"That isn't the woman who was in there yesterday," Jerome said. "She told me that she and her husband owned the place. I'm surprised they can afford help."

"That lady is not the help," Whiteside said firmly. "Maybe the woman in the store was just trying to impress you."

"Maybe," Jerome sighed.

A few moments passed before Whiteside spoke again.

"Scott Lewis ring a bell?"

"What do you think?"

"The cop who gave me the gear told me about the murder. I didn't think much of it until Dirk started mealy-mouthing around. Even then I was just pissed that he'd taken off. But when I went back to go to the john, the owner says to me, 'Would you like to use the telephone too?' and I knew something was up."

"So what was up?"

"You just love playing dumb, don't you? I called the local cops and asked them for the name of the victim. I told them to check it out with Interpol. Paul Kelly didn't check out. So I had them fax his picture to Interpol. Guess what?"

"That's why you were inside so long."

"There's nothing as underrated as a good shit."

"What's all this got to do with Sarah and Dara?"

"Your questions are getting as disingenuous as your answers, counselor. You tell me. You had the newspaper. You recognized Lewis. You didn't say a word to anyone. You made a secret phone call. What am I supposed to think?"

"Why are you telling me this now, Shane?"

"Because I trust Roger."

"What?"

"He's been straight since I was a beat cop. He contacted me before you left for the airport and told me that Dirk spent a long time on the phone to Provo the night before. He also said he didn't trust drug dealers. But he trusted you."

"Or?"

"Or I'd have had you both arrested when we got here and taken care of things myself."

Jerome could hardly see Whiteside's face. He was glad for the cover, and took a deep breath.

"I made a deal with Gunnar. I rat out Dirk and his laundering contacts, he lets me do what I have to do to find out what happened to

Sarah, and lets me keep enough of the stash to finance the search and start a new life."

"Finally I get whole story." Dirk stepped from the marshes behind them.

■

"Please relax. Keep hands in air."

"What's going on, Dirk?" Jerome asked.

"I think funny mute button work, not work. I come. Listen. I sorry Jerome. But family first. You for sure understand. I see now too dangerous to find Ludwig. Too dangerous in Canada, now you friend with police. But I need much money to hide. Too bad Lewis not co-operate."

"But he was dead before you got here. You didn't kill him," Jerome said.

"You have secret. I have secret. Now Lewis dead, you help me get money from account. Then you friend again and I not kill you. Colleague keep you maybe month, maybe two. Then I gone. You go home, forget about me. . . I forget about you."

"That's not going to happen, Dirk," Whiteside said, pulling his gun from its shoulder holster.

Dirk, barely six feet from the pair, fired first, but Whiteside remained standing.

"They're blanks, Mueller. Roger is thorough," he said. "What are you smiling about?"

"He is happy to see his wife." The woman who had opened the convenience store that morning came around the corner bearing an Israeli Micro-Galil assault rifle.

"Put gun down, Inspector. Then I like you meet Juliana, every-body," Dirk said. He walked casually to his wife and kissed her on the cheek. "Good woman, yes?"

"Depends how you define good," Whiteside said.

"You show respect," said Dirk, as angry as Jerome had ever seen him. "Juliana, give me rifle and bring car here please."

She handed the rifle to her husband.

"Drop it, Dirk." The voice came from the marshes.

With all eyes on Dirk, Juliana reached into her shoulder bag. The morning sun glistened on the emerging pistol barrel.

"No," Jerome screamed. He ran towards her. "Sofia."

Had she not hesitated before she moved, the fire from the marshes might have missed her. But two bullets found their mark, striking her leg and chest before she could get a shot off in Jerome's direction.

"Juliana," Dirk shouted. He moved backwards towards his motionless wife, firing at will in the direction of the hidden shooter.

"Stop it, Dirk! Think about Sofia," Jerome pleaded. But no return fire came from the marsh.

Dirk didn't see Whiteside retrieve his weapon. But as the detective raised the gun, Jerome shoved him to the ground and kicked it from his hand. He reached for his own pistol.

"Enough." Dirk said, lowering his rifle. He knelt by Juliana and felt for a pulse. His hand went limp.

Whiteside tried to get up. Jerome, gun in hand, waved him off.

"Dirk, where's Sofia?"

"With nanny at Sheraton."

"Go get her and get the hell out of here. I'll make sure no one comes after you."

"What the hell are you talking about?" Whiteside boomed.

"Go on, Dirk, get Sofia and get out of here."

"What about Dara?"

"That's my problem."

Dirk looked in the direction of the hidden shooter. Nothing moved.

"I have better answer."

In one motion, he lifted the rifle and pointed it at Whiteside. He took two bullets to the head and chest as his hand squeezed the trigger; then he stumbled, pointing the rifle downwards and shooting up the ground before he fell on top of his weapon.

Portland, his jacket torn at his bleeding shoulder, emerged from the marshes. Jerome was at Dirk's side.

"I'm sorry, Buga. I'm so sorry, my friend."

Dirk tried to speak, but couldn't. Jerome leaned his head forward. Dirk reached up and, with surprising strength, forced Jerome's head to his face. He whispered something, turned his head to Juliana's body, and died.

Only then, with Dirk in his arms, did Jerome let death touch him. He raised his face to the sky. The sun's warmth penetrated his closed eyes. Dirk's head felt light, even soft, to his touch. He mourned what they had lost, and he let Sarah go.

■

When he opened his eyes, he saw Dara in an upper floor window.

"Look over there," he said. But the curtain closed in front of her.

"Is that Dara?" Portland asked.

Jerome nodded.

"Surprise," Whiteside said softly. "They know we're here. Time to go, Jerome."

CHAPTER

EIGHTEEN

HE WOULD GO IN ALONE. LET DARA'S KEEPERS BELIEVE HE had no backup. He reached for the communicator in his pants pocket.

"Shit, I left my jacket in the car," he said. "Where is it?"

"A ways down the road. It was so late I thought I'd better move in on foot," Portland replied.

"What happened out there?" Whiteside asked.

"He met some friends at a bar before I could stop him. I spent most of the night waiting for him. When he did, his friends were carrying him. I followed them to his place and broke in after they left. But he was so drunk or high, I couldn't wake him for a couple of hours, and after I did, he didn't know where he was. So I let him sleep some more. I woke him again. Same thing. After the sun came up, I gave it another try and realized it was getting late. So I came back. When I got close to the garage, I turned on my communicator and heard you talking to Dirk."

"You activated it?" Jerome said to Whiteside with a touch of anger.

"Or you'd be dead. Now let's do what we have to do. Forget the jacket, Jerome. Put the walkie-talkie in your shirt pocket."

"The shirt's white. It'll show through."

"Not all criminals are alert," Whiteside said.

"Which reminds me, are the bullets in my gun real?"

"Yeah. I told you. Roger trusts you."

Jerome could hardly believe his ears. "And now?"

"It's still good enough."

"Thank you."

"What about you, Adam, are you all right?" Whiteside had torn up his jacket to fashion a makeshift tourniquet for Portland's left arm.

"Yeah. It's just a flesh wound."

"Can I ask you something now, Adam, just in case — "

"Sure."

"What took you so long? How come you didn't move in when I knocked Shane down?"

"I dropped my gun when I got hit. It took me a while to find it in the marshes."

"Is that all?"

Portland looked at Whiteside. "I wasn't sure what the rules were."

"I'm still not sure," Jerome said. "But if anything — " He couldn't finish the sentence.

"Don't worry. We'll look after the girl."

■

With the garage as cover, Jerome moved back into the marshes closer to the sea. He stayed low as he turned left, traversed the plane of the Island Trust building, and continued until he was certain he could no longer be seen from its windows. Then he crossed to the far side of the street and turned towards his destination, holding the road's edge to minimize the viewing angle. When he could see the front windows of the building, he ran diagonally for the protection the side wall afforded. He stood there, catching his wind; like an overanxious novice in the gym, he'd been holding his breath since he left his companions. In the face of certainty, his hope reappeared and he was no longer afraid: his nightmare would end one way or the other.

Walther in hand, he turned the corner cautiously, staying tight to the front side of the building and trying to keep his eyes both on the open door and the glass behind him as he passed the law firm's window. He hesitated only momentarily before he entered, studying the electronic alarm pad just inside the door as he eased himself up the stairs along the wall. Crouched near the top, he could see that the landing formed part of a functional reception area bathed in unfortunate fluorescent lighting reflected in the mandatory prints of conch, dolphins, beaches, and glistening seas. Each of the three walls away from the entrance had a door at its centre leading, he expected, to the inner offices. Along the side walls were a half-dozen thinly upholstered stainless steel chairs for visitors. Directly in front of Jerome, in the middle of the room, was a receptionist's desk, obviously the domain of a very tidy or very absent employee. A low-backed secretary's chair stood flush against the desk, leaving an ample traffic lane to the open door behind it.

Jerome could see little beyond the desk without standing up. Now on his belly, he crept from the landing toward the safety the heavy furniture offered; to his left, he noticed a bulky sliding door adjacent to the entranceway. He wondered whether he should try to close it behind him, but reasoned that he didn't have the strength to do it and still stay low. He continued on slowly until he reached the desk, where he sat up with his back against it.

"That's far too much effort, Wyndham," said a voice he remembered but didn't recognize that came from the direction of the inner room. "After all, I invited you here, didn't I?"

Jerome dropped to his belly again. It was then, looking up, that he saw the camera mounted over the landing.

"Come on in. But first take the magazine from your gun and throw it down the stairs. When it hits bottom, throw the gun down the stairs too. Do it quickly, before the door closes. Then step in here — behind the desk."

Jerome considered shooting out the camera, but apart from the other risks, knew his questionable marksmanship — dead Rottweiler notwithstanding — made his chances of hitting it slim. He did as he had been told, walked around the desk, through the door, and into the centre of a large rectangular office that ran half the width of the building. The furnishings mimicked those in reception, save for the desk directly across from him, whose elegance left it no less functional in impression.

Dara sat behind the desk, gagged with her hands tied to the arms of the chair. Her dark hair, longer than he had seen it, hung loose about and well below her face, its natural inward fall framing a pallid complexion that hadn't seen sunlight or slept much, an impression brought home by her eyes, reddish and squinting. Her T-shirt, once beige, hung loosely over her khakis and what remained of her figure. She seemed neither frightened nor calm, but lifeless.

"So you're in it with Gunnar," he said.

"Think what you want," Yu said. "But I have to admit, figuring out that it was Gunnar who needed a ride at the murder scene because he didn't drive and that the glare off those pictures came from the tie pin Marta gave him was pretty good detective work."

"Only my daughter's murderer would call it a murder," Jerome said.

"I'm truly sorry. I had no choice. She obviously had your genes. It was bad enough she started snooping through Lafond's books. She also took it upon herself to call in with the information."

His legs began trembling and went to sleep, as they had when he and Heidi stood by Sarah's body in the morgue. Now, as then, only his desperate need to know kept him from falling. He heard himself speak.

"That made her an informant?"

"It put her in the undercover database."

"You and Gunnar ordered Lafond to kill Sarah and make it look like she overdosed."

"Something like that."

Jerome started towards him. Yu shook the pistol.

"Don't be stupid, Wyndham."

"What do you want?" Jerome asked.

"Same thing you do. Money."

"And how do you think I can help you?"

"To start with, cut the bullshit. You've cost me a small fortune already and complicated things immensely by having Lewis killed. Now you'll have to help me empty his accounts as well as yours."

The possibility of negotiation revived Jerome.

"I had nothing to do with killing Lewis."

"Let me paint the picture for you. The same people who are waiting outside to take care of your friends — they watched all four of you arrive at the airport, by the way — have other unique talents. They can draw out death in ways you can't imagine. If you don't cooperate, they'll start with your girlfriend and you'll be watching."

Involuntarily, Jerome started forward again.

Yu pointed his gun at Jerome. "Don't waste your time. I won't shoot to kill until it suits me."

"And what happens if I give you the information? Are you going to leave us alive? I'll be after you for the rest of your life."

"Of course not. But then you and Miss Addario will die quickly and peacefully, and you won't be responsible for the death of Meuller's daughter either."

"You're crazy, Tom."

"I'm glad we're still on a first-name basis. Now, how about it? Where do you want to start?"

The shooting that came from outside the building startled only Jerome and Dara, though it lasted less than a minute. Still, Jerome had heard enough of the sound of pistols to know that it wasn't his companions who were pulling the triggers.

"See?" Yu said. "Just like I promised. My men do nice clean work when they have to."

"Dara," Jerome said. "Remember that night in Montreal, in the park. More than anything, I wish we could have it back right now."

With that, Dara raised her legs and jammed both her feet into the desk as hard as she could. Her chair kicked backwards, striking Yu full bore in the groin. As Jerome moved towards him, Dara rammed her feet into the desk again. Yu's gun went off wildly and fell to the floor, on the opposite side of the desk from the oncoming Jerome. Dara continued to squeeze the chair against Yu, impeding his attempt to recover his gun. He grabbed the chair by its arms and with surprisingly little effort, overturned it. Dara went down hard, tripping Jerome as he neared. Jerome fell over her and scrambled after Yu, who by now had his fingers on the gun. He whirled and fired, hitting Jerome in the chest just before Jerome landed on top of him. Dara, who had managed to wriggle over enough to see what was happening, screamed soundlessly, sure she was hallucinating when Jerome raised his fist and rammed it square into the face of a surprised Yu, who dropped the gun on the floor beside him. Jerome picked it up, pistol-whipping Yu until he felt an excruciating pain in his abdomen. The gun fell to the floor. Yu stabbed him again, this time, in his right side. He fell. Yu grabbed the gun, crawled over to Dara and held the knife at her neck.

"You've got ten seconds to start talking or she starts dying right now," Yu said. "Bit by bit."

"That's not going to happen, Tom. Drop the gun and the knife and slide them toward the doorway without turning around. Then get on your stomach and stay there."

CHAPTER NINETEEN

GUNNAR KICKED THE GUN ASIDE AND PICKED UP THE KNIFE. HIS piston still in his hand, he kneeled beside Jerome.

"How you doing?"

"It hurts. But I think I'll be all right."

Gunnar moved to examine the wounds.

"Untie her, please."

As Gunnar concentrated on freeing Dara while keeping an eye on Yu, Jerome crawled towards the door.

Satisfied that Dara was unhurt, Gunnar turned to the desk and picked up the telephone.

"I'll call an ambulance."

"You won't need one for him." Jerome had picked Yu's gun off the floor. He got up slowly, intent on Yu and oblivious to Dara. From his torn shirt pocket, he pulled what remained of the communicator, staring at it momentarily. With his eyes back on Yu, he raised the gun.

"For you, Sarah."

"That's not what she would have wanted," Portland said quietly from the doorway, where he stood with Whiteside behind him.

"How would you know, Adam? How would you know?"

"I know you, Jerome. That's enough for me."

Jerome sank to the floor, crying quietly. Portland moved in, kneeled, and put his arm around Jerome, who buried his face in Portland's chest. Dara stumbled toward Jerome, stooping unsteadily beside him. Portland stepped back. She took Jerome's face in her hands, pressed her cheek to his and let their tears mingle.

"What happened out there?" Jerome asked Portland after a time.

"Yu set up an ambush. But Gunnar and the locals got them before they got us."

"I don't understand," Jerome said, looking at Gunnar.

"I've been trying to flush Yu out for years. He'd been working with Lafond ever since he first busted the kid, but I could never prove anything."

"That's why you gave him the job at CID?" Portland said.

"I figured promoting him would give him a false sense of security. And keeping him near me was the best way to keep an eye on him."

"How did you know we were down here?" Whiteside asked, with more respect than he had previously reserved for Gunnar.

"It's not too many days of the year that both Portland and Yu don't show up for work in the middle of a crisis. You were gone too. By the way, Whiteside, your bosses were only too glad to hear that you were into something up to your ears."

"Yeah," Whiteside laughed. "They like me but they don't. You know how that feels, don't you, Jerome?"

"All too well."

CHAPTER TWENTY

"I DON'T KNOW WHY YOU'RE COMPLAINING, BUDDY," SAID Portland, chewing contentedly on a garden burger at Weber's in Toronto's Terminal Two. There had been much explaining to do to the Provo police, and Whiteside had remained behind with Gunnar to clear up the mess after arranging medical care and passage for Portland, Jerome, Dara, Sofia, and Maria, the governess whom Jerome and Dara found with the child in the room at the Sheraton.

"I'm complaining because Wyndham used me and I'm complaining because they took me off the story. The embarrassing thing is that Morris had to break the news to me. 'They think you're too close to it. So do I,' he said."

"Are you?"

Buddy inhaled, filling his cheeks with air and blowing it out with a snort.

"I keep asking myself why it never occurred to me that Wyndham planted the note himself. Maybe because I had a preferred ending to the story."

He paused and looked away.

"You know, that Wyndham had a stash and was killing people for it."

Portland couldn't hold back a broad smile. "I'm sure that whoever has the story will do a conscientious job and interview you."

"Great. Everybody will know I'm an idiot."

"Then we all are. I only caught on when he used the same red marker for the note he sent me about the meet. Very clever, really. Once Jerome suspected that Gunnar was involved in Sarah's death, he needed a cover. So he made it look like we were forcing him to rat on Dirk. That let him poke around for a while, but it all came apart when Yu's people caught Dara visiting him at the hospital."

"What about the beating at the prison?"

"We're pretty sure Yu arranged it to discourage Jerome from getting involved."

"I still don't like being part of the news."

"It'll make you a better reporter in the long run."

"Would being a criminal make you a better cop?"

"Probably. Besides, I did some things that came close."

"Did you tell Gunnar about that, Adam?"

"Right away. Back in Provo, first chance I got."

"What did he say?"

"He said, 'Very cute, very cute. Looks like we'll have to tighten up our computer security.' Then he told me to use my own phone the next time I make a social call to you."

"But there was money in that account, lots of it, right?"

"Yes. About $15,000,000. It was all in the names of companies Lewis controlled. Jerome never had a cent."

"So tell me again, how did Wyndham know about the account?"

"Part of the reason he got such a long sentence is because he allowed his office to be used as a clearing house for Lewis's money. I guess he hung on to a little extra information as insurance."

"What do you mean by insurance?"

"To tell you the truth, I'm not sure. Those were his exact words when he told me about it on the plane."

"Do you think he was planning to get some of that money for himself, Adam?"

"No. Unless maybe he needed it to track down his daughter's killers. Come to think of it, that's how he used it."

"You've got to give him credit."

"I do. But I'm worried about him."

"Why? He got what he wanted."

"I'm not sure. He wanted peace. He wanted certainty. He even got another daughter. But one day Sofia will want to know about her parents."

"How do you feel about that, Adam?"

"I don't know. I always thought that if I had to shoot someone, it would be OK as long as I had no choice and I was doing my job. Now — "

"It must be hard to look at Sofia when you're feeling that way."

"I'll try to visit with Jerome alone, at least for awhile."

"What did he tell her, anyway?"

"I don't know. I don't think he knows. I've seen that look on his face before."

"What look?"

"That look that says it's all his fault. It was there whenever he talked about Sarah. It's still there. He believes he's responsible for Sofia's parents' death. Until he rids himself of that notion, he'll have a tough time being up front with her. It's been a lifelong pattern with him. You know, blame yourself, then try to hide it."

"That's not your way, though."

"No."

"What is your way?"

"I knew more about that before all this happened."

"Well, if this didn't teach Wyndham not to take it all on himself, what will?"

"Maybe Dara."

CHAPTER

TWENTY-ONE

JEROME AND DARA RETURNED TO TORONTO IN TIME FOR THE baptism of Heidi's son. The two quiet months they had spent with Sofia and Maria in Adam's cottage on Georgian Bay were not without difficulty, but went a long way to a fresh start. Sofia's English, a product of immersion schooling, was surprisingly good, and the little girl had taken to helping them out with the homework for their Spanish correspondence course.

Over Jerome's objections, Dara had insisted that they tell Sofia of her parents' deaths as soon as they returned to Toronto from Provo. The tragedies were "a terrible accident," Dara explained.

"What kind of accident?" Sofia asked.

"A shooting accident," Dara said. "There were people with guns."

"Were they bad people?"

"The people responsible for your parents dying were bad people."

"Why didn't they like my mother and father?"

"They didn't know them very well."

"But my mother and my father, they were bad too?"

"No. They died because they loved each other."

"I love them. Will I die too?"

"No, sweetheart, there will be no more people with guns."

"Will you be my parents?" Sofia asked.

"If you want us to," Dara said.

"Only if Maria can stay with me."

"Of course."

"Forever?"

"Forever."

"That's what my mother said before we went to see Daddy. I only saw him for a few minutes."

She was quiet for a long time before she cried, and then she buried her face in Maria's lap. After that, she'd run off when the tears came; sometimes they heard her sobbing quietly in her bed at night. But in their last few weeks at the cottage, she had many questions for Maria; often, the answers made them both cry. On the way home in the car, she finally talked about her parents. They shed their first tears as a family.

For all the sadness, their vacation hadn't been without laughter and fun. With any luck, joy would come later.

Sitting beside the little girl in the church, Jerome realized that Dara had been right. Being upfront gave time a head start on taking care of the future. Maybe he could learn to share the waiting with the people he loved.

"What is the name of this child?" the minister asked.

"Adam Jerome Carson," Heidi replied.

Sarah lived on for them all.

ACKNOWLEDGEMENTS

To Jean Cumming, for all your help.

To Mom, for being there always.

To Melissa, Mark and Tashy, for the joy.

To my publisher, Jack David, who continues to believe in people and principles others have long abandoned; to Michael Holmes, my editor, for letting this book be mine, and so teaching me what writing is really all about; to Amy Logan, my publicist, for enthusiasm from the beginning to the end; to Mary Bowness, for putting up with me and getting this book in print; and to everyone else at ECW, a very special place where thanking anyone is thanking everyone.